THE SIBLINGS
BOOKS

SIBLINGS Kit's Story is part of a cycle of novels set mainly in the present day, of which SIBLINGS Emma's Story and SIBLINGS Holly's Story are part. Although each work within the cycle presents an independent, self-contained story, they are all connected through characters and storylines, creating thematic and narrative links.

Each individual book in the SIBLINGS series can be read in any order, enabling the reader to explore the labyrinth of stories along different paths which, when woven together, complete the heart of the narrative.

First published 2023 in Great Britain.
This second edition is published 2025 by The Queen of Hearts
Publisher and includes minor updates while staying true to the story
readers first enjoyed.

ISBN 978-1-0684171-0-8

British Library Cataloguing in Publication Data
A catalogue record for this book is available from the British Library

SIBLING Books: Reader Feedback

A compelling story of dysfunctional families and flawed characters where, in the case of Kit's Story, the setting of a cruise ship magnifies the tension of sibling rivalry, greed and long-buried secrets.

Kerry Fisher, million-copy internationally bestselling author

My goodness! What a page turner. I haven't been pulled into a book so fast for a long time. I can't wait to read the next in the series. They are such well-rounded, down to earth characters. I like that they are one of us, one of the girls. In 'Siblings Kit's Story', Kit is identifiable, with the vulnerabilities that hang about like stubborn stains after dysfunctional relationships. She's given a taste of luxury living and a taste of new love, but doubting herself, she doesn't know what to do with either. How human, even though she is stronger than she thinks and is moving on. The setting is inspired, a great way to present the different characters and used superbly to add suspense as it is moving from one place to another

A.C. Bourne, Bookshop Owner, Polly's Bookshop, Spain

A gripping novel about love, loss and secrets that took me on an emotional journey. I was hooked from the start and can't wait to read the other books in the trilogy.

Amy Parker, author of Refuge

Gripping. I don't read a lot as I am short on spare time, but this was recommended to me by my mum, and I wasn't disappointed! I was gripped from the first page and could barely put the book down to go to work. A thrilling tale yet full of real believable characters and interesting family dynamics which I'm sure many can relate to in one way or another. An extremely satisfying ending too. Can't wait to read the next one!

Vicki

Hooked from the start I had to restrict how much to read at once as you could feel the tension growing in the character. So many twists and turns and things that related to experiences in my life which brought this book to life for me. A roller coaster of a ride reading this book and one I did not wish to come to an end. You think you know what will happen next but there are so many twists it kept my attention to the very last page.

Lilly

I really enjoyed reading Siblings. It has great character development and an interesting theme. I kept reading eagerly waiting to find out how the sister named Kit was going to overcome a lot of heartache and abuse in her life. Looking forward to reading another Siblings book.

Patricia W. United States of America

An emotional journey on several levels encompassing the tricky themes of family and identity, love and loss, penned with much empathy and understanding. This promises to be an intriguing and enjoyable trilogy.

Faringdon Writers

ABOUT THE AUTHOR

Hilary Coombes is an award-winning English novelist whose SIBLINGS trilogy explores the complex emotions of adoption something she's experienced firsthand. A former librarian, teacher, and journalist, she's spent a lifetime immersed in words (with a brief detour selling ice cream on a department store rooftop).

She writes romantic fiction with a gritty twist, promising to tug heartstrings and bring smiles. This is her fourth novel - discover more at **hilarycoombes.com**

Keep in touch with Hilary via the web:

WEBSITE: **https://hilarycoombes.com**

FACEBOOK: https://facebook.com/hilary.coombes.94

BLOG: medium.com/@HILARYCOOMBES

TWITTER: http://twitter.com/HILARYCOOMBES

DEDICATION

For Keith
My partner in life,
every chapter is richer with you by my side.

And for my grandchildren,
and the wonderful people who love them.
You keep me young at heart.
Thank you for filling my story with love.

ALSO BY HILARY COOMBES

For Adults

The Hen Party
Beyond Promises
Short Love Stories
SIBLINGS Emma's Story

For Children

Martha and the Squirrels

SIBLINGS
Kit's story

by Hilary Coombes

KIT

The trip to New York had seemed such a long time coming and there were times when I believed it would never happen. However, at last, there I was on that wet June morning, waiting on the quayside of a windswept Southampton Cruise Terminal. I glanced for the umpteenth time at my mobile. Still no message from Jess.

'Where the hell are you?' I muttered to myself, as I watched the dark clouds turn thunderously black. As the wind picked up intensity, some passengers magically produced an umbrella against the thousand tiny spikes of raindrops that began to hammer the earth.

In desperation, I rang his number again and as I left an angry message, my eye was drawn to a tall, thin man nearby, who was totally ignoring the rain that was sending other passengers scurrying for cover. He was slowly squatting up and down as though to sit on a chair, but there was no chair. Then, he started skipping without a rope. I looked away, thinking he must be an exercise fanatic.

The huge ship towered over me, its fifteen passenger decks making me feel small and insignificant as I tightly clutched the precious box to my chest to shelter it from the cloudburst. Its commonplace brown-paper wrapping concealed its importance. Nobody would ever guess that my life was in this box. The noisy loading of new cargo jostled for supremacy over the excited chatter of hordes of cruise passengers about to board, many of whom had porters carrying their Porsche designer cases behind the fur-clad owners. I could almost smell the excitement, especially from the passengers who were carrying their own luggage.

Suddenly, my view of the horizon was blocked by the exercise fanatic. I blinked as he pointed his mobile phone at me and took a photo. It was over in a second but it caused a shudder down my spine. There was something about him that made me uncomfortable, but before I could speak, he gave me a creepy smile and ran towards the ship.

I did not relish the thought of doing this journey alone, even though being incarcerated with my brother wasn't a congenial option either. Where was Jess? Would he even come? I'd texted him countless times and left voice messages. All unanswered. I looked at the deep, black water by the side of the ship. It mirrored the gloominess I felt at the thought of spending six whole days with Jess. Charismatic, unscrupulous Jess. A brother I didn't particularly like.

My suitcase had already been stowed. I felt committed and, of course, Mother had been aware of that; she knew I'd go through with the hare-brained instructions.

The rain was beginning to invade my thin cotton jacket and I was about to run for the entrance when I saw the unmistakable outline of Jess in the distance. I didn't know whether to be relieved or angry. As he drew near, I could see that his normally slick, black hair had been tousled by the wind, and it was odd to see him minus his smart, conventional outfits. Nevertheless, his familiar ambling gait gave him away despite his natty leather jacket and slim-fitting black jeans. Even I have to admit that the clothes suited him. It was no wonder that women threw themselves at him.

'Well, you took your time, didn't you?'

'Sorry, Sis,' Jess shrugged, brushing off my annoyance. 'You know what it's like, but I'm here now.'

'For goodness' sake, let's get on board. My clothes are soaking, thanks to you.'

I ignored Jess's disarming smile and marched ahead. It wasn't until I reached the huge atrium of the ship that my temper cooled as my wet shoes squelched all over the floor. I turned to Jess.

'As you approached the ship, did you see that weird man who took my photo?'

'No sorry, Sis, but why on earth would anybody want a photo of you? You're not exactly supermodel material.'

'Thanks a lot.'

His tone softened. 'Maybe he was taking the scenery behind you or something.'

'Maybe, but he was odd and his smile was creepy.' The memory absorbed the chill of the atmosphere and I suppressed a shiver.

We joined the long queue of passengers waiting to be given the pass key to their cabins and shuffled slowly forwards.

Jess frowned. 'You'd think they'd have a separate queue for first-class travellers, wouldn't you? They could at least have dedicated staff waiting for us.'

I shook my head, unable to suppress a smile that escaped. 'Jess, you haven't changed one bit.'

'Well, we're important passengers.'

'You're incorrigible.'
'Never mind, Kit. You're stuck with me.' His grin reached from ear to ear and, as he ran his hand through his tousled hair, I knew I couldn't remain angry with him for long.

I fished about in my bag for the boarding pass. 'I'm not looking forward to this trip. Are you?'

'Think of it as a means to an end, Sis. In under a week, all the aggravation our parents have thrown our way will be behind us.
We'll be free. We'll be rich. You'll be able to do anything you want.'

'I'm okay as I am. I don't need riches.'

His eyes twinkled but his voice dripped with sarcasm. 'Oh yeah. Why don't I believe that?'

Jess waved our blue boarding cards at a member of staff, who seemed to be doing nothing except gaze at the queue.

'Hey,' he shouted. 'Why are we being kept waiting?'

She stepped forwards and glanced at the cards. 'I apologise, Sir, Ma'am. You shouldn't be in this queue. Didn't you see the notice for first-class passengers as you boarded?' The woman blinked continuously as she searched our faces, waiting in vain for one of us to reply. 'Please wait here and I'll have a member of staff with you straightaway.'

Jess stuck out his chin and nodded at me as the woman scurried away. 'What did I say? I knew we shouldn't be waiting in line.'

I glanced at the many passengers slowly shuffling towards the reception desks. It was then I noticed a raised camera pointing at me. 'Jess. Look. There's that creepy exercise man I told you about, only he's using a camera this time, not a phone.'

'You're becoming paranoid about this poor bloke. He's probably just taking pictures as a record of his holiday. Look, he's taking pictures of the reception desks now – don't tell me that's suspicious, too.'

'No, I suppose not. The horror of this trip must be getting to me.'

'There's plenty of time for horror once we're in the Atlantic. These first few days can be when we relax. Yes?'
'Yes, I suppose. It's just that he's odd. Honestly.'
'We can all be odd sometimes. Perhaps he's just a bit nervous, that's all.'
I remained silent and tried to convince myself that Jess was right. Perhaps I was being paranoid.

I felt Jess's elbow in my side. 'Look, here come the troops ready to escort us to our staterooms. We'll probably go separate ways now, Kit, so shall we meet tonight in our restaurant, about eight?'

'Which restaurant is ours?' I hated admitting to Jess that I didn't know, but all the problems with Mother, plus the strange photographer, had banished my normal efficient memory to a place out of reach.

'The most exclusive one, of course. It's the Hibiscus something or other. I'm sure it will be printed somewhere in your stateroom.'

I nodded. In truth, I'd been looking forward to the peace I hoped my room would hold. It had been a tiring day. In fact, it had been a depressing, tiring few months. However, as Jess pointed out, it would soon all be behind us.

-o-

Once safely inside my stateroom, I walked around the spacious area, which was perfumed with freesias and freshly laundered sheets. I inspected the empty storage cupboards and walk-in closet that contained my complimentary white cotton bathrobe and slippers. I was amazed that it had all been personalised with my embroidered initials. On entering the Italian grey marbled bathroom, I wondered who on earth would need a marbled bath as well as two separate sinks and an enormous shower. I held the various soaps and shampoos to my nose, breathing in the expensive fragrance. It was certainly very different to the supermarket own brands I used.

I flung myself down onto the crisp, white, king-sized bed and the peace of the room embraced me. The strikingly papered walls and antique-filled room consumed all my senses. At last I appreciated the fact that Jess had insisted we choose the best staterooms available. *The parents want us to come on this journey, so let them pay for it,* he'd said when I'd pointed out that much cheaper ordinary club cabins were available.

I picked up an embossed folder on the bedside cabinet, but I'd hardly glanced at the first page when I heard a soft knock on the door. I frowned because I'd no wish to lose the peace. It couldn't be Jess because he wouldn't knock like that – whoever was in the next room would hear his thunderous knocking. I inched the door open and was surprised to find a smartly dressed man wearing a black suit, immaculate white shirt and black bow tie. His smile was infectious.

'Welcome on board. I am your butler, Ma'am. My name is Juan.'

He extended a white-gloved hand in my direction. I tentatively shook his hand and remained silent. In truth, I'd forgotten that Jess had insisted we both had a stateroom butler.

'I've come to unpack your luggage, Ma'am, and to stock your ensuite bar with any particular drink preferences that you wish.'

'Thank you.' The words seemed inadequate even as I uttered them, but I'd no idea what to say and found the whole experience embarrassing. I hesitated. 'It's okay, Juan, my drink preferences are probably already in the fridge. I've simple tastes. And I can unpack my luggage.'

His white teeth gleamed. 'It is my job, Ma'am, and one I would very much like to do for you.'

His politeness disarmed me and I was at a loss for words.

'Ma'am, may I suggest that you relax on one of the balcony recliners? You will be able to see our ship leave the dock from there – that is, if you do not wish to join other passengers on the upper decks. I will bring you iced water or a pot of tea, or something stronger if you prefer.' The gleaming white teeth again.

I returned his smile and thought that maybe I should unwind while I had the chance. I knew that once the ship was out in the Atlantic, my stress was going to increase. I closed my eyes and reclined into the thick cushioning of the balcony lounger. Drowsiness arrived quickly and I ridiculously found myself wondering if this was the weariness a new mother experienced – not that I'd been lucky enough to be in that position, thanks to my ex-partner. My reflection nowadays no longer said 'attractive woman' but was more 'nice girl, pity about the faded skin and world-weary, dark-circled eyes'. The many tears I'd shed over Tom had obviously taken their toll. I suppose if you added the confrontations with Mother, it was no wonder. I'd once believed that my relationship with her had taken a turn for the better, but that thought was now submerged without trace.

The ship's long, deep blast of the horn interrupted my daydream. I re-entered my room to find that all my belongings had been tidily put away in the various drawers and cupboards, and my toiletries had been unpacked neatly in the bathroom, although it embarrassed me to see my supermarket special offers on display.

On the table, there was now a cut-glass bowl filled with every conceivable fruit, as well as a bottle of champagne cooling in a beautiful silver ice bucket, which, to my inexperienced eye, looked as antique as some of the furniture in the room. I hesitated to guess how much it cost, probably more than my weekly rent. Juan had left me a printed list of his duties, which encompassed everything from bringing me board games or books, delivering fancy canapés and dealing with every possible minutiae of my trip. I obviously had no need to leave the room unless I wished.

I glanced out of the balcony doors at the moving scenery outside. Not very beautiful scenery, it had to be said, but then which dockside could be classed as beautiful? The view highlighted my sadness, which no amount of opulence could dissipate. I know that for the past few months I'd been hiding from the truth, pretending that everything was fine. But it wasn't fine. It wasn't fine at all. I was hanging on to the hope that once this terrible journey was behind me, it would be the turning point in my life. But would it?

As the kettle boiled, I struggled with the thumb-size carton of milk, which refused all my efforts to open. Exasperation took over and I banged my fist on the worktop.

'Damn you, Mother! Why the hell are you putting me through this?'

And with those words reverberating around my room, I slammed the door and made my way to the upper deck where I mingled with the fellow passengers waving goodbye to the cold, dank country that was England.

-o-

When I reached the upper deck, I scanned the horizon for Jess and felt a flood of relief that he wasn't in sight. In fact, there were very few people on deck at all.

The persistent rain had driven most passengers inside and I didn't blame them. I pulled the hood of my cagoule over my head and raised my face to the sky. A thousand tiny spines of raindrops melted into my cheeks as I walked towards the railings, where a small group of women were huddled against the wind. Despite the terrible weather, they were laughing.

The tallest woman smiled at me. 'Hi, you must be going our way for the next six days. D'you think we're going to get this weather all the way over?' I was soothed by the older woman's friendly face.

'I hope not.'

'Are you travelling alone?'

'No, I'm with my brother.'

This brought squeals and giggles from the other three women, who looked younger than their tall companion.

'OMG, a man!' one of them shrieked, competing with the howl of the wind. 'Please tell me he's single?'

'No, he has a partner.'

'A partner, eh? Not a wife. Yeah, no problem then,' the woman squealed.

I thought of feisty Lily back home in Bristol and decided this woman had no idea what her opposition would be.

'Did you know,' the woman continued to yell at the top of her voice, 'that in the jungle the alpha male lion claims sexual rights to all the female lions and fights off all other males to enforce that right.'

I smiled inwardly at the thought of Jess fighting off men for sexual rights, as if he needed to. He's handsome in an understated way; those broad shoulders and muscles he's fostered after years of working out in the gym all add to his allure. Woman, overall, like what they see and once he's charmed them with words, they're usually his. No fighting of any opposition needed.

'Oh, shut up.' The tall woman was talking again. 'Take no notice of Cassie, she's had too much to drink. My name is Lou, by the way. The name on my passport is Louise, but my friends call me Lou and I prefer it that way.'

'Hello, Lou. I'm Kit.'

'Nice to meet you, Kit. We'll probably never bump into each other again on this huge ship, but if we do, then we must have a drink and say hello properly, and if I see you with your brother, I'll rush this lot in the opposite direction.' She laughed and inclined her head towards her friends, who were clutching the ship railing as though their very lives depended on it. 'They're all looking for a single man – well, perhaps even the word single isn't necessary. They'll be all over him.'

I watched the women fight their way through the rain towards the door. My heart felt lighter at having had a normal conversation with someone who had no clue of the mess that was my life. They had no knowledge of the problems my parents had caused nor the reason why I was on this ocean cruise liner to New York. They knew nothing of the little box wrapped in its boring brown paper. No, they had absolutely no idea at all and I was glad about it.

I hoped I would meet Lou again, but very much doubted it given the size of the huge ship. However, with my luck, it was probably not big enough to stop me bumping into Jess – and with that thought, my small bubble of happiness burst.

I've lived a simple life for many years – in fact, some might call it boring – but, in my way, I'm happy. I've buried memories of the catastrophic life I led with Tom (well, almost buried), at least the crying is behind me now. Nowadays, I'm far more comfortable in my skin if I avoid men. I'm tired of being hurt and every partnership I've ever been involved in has ended badly.

That evening, I shuddered as I waited to be seated in the elegant, chandeliered dining room. The little confidence I had gradually melted away with each passing Dior-dressed passenger.

'Ma'am.'

I realised the impeccably dressed maître d' was addressing me. 'Oh. Um. Yes.'

'Your name and stateroom number, please, Ma'am.' The maître d' held a clipboard and, judging by the thinness of the paper clipped to it, only a small fraction of the many passengers on board would be dining in this restaurant.

'Kit. Kit Langford.' I took the card out of my diamanté evening bag. 'Stateroom number 7109.' I disliked the word 'stateroom', which suggested connotations of grandeur. I replaced the card and quickly let the bag drop to my side again. It might sparkle but I believed the maître d' would know that rhinestones glittered just as much as diamonds.

I glanced around the room at the array of people attired in designer evening wear – my experience working in Harvey Nics' fashion department meant I knew the real thing from a copy. The woman stood in front of me was wearing the latest blue-and-white chevron striped mini by Balmain, which alone would have cost almost three months of my salary. Although the garment would have suited her far better had she bought it two sizes larger.

I brushed my hand down my dress. It'd been a fantastic knockdown price and by the time I'd deducted my staff discount, I hadn't been able to resist it. When I tried it on in my stateroom earlier, I'd felt a million dollars, but that was before I'd walked into this exclusive restaurant. My discomfort increased as a perfectly dressed waiter seated me next to an elegant woman wearing a feather hat creation. The woman eyed me cautiously before speaking.

'Good evening.' The clipped tone of her voice caused my stomach to lurch and I wrung my hands together under the table before replying in the most cultured voice I could adopt.

'Good evening.'

The table fell silent for a few minutes as we both surveyed the dining room. Eventually, the feather creation nodded in my direction once more. 'Have you travelled to New York by liner before?'

'No, this is my first time.'

'You are going to find it immeasurably interesting and they look after one tremendously well on this liner.'

'I've been impressed so far.'

The feather bobbed up and down as the woman nodded her assurance that it was so. 'Who are you wearing, darling?'

I looked down at my dress as though to find someone there.

'I favour Zuhair Murad, the Lebanese fashion designer for my frocks. Do you know him?' the woman continued.

I shook my head and swallowed hard. I wondered whether my hot cheeks were very red.

'What is your name by the way?'

'Kit. Kit Langford.'

'Oh, how decidedly odd; you are the second Langford that I've met today. There was a charming gentleman by the name of Jesse Langford in the cocktail bar a little earlier. You must be related?'

'W-well, maybe. I'm not sure.'

'You are not sure! How can you possibly not be sure? Are you travelling with anyone called Jesse?'

I'd no idea what story my brother may have told this stylish woman and knew it was prudent not to divulge too much. 'Yes, I'm travelling with my brother, but maybe he's not the Langford you met.'

'Come, come. It's not a common surname. Is his first name Jesse?' The woman raised her chin in an enquiring manner.

'I call him Jess.'

'Then it must be him. Surely? Anyway, we'll know in a minute, because he arranged that I join him at this table tonight and I believe I now have his sister here, too.' A paper-thin smile appeared. The clipped voice continued. 'You two do not resemble each other.'

'No. Probably not.'

'It matters not. My name is Lady Allegra Manster, but do call me Allegra. All my friends do and as we might share this table for the next few days, then we must surely fall into this category.'

Allegra studied the menu and I followed suit, enjoying the feel of the smooth silk finish of the paper rather than the words printed upon it. She suddenly turned to me and, in pared-back tones, announced, 'Look, they have Huevos Florentina – don't you just adore them, darling?'

I gulped and hoped that she did not see this involuntary reaction. I answered with a one-word affirmative, before quickly hiding behind the menu once more. How Jess could possibly feel at home in these surroundings I'll never know. I do know, however, that ostentation sits uneasily on my shoulders.

Jess looked at me in surprise as he approached the table a few seconds later, but he kept his beguiling smile for Allegra.

'Good evening, Allegra, you look even more beautiful than you did an hour ago, which I would have thought impossible. And hello, big Sister, you're early for once. I see you two have met.'

Allegra smiled. 'Yes, isn't it strange, meeting two Langfords in one day?' She did not add that there was no way she'd have contemplated sharing a table with the mousy big sister unless she'd met the handsome brother first.

-o-

My hands were still shaking when I returned to my stateroom much later. I'd hardly eaten any of the food placed before me and the waiter had shown tremendous concern, offering for the chef to make me any dish I desired. It was no use; I was too tense and too stressed to eat a single morsel. Eventually, I pleaded a horrendous headache, which, in fact, was the truth. I knew I wouldn't be missed.

After polite farewells, Jess and Allegra resumed their positions of physical closeness. I knew Jess's stratagems of old and had to admit that he was excellent at making a person feel important and special when he wanted to. My brother had inherited the lion's share of charm and I wondered why I'd missed the genetic handdown in this area.

The quietness of my stateroom was a panacea. I tossed my bag on the bed and quickly stepped out of my dress – a dress that only a few hours ago I'd loved, but now I hated it. I knew it was the only dress I had that was remotely suitable for the restaurant, but being forced to wear it for the following five nights was sure to be noticed. Although, if I wore the little black M&S dress I'd brought, that, too, was bound to be noticed and for all the wrong reasons.

The pounding in my head made it a priority to find the paracetamol tablets I felt sure I'd packed. With every drawer open, every cupboard searched, I drew a blank and under my breath was beginning to curse Juan and his insistence on unpacking my luggage. I picked up the phone and rang the number printed on the paper that Juan had left.

'Good evening, Ma'am, how may I help you?' The woman's friendly voice was soothing and I'd hardly put down the phone when I heard a quiet knock at the door. I quickly grabbed the white towelling bathrobe that had been folded so prettily in the bathroom.

Juan's reassuring voice greeted me. 'Good evening, Ma'am. Housekeeping has been in touch. May I come in?'

I held the door wide open and nodded. Juan wedged a small wooden jamb under the door, ensuring that it stayed open while he was in the room.

'I am sorry, Ma'am, but I cannot recall putting away any paracetamol tablets, but my memory can be a little dim at times,' he smiled pleasantly. 'I will search for you, but just in case I am unable to find them, I have taken the liberty of bringing a new packet with me from the pharmacy. I hope that this is in order?' Juan's efficiency and kindness were the antidote to an otherwise terrible evening.

Two paracetamol and an hour later saw me lying on top of my stately bed, willing the pain in my head to diminish. The more it pounded, the more it reinforced my decision not to spend another night in that awful dining room, with or without Jess and Lady whoever she was. I glanced at the little brown paper parcel perched solidly on the desk and wondered for the umpteenth time why my life should be entrenched in this nightmare journey.

The gentle hum of the ship's engines eventually soothed my mind and by the time my eyes were struggling to remain open, I'd made my tentative plan. A plan I decided would be best for me. After all, I cared little for the money involved.

Tomorrow, I would seek out Jess and talk to him about it, but I imagine he'd resist any deviation from the rules laid down by our parents. That – as he was bound to point out – would bring the solicitor hot down upon us.

A gentle tapping on the stateroom door broke into my half-sleep. I could see daylight peeping under the thick, green velvet curtains that hung in generous folds around the glass balcony doors. I rubbed my eyes in disbelief. Surely it couldn't be morning.

'Good morning, Ma'am.'

Juan opened the door a tiny fraction but stood behind it in the corridor.

'Ma'am, I am sorry to disturb you, but there is not a "Do Not Disturb" sign on your door and I didn't know whether you wanted breakfast in your room. Some people forget to tell me, and as we only met briefly yesterday, there was very little chance for you to make your wishes known. I thought that perhaps you might be waiting for breakfast.'

'One moment, Juan.'

I climbed out of bed and pulled aside one of the heavy curtains. I was greeted with the sight of a bright, sunny day, which made me blink. The dreamy blue sea was certainly its own master in this area, for it filled the view without a single interruption.

I quickly pulled on the bathrobe and made my way to the door.

'Juan, what time is it?'

'It's almost eleven o'clock, Ma'am.'

'Eleven! Good God.'

Juan nodded politely. 'I am sorry to disturb you, but perhaps you'd like me to bring you some fresh fruit juice, and I can recommend the coffee and croissants. Our breakfast chef is French and the croissants are mouth-watering. Or perhaps you would prefer something a little different? Many people ask for the tantalisingly delicious Moroccan baked eggs, but whatever you wish, Chef can make for you.'

I stood in the doorway, mouth slightly agape. Whether it was astonishment at the breakfast on offer or whether it was because I'd not quite woken up, I didn't know.

I coughed unnecessarily. 'Juan, I think I'll just have orange juice and coffee, if that's okay.'

'Of course, Ma'am, and I am sorry to have disturbed you. I will return with your breakfast as soon as possible and, meanwhile, I have been instructed by the captain to give you this packet.'

I rubbed my thumb across my forehead and felt like pinching myself. Surely this couldn't be real. Last night I had sat in a glittering restaurant with Lady somebody or other, who'd been wearing a feather hat. This morning, my butler – *my* butler – had offered any breakfast I desired because a chef would cook it just for me. Now I'd been handed a large, white, embossed packet that oozed sophistication. It was almost too good to open.

My name was beautifully written in blue fountain pen, the formation of the font not unlike that of the calligraphy I'd dabbled with all those years ago at Girl Guides.

I had no idea what to expect and speculated it might be an invitation to sit at the captain's table sometime during the crossing. I've seen this kind of thing on TV and as I was in one of the most expensive staterooms, then no doubt they'd be obliged to invite me.

I carefully opened the packet and two smaller sealed envelopes immediately fell out. I chose the smallest one and ripped it open. My face prickled with heat as I quickly scanned the words. *What on earth?*

I sat on the bed to re-read.

My dear Kit

This is the first of two letters you will receive from me during the crossing. I want to thank you for undertaking what for you must be a very unpleasant task. However, once you reach New York, the reason for everything will be clear and I hope that you will forgive me for not explaining things beforehand.

The captain has been instructed to hand you the second letter much later in the sailing. Prepare yourself for it because it will contain unexpected and perhaps disturbing information. Love Mother x

I shook my head. *For goodness' sake, Mother. Haven't you done enough damage? Will I never wake from this nightmare?* I reached for the second envelope.

Dear Miss Langford

My fellow officers and I very much hope that you are enjoying your passage to New York. I am sure that you will have discovered the many positive experiences and delightful advantages of joining us on board the Queen Anne.

It is my duty to inform you that before we set sail from England, Mr Jones-Regal, Senior Partner with Regal, Smith and Cooke, Solicitors, Bristol, approached me. I understand that he is your legal advisor. He has lodged with me, as Ship's Captain, certain documents that I am to give to you and your

*brother, Mr Jesse Langford, at a specific time during
the journey.*

*I have been charged with the responsibility of
overseeing the procedure that you and Mr Langford
are to carry out while on board. When I am satisfied
that every condition has been accomplished, I am to
contact your solicitor and confirm that it has been
done. It is at this point I have been instructed to
release to you and your brother two envelopes that are
in my safe keeping.*

*Let me know if there is a specific area of the liner
you wish to use. If not, might I suggest a quiet area
on the lower stern deck.*

*I trust that this will be agreeable to you. An identical
letter has been given to your brother, Mr Jesse Langford.*

*It is my sincere hope that you will enjoy your
journey with us, and I feel sure you already know
that all my staff are dedicated to this purpose.*

Yours sincerely

Captain James Charles Hurley

The Queen Anne

I was still sat on the bed clutching the letter when Juan
returned with breakfast.

'I have taken the liberty of bringing a plate of toast,
Ma'am, just in case you'd enjoy a little something to
accompany your coffee, but I can take it away if you prefer.'

'No, it's okay, Juan. Thank you.'

'Please don't forget, Ma'am, that if there is anything I can
do to help you enjoy a wonderful crossing, you only have to
say.'

'Thank you, Juan.' I answered on automatic pilot for, in truth, my head was still reeling from the words I'd read in the captain's letter. Why hadn't Mr Jones-Regal mentioned any of this when Jess and I had visited him at his Bristol office? I disliked the man even more now, although he'd never hit my radar as being a pleasant person in the first place. He was certainly in the pocket and working from the instructions of my parents.

I stared at the small box that I'd placed carefully on the desk; its brown paper wrapping still in pristine condition. Nobody could possibly guess the importance of that box to this journey.

I needed to talk with Jess and wondered whether he'd be in his stateroom. While waiting for him to answer the phone, an avalanche of conflicting emotions overwhelmed me. I wish I could run away, hide from the world and shut out the past year, but how pointless was that? I chided myself. *Pull yourself together. If you're not careful, you'll be crying your sorrow into the sea.*

'Hello.' The curt female voice on the other end of the phone caused me to apologise. 'Wait. Don't put the phone down; you may have the correct extension. What is the number of the stateroom that you wish to contact?'

I hesitated. 'Stateroom 7232. Mr Jess Langford's stateroom.'

'This most certainly is Jesse Langford's stateroom, and I recognise that voice. It's Kim, isn't it?'

'It's Kit.' I had no need to wonder why Allegra was in my brother's room. 'Is my brother there?'

'He most certainly is.' Allegra giggled. 'But I'm afraid that he cannot come to the phone right now. I will ask him to phone you. A little later, when he's free.'

The line was dead before I could reply. I sat on the bed wondering what to do. Not being able to discuss things with Jess was frustrating. I picked up the daily activities paper Juan had left with the breakfast tray. I certainly had no wish to listen to a talk on flower arranging or antique jewellery, which were on offer right now, and the thought of aimlessly wandering around the liner, looking at the many boutique shops, did not appeal either. I looked at the unrequested toast, now stone cold. Toast was something I always avoided; even the thought of it has the power to make me shudder. I ignored the rumbling in my stomach and escaped to my balcony to watch the sea glide effortlessly past while I drank the coffee. There was now no sign of the rain that had resolutely remained with the liner as we'd left English shores.

The sea breeze caressed my face and I settled on the balcony recliner. It was good coffee, but the imaginary smell of toast grew uppermost in my mind and, with it, a thousand memories came flooding back. Memories I'd managed to keep buried for a very long time.

I squeezed my eyes tight shut, trying to block the dreadful memory of the toast incident from surfacing, but it was of no use. It had already escaped and was now waiting in full technicolour to remind me of the worst day of my childhood.

A younger version of my mother appeared in my mind's eye as clear as a picture. Her body, slim as a willow, clothed in a unique way, unlike other mothers. As I grew older, I realised that her clothes were always classic and designer-inspired and her immaculate soot-black hair must have been dyed. Her heavy perfume invariably arrived before her and I hated its aroma.

For me, it's Mother's face that has left the most indelible impression. A face that wore a permanent expression of disgust, especially when she looked at me. I cannot recall Mother ever smiling at me, but she didn't smile at Jess either so at least she was even-handed in her dislike of both her children.

It'd been an unusual day, one when Mother had prepared our breakfast because yet another live-in au pair had just walked out. Preparing breakfast for anyone was way outside what Mother thought she should be doing, but as we were so young, she had no option.

The plate containing thin, cold toast with blackened edges had been placed between Jess and I. Jess was unable to reach so I handed him a piece of toast, then chose a piece for myself and placed it on the empty plate in front of me.

Mother glared at me suspiciously. 'Do you intend to eat your breakfast, young lady?' she asked.

I'd no wish to anger Mother, as I knew that could lead to being shut in my room for hours, but the cold, burnt toast was totally unappealing. I raised it to my mouth and nibbled the edges.

'Go on then, take a big bite.' Her eyes bored into mine.

I bit into the side, trying to suppress the horror my taste buds were shouting; the awful burnt smell invaded my nostrils and brought a feeling of nausea, thick and fast.

'Why are you making such a face?'

Mother was so close that I felt her breath on my cheek. It was a breath tinged with a distinct, sweet odour. A smell I'd been unable to recognise, but one that Mother always reeked of.

'Anyone would think I was feeding you mangy worms. You ungrateful child!'

I gulped and tried to take another bite, but the thought of mangy worms, plus my rising terror at Mother's increasing anger, took over. I spluttered half-eaten pieces of toast over the table in front of me.

Mother's piercing scream startled Jess and he immediately joined the cacophony of noise that filled the room. It felt as though my heart was beating outside my body. A body now too frightened to move.

She grabbed my arm and squeezed so hard that I burst into tears, causing Jess to clamber down from his chair and scramble under the table.

It was then it happened. And its memory was as raw and embarrassing thirty years later as it was at the time. As my terrified eyes stared up at Mother, I felt a warm stream run down my legs and gather in a pool at my feet. She let my arm go and looked down at her own unshod feet, which were now paddling in the warm puddle. She glared at me and the hard glitter of her shiny eyes increased my panic.

I didn't see her hand coming, but my cheek certainly felt it. It was then her face drained of all colour and her hand fled to cover her mouth. Tears filled her eyes and her dilated pupils stared at me as though she was seeing me for the first time.

'You shouldn't have done it,' she stuttered.
There was a raw panic in her voice that I'd never heard before. She immediately ran out of the room, leaving me shaking in front of my transgression. A wide-eyed Jess, who was sucking his thumb under the table, watched as my tears joined the puddle on the floor.

I'm grateful that I've managed to erase everything else from my mind about that dreadful day and thankful that Jess apparently has no recollection of it; at least he's never mentioned it if he has.

With adult eyes, I wonder whether that was the day Mother discovered that our father was seeking a divorce. She'd always been strange; she'd shout at us for no apparent reason and sometimes even throw objects at the walls. But that day had been a new experience in my childhood and one I didn't want to repeat.

Father was frequently absent from home. He was always away on business around the world somewhere or at least that's what we were told. Although this made very little difference to me, because Jess, even at that young age, was the more amenable child, so when Father was home he spent his time with my brother rather than me. In truth, however, he spent very little time with Jess either. It was only when Jess became a man that Father took a greater interest in him.

I made sure that nothing like the toast incident ever happened to me again. At school, I was the child who would always give way or step down quickly if it looked as though an argument might develop. I didn't answer adults back; in fact, I rarely stood my ground with other children. I became known by my teachers as a well-behaved, dependable child, one who would always do as I was told – and, to my misfortune, it was this asset that attracted Tom many years later, but that was another story and not one I wanted to dwell on today. The toast episode was more than enough memories for one day.

JESS

I watched Allegra pull her dress down over her naked body. She turned half laughingly towards me.

'Well, thank you for an amusing night, Señor.'

'Amusing, eh? Is that what you call it, Señora.' I laughed, stretching my tanned arms behind my neck as I lay back on the crumpled sheets.

'I could think of a few other adjectives that might suit, but Señor might need a little more practice before I could use them.' She pouted at me.

'Practice! Get out of here, wench, before I teach you a thing or two.'

'Promises, promises.'

I found myself smiling to an empty stateroom. Sex was so easy; why did some people have such trouble achieving their desires?

I was halfway through my shower before I remembered that Kit had phoned, at a rather awkward time as it happened. I smiled again. Trust Kit.

Sometimes, I feel sorry for Kit – she's my only sister, after all. I don't think she's ever been truly happy, even when she was with Tom all those years ago. It's far too easy to put on Kit and I'm afraid everyone does, me included.

Thinking of Tom has brought back a memory I'd quite forgotten. It was when Kit first met him. She was besotted with him and Lily thought I should do the brotherly thing and invite them to dinner, so, against my better judgement, I did. Oh my God, the man was so full of himself. Smarmy, I thought, but judging by the way Kit looked at him, she didn't see it.

Once they'd gone, Lily said something I've felt guilty about ever since. Guilt is not something I naturally harbour, so this was unusual for me. We were in bed and Lily was in a mood. She didn't want to make love, she didn't want to go to sleep; the only thing she seemed keen to do was talk about my sister and Tom.

'He's not good for her, you know,' she announced.

'What. Why?'

'Just look at him; he's a bully and exerts power over her already.'

'You're imagining things.'

'I'm not. You must have noticed how she never answered any question without looking at him for guidance or approval first.'

'You're imagining it.'

Lily raised her voice. 'I'm telling you, I am not. Did he ever look you straight in the eye? No! And just look how arrogant he is. I don't know why Kit can't see it.'

'Perhaps because it's not true. He's got an inflated view of his own importance, I'd agree with that, but that's about it in my book.'

'I despair. I'd put money on him being married with a little wife and half a dozen children secreted away somewhere. He's certainly old enough.'

'Now you're talking rot. I'm sure he'd level with Kit if that were the case. And if you're right, perhaps she already knows.'

Lily ignored me and carried on. 'And another thing, he's a guy who obviously likes women. Look how he flirted with me.'

'That was something I did notice, but I thought it light-hearted banter.'

'Light-hearted, it may have been, but if you hadn't been here, it would have been much more. I'm sure of that.'

'Whether you're right or wrong, there's nothing we can do about it, Lily.'

'Oh yes there is. You're Kit's only brother and you should warn her that Tom's not all he seems.'

'I can't do that.'

'Why not? I'd say something if she were my sister.'

'Kit and I don't have that kind of relationship.'

'That's a weak excuse. I'm telling you, Jess, if you don't warn her and something happens between them, which it most certainly will, you're going to be very sorry that you kept quiet.'

I ignored Lily at the time, but it turned out she was right, and more than once I'd wished I could go back and warn Kit not to be too trusting.

I wasn't necessarily proud of the way I lived, but at least I acknowledged my ruthlessness with an easy mind. It's just the way I was. Here today, gone tomorrow, like the women in my life – apart from Lily, that is, and she was on borrowed time.

Father had always told me to never give my heart away. *Play the field, Son,* he'd say when we shared a midnight whisky or two. I was Father's favourite child as much as either of us could boast this title, for there were times when he could be distant with both of us.

I shrugged at my mirror image and grinned. I suppose not everyone could have my personality. However, we are all born equal, with the capability to be happy or sad; it was what we did that determined which way we go.

My mind wandered back to Allegra. As well as providing a bit of fun on this dreadful voyage, I realised she could be very useful to me, especially when we docked in New York. She was titled, rich and had many contacts in the Big Apple; being introduced to the right people would be very advantageous indeed, especially as in New York I would be very rich – Father assured me it would be so. Why else would I have agreed to come on this ludicrous debacle of a cruise, with my sister of all people?

KIT

I was longing to discuss the captain's letter with Jess that morning, but it proved impossible to find him. I'd scoured every deck and left several messages on his phone.

As I searched the ship, I had a sensation of being watched. My increasing heartbeat invaded my ears. *This is stupid*, I told myself, but I couldn't stop the flutter going on in my stomach. When I reached one of the many quiet corridors between cabins and social areas, I stopped and listened. I was sure I'd heard footsteps. Why the hell I didn't look behind, I had no idea. I broke into a run, not stopping until I reached the art gallery where a group of passengers were studying the art for sale. A nervous giggle escaped as I looked behind – of course there was no one to be seen in the corridor from which I'd just come. I exhaled but that didn't stop my heart from beating wildly. Why on earth was I doing this to myself? It was madness.

-o-

It was mid-afternoon before I caught up with Jess. The lido deck was crowded, but Jess's muscular shoulders and jet-black hair peeping from the back of a sunbed caught my attention. As I rounded the recliner, I was taken by surprise and involuntarily let out a small gasp. He might be my brother but I had to admit he was attractive. You could almost call him beautiful. He wore an open vest, no shirt and at his throat, a head of curling hair escaped.

'Hello there, Kit,' he said, in a voice loud enough for those around him to hear.

'Where've you been, Jess? I've looked everywhere.'

'Oh, sorry.'

'I've been leaving you mobile messages on and off all day and I rang your stateroom this morning. Didn't you get a message?'

Jess raised his shoulders and held his palms upwards. 'Yes, I was told, but you know what it's like, Kit. Things get in the way, don't they?'

I did not know what it was like and pursed my lips together. 'So, where've you been all day?'

'I sat alone in the private Kings Grill for breakfast. Eggs benedict and breaded haggis balls, and it was great. Where did you eat?'

'It doesn't matter. Anyway, why didn't you answer your mobile?'

'Now, there I've a confession – for your ears only, of course. D'you remember Allegra? The woman who dined with us last night.'

I nod. *Who could possibly forget her?*

'I've turned my mobile off in case she decides she'd like to accompany me during the daytime hours. Don't get me wrong; Allegra's a lovely woman and lots of fun, but she's only for the night, to my mind.'

'Jess. We need to talk.'

He looked surprised. 'Do we? What about?'

'The letter.'

'What letter?'

'Didn't you get a letter from the captain this morning?'

He looked bemused. 'I don't know. I haven't bothered to look at anything that's put under my door. I'm on holiday, after all. Well, kind of on holiday. At least I'm trying to imagine that's what this is.'

'I think you'll find one of the things put under your door is a letter from the captain. Juan gave me mine this morning.'

'You dark horse, you've met a man then. Who is this Juan?'

'No, I've not met a man.' I roll my eyes and exhale sharply. 'Juan is my butler.'

'On first name terms, eh? I don't even know what my butler looks like.'

'You wouldn't.'

'What do you mean by that?'

I realised this conversation was getting me nowhere. 'Look, Jess, we've both had a letter from the captain. He wants some information from us. Our parents' solicitor is involved. You need to read this letter and then talk to me about it. Okay? I'm now going to my room to make a cup of tea.'

I could tell by his face that I now had his attention, and it wouldn't be long before he was in touch.

-o-

I sat behind the glass patio doors of my stateroom, watching the waking of the slumbering sea titan as I drank my tea. No longer did it appear as a millpond, little waves topped with white froth were being tossed about as though in a tennis match, but none of this affected the tranquil smoothness of the huge liner as it made its way slowly across the grey water. There was a knock on the door. I knew who it was before I rose to answer.

It was a different Jess that sat opposite me watching the sea, his devil-may-care attitude had gone and was replaced by a frown. 'So, what do you make of this?' His voice was low and serious.

'I don't know what to make of it. I didn't think anyone knew about our mission.'

'I thought it would be cut and dried. Carry out their wishes and be rewarded for being good children.'

'Mm, I know, but I've been thinking about it. Thinking all day, to be honest. That was when I wasn't looking for you.'

'Oh, don't start that again.'

I realised that to go down the angry path would be of no use, but I was still annoyed with Jess for being so laid-back about everything. In fact, a lifetime of his laid-back attitude was beginning to weary me. 'I was thinking, perhaps the solicitor is legally obliged to get proof that we carried out our parents' instructions. Involving the captain would very easily fit into that requirement.'

'It's a good point.'

'It's the second part of the letter that intrigues me. The handing over of certain documents at an appointed time. What's that about?'

'I don't know.' Jess rubbed his chin. 'Did Father ever mention anything about this to you?'

'No, but why would he? He barely spoke to me. You were always his favourite, Jess. You know that.'

Jess nodded slowly before standing and pacing backwards and forwards across the stateroom. 'What on earth could these documents contain?'

'I've no idea, but getting anxious won't help, will it?'

Jess returned to the chair. 'You don't suppose they've decided to change everything they've promised, do you?'

'I've no idea, but I suppose we'll find out soon enough. In the meantime, there's nothing we can do. We should probably try to enjoy being on board - walking around today I realised that everything you could possibly want is here. Did you know there are five different themed areas? The

Asian one houses   hundreds of plants and trees. Imagine that: we're in the middle of the ocean and there's all this greenery. Then there's an observation pod where you can rise four hundred feet -'

'Stop, Kit. Stop. This is more than just a pleasure cruise.'

'But, Jess, if they've changed their minds, we might as well enjoy the journey – and at least our airfares back to the UK are paid.
We've nothing to worry about.'

'I can't listen to any more.' He pecked me on the cheek and rose to leave. 'I need to think. This is important.' His actions amazed me. It'd been a long time since he'd shown any form of tenderness towards me.

I called his name just before he reached the door and he half turned.

'I want to say something, Jess, but I don't want you to fly off the handle if you don't like what I say.'

He looked at me with utter bewilderment.

'It's Allegra. I think you should be careful. I don't trust her. There's something about her, Jess. I don't think she's what she seems.'

'Nonsense. You're imagining it. Are you sure that you're not just a little bit jealous?'

'No, I'm not jealous. I just want you to be cautious.'

For a few seconds, my eyes held his. 'Don't worry, big Sis, you're talking to a man of the world here. I can handle myself.'

'I hope so.'

Jess smiled softly. 'I'm fine. Don't lose any sleep over me.'

'Just be careful, that's all.'

He laughed. 'I'll see you in the dining room later. Yes?'

'Maybe.'

But he was halfway into the corridor when I spoke, so he probably didn't hear.

That evening, I purposely walked past the exclusive dining room to which my gold-embossed key card gave me full access. In fact, my card gives me access to virtually everywhere on the ship, from the exclusive observation deck to the so-called 'Rebellious Cocktail Lounge'. It was an access that many passengers on this liner would probably love, but it wasn't for me.

Walking briskly past the lounge, I made my way to the Seattle Bar where I planned to order a mojito and put off the decision as to which restaurant to visit.

My eyes did a double take when, in the distance, I saw the outline of the exercise fanatic that had accosted me before the ship sailed. I watched him, mesmerised, as he hopped first on one foot then the other, back and forth. I didn't know whether to be suspicious of him or feel sorry for him. I quickly headed for the bar before he spotted me.

As the barman poured my mojito, I heard a familiar voice. I turned and saw the woman I had met on the rain-soaked deck on the first evening. The three younger women were also with her and they were still giggling. Looking at these normal women, who were not out to impress anyone, made me feel happy. I turned back to the bar, but before I could pick up my cocktail, I heard my name shouted across the room.

'Hello, Kit. Remember us? Where's your handsome brother?' I saw a brightly dressed, attractive young woman grinning at me. 'Come and join us and bring that invisible brother of yours.' The young woman's words caused the rest of the group to giggle again.

'Take no notice of Cassie,' Lou's familiar voice shouted as she dragged an empty chair into their circle in readiness. 'Come on. Join us.'

'Nice to meet up with you all again,' I said as I put my mojito on one of the many coasters.

'I didn't expect to see you again.' Lou smiled. 'It's such a big ship. I wonder what the chances are of us bumping into one another again?'

'One in a million, I think.' Lou had used the word 'ship' instead of 'liner' and I felt comforted. She had no need for pretence.

'Where's your brother?' Cassie piped up, eagerly.

'Cassie is up to her usual high spirits, as you can see.' Lou laughed loudly before sweeping her arm in a circle towards her friends. 'This is Lucy, this is Amy and, as you already know, this is Cassie. I must tell you, she's the noisiest of the group, but you're harmless, aren't you, Cassie?'

Cassie grinned from ear to ear. 'Oh, come on. Seriously! When I meet Kit's brother, he might not agree.'

I thought of my brother and smiled. I couldn't imagine him being overwhelmed by any female.

'So, Kit, what have you been up to today?'

'I explored the ship.' I thought it best to leave my reply at that for I'd no wish to get involved in a conversation about posh restaurants or captain's letters.

'We've been exploring, too. Then, we spent the afternoon on the covered sun deck. It got a bit too windy for the open decks.'

I nodded. 'My but...' I managed to swallow the word I was about to say, sensing that to utter the word 'butler' here would have been suicide. I tried again, hoping that they wouldn't notice the slight word change. 'My brother told me it's likely to be windy from now on, all the way to New York.'

'Really? I was hoping for a bit of sunshine.' Cassie smiled. 'I want to get a tan.'

'Oh, I think it could well be sunny as well as windy. After all, we'll be in the middle of the Atlantic Ocean. It's bound to be a bit windy.'

Nodding heads agreed with me.

Lou changed the subject. 'Which restaurants have you used so far? Can you recommend any?'

'To be honest, I ate in my room last night and this morning I didn't wake up until really late.'

Cassie patted the side of her nose. 'Ahh, it was a good night then.'

'It certainly was.' Another lie. I was becoming adept at them.

'We tried the Manhattan Steak Restaurant last night. We enjoyed it; there's so much food on offer. I admit I ate far too much,' Lou said.

'Trouble is…' Cassie pinched a microscopic roll of fat at her waist, 'if I eat as I did last night, then I'll become huge.'

Lou laughed. 'We're only on the ship for six days, Cassie. That's not long enough to worry about.'

'Well, I don't want to take a step down the slippery path.'

'Amy met a lovely man on deck today. Didn't you, Amy?' Lou smiled. 'We've christened him "Mr Romeo".'

Amy's eyes met mine. 'Oh, Kit, he was divine. Makes my knees go weak just thinking about him. He has the kind of face that stops you in your tracks and as for his body, well—'

'Whoa, girl, whoa!' Cassie squealed. 'Spare us the details, please. I don't want to think about testosterone-filled men before my dinner. After, maybe.'

A chorus of laughter rose from the table.

'Back to the subject of where to eat, girls.'

I could see that it was Lou who kept them in some kind of order. 'I don't want to go back to the Manhattan Steak Restaurant nor the self-service, although the food there was fine for a lunchtime. It's nice to be waited on and sit at a table with a proper tablecloth.'

Amy looked at me. 'You'll join us for dinner tonight, won't you?'

'I'd love to.'

'What about your brother?' Cassie had a half-smile on her face. 'Do you think he'd like to join us?'

'Cassie, shut up. You and men – what is it?' Lou sounded as though she meant it, and I wondered whether the bonhomie might get her down as the days passed.

'We talked about going to that posh restaurant tonight.' Amy looked inquiringly at the group. 'You know, the one where people who believe they're better than us go.'

Lou was practical. 'I don't think we'll get in.'

'Nonsense.' Cassie giggled. 'All we need to do is chat up the man in charge; he's bound to succumb to a bit of flirting.'

I smiled and tried to imagine the maître d' succumbing to a bit of flirting. It was more likely that pigs might fly. We chatted around the topic all through a second cocktail and as the decision was stalemate, it was decided to write the name of each of the restaurants and put them in a glass. I was given the honour of picking out one piece of paper.

I hesitated, surreptitiously trying to glimpse any of the words on the pieces of paper. I hoped against hope that I didn't chose my exclusive restaurant. To bump into Jess and Allegra didn't bear thinking about.

'Come on then, where are we dining tonight?' Cassie asked, her face full of expectation.

My heart sank. 'It's Le Blanc Hibiscus restaurant.'

'Great.' Cassie clapped her hands. 'I've read about it in the information pack and I wondered what those tables of lights were all about – now I'll get to see them. We might even sit inside one.'

I winced as I remembered the 'Tables of Lumière' – the luminescent curtain of shimmering fibre optics cocooning some of the tables in the restaurant. It was obviously aimed at couples, because they could see out but were screened from view. The previous evening, Allegra had asked the waiter whether she and Jess might be moved to one of those tables. The waiter had looked at me, before answering, 'I am sorry, Ma'am, those tables only have room for two people.'

'But that is exactly what I want! A small soirée for two.'

At the time, I'd been embarrassed. Later, I was angry. Very angry. How dare Allegra humiliate me in such a way and, even more demeaning, why had Jess said nothing?

An unease settled in my chest as we made our way to the Le Blanc Hibiscus restaurant. 'Where shall we go if we can't get in?' Lucy said, as we approached the ornate glass doors.

'Don't be a wimp, we'll get in. Just you wait and see.' Cassie sucked in her stomach before pushing open the doors, but it was then obvious that the palatial entrance area to the restaurant took the wind out of her sails. It was either that or the sight of elegantly dressed individuals waiting to be escorted to their tables.

'Jeez,' Amy whispered under her breath. 'I didn't expect this.'

'These women are wearing some impressive dresses.' Cassie cupped her hand across her mouth before whispering to me, 'They didn't get those down the market, did they? Mind you, I think they've eaten far too many steak and kidney pies to look good in any clothes… some would look better wearing a tent.'

I couldn't help the smile that spread across my face.

'I don't think we're going to get in here. Let's go,' said Lou, but her comment was totally ignored by her young friends.

'No, we're as good as any of this lot.' Cassie had regained her confidence. 'Come on, join me in the queue.'

It was then I saw Jess hold the door open to allow Allegra to walk though. I quickly looked away and saw Cassie nudge Amy before announcing a little too loudly, 'Look, it's him. Mr Romeo.'

Amy cheeks bloomed red. 'Shush, Cassie.'

I was sure Jess and Allegra must have heard Cassie's remark, but it was Allegra who took charge. She swept past, the sound of her silk dress rippling under the spin of movement. Her chin was held so high that only those of height would be able to see the look of distaste on her face. Jess adopted a very unusual meekness as he followed in the wake of Allegra's striding steps.

'We have a booking for one of the lumière tables this evening.' Allegra's voice rang around the entrance area as she commanded the attention of the maître d'.

'Certainly, Lady Manster.' He nodded at Jess and turned to lead them from the foyer. 'Please follow me.'

'Get her!' Cassie announced in a voice so loud that it turned the heads of those waiting in the entrance lobby.

'Amy, I reckon you're best off without Mr Romeo. He's obviously a two-faced flirt, with a big ego.'

'I'm going. I don't want to eat in this restaurant,' Amy said and strode towards the door.

I saw my chance to escape any further embarrassment and quickly joined Amy. Seconds later, we were all stood outside the restaurant and it was to my relief that Lou took control and steered the little party away from the area.

Much later that evening, as I prepared for bed, I thought that although I enjoyed the company of my new friends, it might be better if I kept myself to myself from now on. Much less complicated. I looked towards the box on the desk, still wrapped in its brown paper, and nodded. Yes, far less complicated.

I hadn't slept well. In fact, long before Tom and I went our separate ways, a good night's sleep was something to be cherished. Somewhere between the state of dreaming and waking, I opened my eyes. I was now in the habit of letting the early sun invade instead of hiding it behind the thick cabin curtains. The first thing I saw was the pattern of the sea shimmering on a little patch of wall on my terrace. I purposely let my eyes lose their focus, which was a stupid thing to do for it allowed the memory of Tom – goodlooking, smooth-talking Tom – to invade. Before I knew it, I was back in 1990, watching him with his back to the sun on the terrace of his London apartment.

The atmosphere of sex we'd enjoyed earlier that morning still lingered in the air. The bright sunshine flickered patterns from a shiny terrace lantern onto his naked body. A body that for me was so beautiful it triggered strong emotions that overwhelmed me, causing me to blush. I was powerless to resist him and we'd reached a point in our relationship when we lived only for the day's encounter. There was no tomorrow or yesterday. Passion filled every craving.

When I first met him at the gym, it'd been the twining cords of muscle wrapping around his entire body I'd been attracted to, plus his strong arms, solid thighs and that firm abdomen, which men half his age envied. I remember the first time I took Tom home to meet Mother.

The visit had been arranged under duress, for in truth I'd no wish to let either of my parents within a mile of him. I could guess what their reaction would be. It was only a sense of duty that kept me in touch with my family, and a feeling of guilt encompassed me if I didn't visit or phone every couple of months.

Even now, all these years later, just remembering the embarrassing afternoon of Tom's first visit made my face flush as I tried to push the memory away. I knew Tom was a strong individual and trusted that this would get him through that first meeting with Mother. Plus, of course, he was such a smoothtalking man there was a chance that Mother might quite like him.

Mother's latest domestic help opened the front door. A large, robust woman, who cared not that my mother condescendingly addressed her as 'my good woman'. Mother heard me enter the hallway and immediately shouted instructions that could have been heard next door.

'Show them in. Show them in.'

We followed the direction of her voice and were greeted by the sight of Mother gracefully perched on the arm of a chair. She didn't stand when she saw us, neither did she smile; however, her eyes slowly looked Tom up and down.

'I can see why my daughter fell for you even though you're much older than she is,' she said in a monotone. 'As well as that handsome face, you obviously keep your body in trim. I expect you've had lots of younger women throw themselves at you.' She turned and looked at me. 'Kit, do you realise our visitor is still wearing his outdoor clothes? And just look at his boots.'

Tom looked at me wide-eyed before gazing down at his boots, which, in all honesty, were hardly wet. He quickly recovered his equilibrium 'I'm sorry, Mrs Langford,' he gushed as he threw her a charming smile. 'It's a bit damp out there.'

'I'm aware of that. It's not your fault that you were ushered into my newly carpeted lounge wearing wet boots.' She looked at me with disdain.

Tom quickly removed the offending footwear, which I then carried to the hallway along with his coat.

'So, you are Tom.' It was a statement rather than a question.

'My daughter has told me all about you.'

I squirmed. Mother made it sound as though I shared intimate details with her, which was the opposite of the truth. In fact, all she knew was his name and that I was bringing him to meet her.

Tom engaged his easy-going manner. 'It is good to meet you, Mrs Langford. Kit speaks very highly of you.' A lie recognised by both women in the room.

'Wine?' Mother held aloft the bottle she'd obviously already half-emptied.

'Thank you, Mrs Langford, that would be very nice.'

'I don't suppose you want any, do you, Kit? You don't approve of drinking in the afternoon.'

I felt my hackles rise. 'No, Mother, you're wrong. I would love a glass of wine. Thank you.'

She raised her eyebrows. 'My, my, the little tiger has reared her ugly head again.'

I glared at her before snatching the glass from her hand. 'I've no idea what you mean.'

'No? I can explain, if you wish.' She looked towards Tom, whom I could tell was a little bemused. She beamed at him. 'Would you like me to explain, Tom?'

He shot her another disarming smile. 'I would far rather you told me all about yourself, Mrs Langford.'

'Yes, perhaps it would be a little more interesting for you, I agree.'

I sat tight-lipped as I watched Mother charm Tom with carefully chosen anecdotes from a life that I'd never witnessed. In these stories, Mother always seemed to be free and easy and very popular. Father was never in any scene.

'My goodness, what an exciting life you've led, Mrs Langford.' Tom brushed an invisible speck of dust from the knee of his trousers.

'Oh, do call me Sylvia. All my friends do. Tom, will you ring for the woman to come and open another bottle of wine for us?'

'Of course, but I can do that if you wish.'

'How kind you are.' Mother smiled as she retrieved the corkscrew from a small drawer concealed underneath the coffee table.

'Would it be rude of me to say that I can see from whom Kit inherits her charming manners.'

'Kit! Manners? Good heavens, Tom, are we talking about the same woman? As a teenager, Kit had the manners of a gorilla. In fact, she almost drove me to a nervous breakdown. She must have changed an awful lot since she left home.'

'I can't believe that, Sylvia. Kit has a lovely demeanour.'

'I'm going to have to put you right about a few things. I can't have you believing everything she tells you. Has she ever explained why she doesn't visit me as often as a loving, dutiful daughter should?'

Tom's face clouded. 'I must admit I don't visit my elderly mother as often as I should. I'm afraid we youngsters have such busy lives nowadays.'

'Youngsters.' Mother's voice raised a notch. 'Come now, Tom. Don't let's fool ourselves that you are a young man.

Charming as you are, you must be nearer my age than Kit's. I imagine she's just a trifle to you, a young woman who shares your bed at night. She was always needy as a child.'

My mouth dropped open. Mother had just voiced something that I'd kept tightly locked away.

'Age isn't important, Sylvia. Kit and I get on very well and despite you believing the opposite, I'm not nearer your age. Far from it.'

Mother ignored him and looked at me. 'I think it is time you left, Kit, and you had best take…' – she paused momentarily – 'this person with you.'

As we silently left Mother's house that day, a boundary line had been crossed for me. Mother had voiced something I'd deeply buried. Now, I could no longer ignore it.

For most of my life, I'd dated older men. One of my friends had once remarked that I must have been looking for a father figure. After Tom's visit to Mother, I saw him through different eyes. I loved Tom and until this moment felt sure he loved me, but did he? Mother had thrown my feelings into disarray again.

Was he simply a substitute father figure for me? And, more importantly, was I just a sexual trifle he played with and would drop when he became bored? The shudder that travelled down my spine seem to reach my very toes and I realised I was sweating with dread.

Three months after our visit to Mother, I moved in with Tom. It was a wonderful moment because it proved his love for me. Why did I ever doubt it? As he carried me over the threshold that cold October morning, I promised myself I'd be the best partner a man could have. And what a romantic gesture on his part at the beginning of our life together. Mother was wrong about me being a trifle to him. We were going to live happily together forever. I knew it.

In those first giddy months, the apartment was a hotbed of lust and often I arrived at work half-asleep. At first, my fellow shop assistants covered for my lackadaisical work ethics, but the day I landed everyone in trouble because I'd undercharged a cash customer by three thousand pounds was the turning point. We were all called into the manager's office and given a stern warning, as well as saying goodbye to any bonus payment for that year. From then on, there was a coldness and the workplace became less pleasant.

As time passed, making love to Tom – although still fun – was changing and the intoxicating drug of sex was beginning to lose its shine. Lately, things felt one-sided and it wasn't Tom who was on the losing side. A little voice at the back of my head told me something wasn't right and I should talk to Tom about it, but I did nothing, fearing he'd think me a nag.

I studied Tom as he waited for the coffee machine to produce our drinks. He was standing one leg in front of the other, one arm in his trouser pocket, the leather belt on his trousers accentuating his narrow waist, and the white T-shirt clinging to his muscled shoulders. There was no escaping the fact that he was handsome, but since the visit to Mother, our age difference jumped out at me at every opportunity.

I took the coffee mug from his outstretched hand. His seductive aftershave drifted towards me, but I shuddered as it reminded me of his roughness the last time we had had sex.

'Penny for them, Kit. You're very quiet today.'

'Oh, it's nothing.'

'It must be something when my little songbird is so quiet.' Recently, Tom had taken to calling me his 'little songbird', but when he did, I knew an argument could easily develop unless I handled things carefully.

'So, what is it?' Tom stared at me, expectantly.

'I've a pounding headache, to be honest.' I hoped the lie would diffuse Tom's obvious rising anger.

'I was about to tell you something very important that concerns us, but never mind. It can wait.' He patted my hand. 'My poor chickadee.'

I smiled weakly.

'I tell you what, why don't you go and have a lie down? Make the most of a quiet Sunday afternoon and, if you feel better, I'll come and join you later.' He smirked. 'Maybe we can make that baby you so want.'

I winced. Tom had made it sound as though it was only me that wanted a baby, whereas it had been a mutual decision. At least, that was my interpretation of the conversation we'd had a year ago. I wished he'd never raised the baby topic, though, for my monthly disappointment was becoming unbearable and I'd no wish to be reminded of it. Recently, my life seemed to revolve around the wish to get pregnant. I had read that the average woman was born with around two million eggs and steadily loses them as she ages.

In her thirties, she has somewhere between eighty and one hundred thousand. It was no wonder I was aware of the ticking of my biological clock.

Tom took great enjoyment in 'making his little songbird sing', as he so poetically put it, but lately it had brought me little joy. Sex had become an emotional labour, something I needed to do if I was ever to conceive a baby. However, I realised that if I didn't give Tom the sex he demanded, he'd quickly adopt a black mood and pick a fight with me.

My Sunday afternoon lie-down had hardly begun before Tom climbed into bed beside me. 'How's my chickadee now?' he crooned as he wrapped his arm around my waist.

'Much better.' I knew any other answer would annoy him, although I was screaming inside. How could he possibly believe a headache would disappear so quickly?

'Good. I think it's a good time to make my little songbird sing. Don't you? Would you like that?'

There was one answer he wanted to hear and I'd be foolish not to give it. Tom was good to me and I believed sex was the best way to repay him. Apart from which I yearned to hold a baby of my own, to become pregnant before it was too late. Sometimes I wondered whether Tom felt the same; I couldn't blame him if he didn't. Why should he? He was the father of a fifteen-year-old girl from his first marriage, so he'd already experienced the joys I longed for.

'Was that good, chickadee?' His warm breath tickled my ear as he propped himself up on his elbow.

The finale had been over quickly, but nevertheless I nodded and ran my fingers through his hair.

'You're a good girl, Kit,' he mumbled and slumped back onto his pillow. 'A good girl.'

I watched him drift into the world of dreams, his head now lolled across my chest. He looked vulnerable and childlike. My tears gathered and threatened to overspill and I'd no idea why. I fought the emotion – I didn't dare set it free.

Tom's roughness during our lovemaking had become worse; there'd be bruises to hide again tomorrow. I pretended the bites Tom inflicted didn't hurt and that my screams were from ecstasy, not pain. Briefly, in those moments, I had nothing but antagonism for him, though it was nothing like the searing dislike I directed towards myself. Mother had it right; I'm no good and made everyone around me unhappy, so I must put up and shut up.

My eyes closed and the sound of Tom's steady breathing cocooned me to that blissful place where my brain allowed relaxation. My mind drifted through fragments of conversation and Tom's words abruptly butt their way in… *I want to tell you something very important that concerns us. Concerns us. Us.* I played with the words over and over in my head. Was Tom fed up with my constant conversations about becoming pregnant? Was he about to leave me? Would nobody ever love me?

My heart beat wildly in my chest and the headache I'd fabricated earlier now manifested itself, pounding and throbbing, like a toothache in my brain.

There'd be no sleep for me that afternoon.

-o-

All through the next day at work, my mind returned again and again to Tom's announcement that he had something important to say. It tantalised me and caused time to pass slowly, even though we were busy.

Winter darkness had fallen by the time I headed home and as I sat on the crowded bus, I battled with my eyes to remain open.

'Excuse me.' A loud voice attacked my ears. 'Excuse me.'

I opened my eyes and turned towards the voice, the stiffness in my neck sending a sharp pain through my shoulders.

'It's your shopping. It's hurting my legs.'

I looked at my huge bag of groceries nursed on the lap of my fellow passenger and felt my face flush. 'I'm so sorry. I'd no idea…' I noticed the liver spots on her hands as I grabbed the offending bag. My white-haired companion's face softened. 'I've fallen asleep on the bus before now. It's the monotonous pace of the bus that does it.'

'My shopping's heavy. I didn't mean to park it on your lap. Again, I'm so sorry.'

'It slid over once your head slumped on my shoulder.' The older woman smiled sympathetically. 'Don't worry, my dear. You must have needed that sleep.'

I fiddled with the shopping bag on my lap, making sure it stayed in place.

'I thought all you young people shopped online nowadays,' she said, not unkindly.

'I usually do, but somehow I didn't get around to it and I needed something for tonight's dinner.'

'And what did you buy?'

'The plan was chicken and fresh vegetables, but I got carried away and kept adding things. By the time I'd finished, I could hardly lift the bag. Still, I've enough food to last me several days now.'

'I prefer to buy my food at the supermarket. You can choose for yourself then, but I do understand the appeal of online shopping. Not that I'd know how to do it.'

An easy silence fell between us and it was some time before my companion spoke again.

'This bus is very slow tonight. Traffic's bad, isn't it?'

'Mm. It always seems that way when you need to get home quickly, doesn't it?'

'That's true.'

'I, too, need to get home quickly as my daughter's coming tonight.' The woman wiped a paper tissue across the steamy window and peered out. 'It's still wet and depressing out there.'

'Just about matches my mood.'

'Oh dear. You sound fed up.'

'I can't seem to get pregnant.' My face reddened as soon as the words were out. Why the hell had I said that to a stranger! The woman's eyes and mouth were momentarily frozen in an expression of stunned surprise.

'I'm sorry, I shouldn't have said that. What on earth must you think of me. First I fall asleep on you and now I've poured out my troubles. You must think I'm a complete idiot!'

'No, my dear, you're not an idiot.' The woman smiled, consolingly. 'You're just a normal woman wanting what many women desire.'

'Yes, but to blurt it out like that.' I rubbed my hand across my forehead.

'Does your partner want a baby, too? Oh dear, that sounds insensitive. I shouldn't ask such a personal question.'

'It's okay. It'd be nice to talk to someone other than Tom about it.' My eyes met those of the stranger. 'Tom is my partner and, yes, he supports me… I think. At least, he did at first. He's a good man and is forever telling me that he loves me and wants to protect me. I know he's looking out for me, but lately I wonder whether he's fed up with all my baby talk. Perhaps I've been going on about it a bit too much.'

'You make it sound as though you've been wanting a baby a long time.'

'We've been trying for a baby for well over a year now.'

'That's not long, my dear.' I felt the woman's warm hand cover mine. 'It was five years before my Alice came along.'

'Five years. How on earth did you cope with the waiting?'

'Somehow you do. It takes a little while for some people to conceive. Did your Mum take a long time to conceive you? I've heard that these things can run in families.'

'Don't ask. She's not interested and I doubt she'd tell me.'

'I'm sorry to hear that.'

I shrugged. 'She doesn't like Tom for a start; she thinks he's too old for me. She doesn't think much of me either, if the truth be told.'

'We're not all capable of showing our feelings. Maybe she loves you but is unable to tell you.'

'You don't know my mother.'

'That's true. I spoke out of turn, I'm sorry.'

'Being able to talk to someone openly about these things is therapeutic for me; so please don't be sorry.'

'Have you tried IVF?' The woman smiled encouragingly. 'My niece gave birth to a bouncing baby boy through IVF treatment.'

I could feel tears prickling the back of my eyes. 'We've tried it all, starting with pregnancy hormones, then on to IUI.

We've been told that there's no reason why we shouldn't conceive. Yet month after month, I fail.'

'I'm sorry, but I've no idea what IUI is. When you get to my age, it's difficult to keep abreast of everything.'

'It's quite simple. They place healthy sperm as close to the fallopian tubes as possible. Gives them a bit of a head start in the race towards the egg.'

The woman winced. 'Sounds painful.'

'No, not really. More embarrassing than painful.'

'Poor you.'

I shrugged. 'I hoped it would all be worth it. IVF treatment was the worst; I hated giving myself daily hormone injections.'

'And where are you now with treatments?'

'We've used up our free allowance, so Tom and I are considering whether to pay for additional treatment.' I looked down at my hands, knowing this was a lie. It'd been a one-sided conversation. Tom had absolutely forbidden me to spend any money on 'such stupidity' as he'd eloquently put it.

'I'm presuming your partner had to have tests as well as you?'

'Yes. Tom's fine. Lots of healthy sperm. It's me that's the problem.'

'I think you're judging yourself too harshly. Maybe you simply need to relax more, learn how to deal with the stress of it all. There must be groups set up to help people do this.'

'Yes, there are.' I shuddered, remembering Tom's reaction when I suggested we join a group.

The woman smiled. 'If I were you, I'd seek help. Find those groups that support young women in your position. Go to their meetings, talk it over with like-minded people and try to stop worrying about it. Perhaps that would be your key to success.'

'Maybe you're right. I must do something – even the sight of a pram is enough to send me into floods of tears.'

The woman unexpectedly put her arm around my shoulders. 'I get off at the next stop, but I do wish you every success. I don't think I'll ever forget our conversation and sometime in the future, I'll think of you nursing that baby of yours.'

I looked at the woman who no longer felt like a stranger. 'You're the first person I've ever told about this; you've no idea how helpful you've been.'

'I'm glad. Good luck, my dear.'

I ran my hand over the steamy window and attempted to wave to my companion as she walked along the pavement, but it was too dark. All I could see was my own reflection in the glass.

It was then I noticed the young woman sat in the opposite seat. The woman who was cuddling a tiny baby, swaddled in pink. My nose prickled, signalling the onset of tears if I wasn't careful. I frantically searched about in my mind for a distraction and once more dredged up Tom's impending news. Was he about to leave me?

As soon as I got home, I rushed around, hastily preparing dinner. I'd no wish to infuriate Tom by having nothing prepared when he arrived home.

I was chopping carrots when I heard his key in the door.

'Hello. I'm in the kitchen,' I called, unnecessarily.

I glanced at the chicken pieces in the oven; they'd not yet started to brown, but I doubted Tom would notice. The glass of red wine I'd already poured him would help gloss over the delay.

He put his arm around my waist. 'Hello, my little chickadee. How are you tonight?'

'I'm fine. You?'

'Oh, I'm the same as usual. It's been another busy day. Glad to be home with my gorgeous baby at last.' He kissed my neck and then took a big gulp of wine.

I read somewhere that alcohol diminished the chance of conceiving, so I didn't join our seven o'clock wine ritual nowadays, not that Tom realised.

'Dinner won't be long.' I gave a false smile. 'It's one of your favourites: chicken and braised vegetables.'

'Okay. I think I'll have a long, relaxing bath before dinner,' Tom called over his shoulder, not waiting for a reply.

By the time he returned, the table was laid and the dinner almost ready to be served. I fussed about lighting candles, wondering whether Tom would tell me his important news.

Conversation over dinner was predictable. Tom talked about his work, his football team and the need for me to be more careful with his money. I dearly longed to say 'Whose money?' since I contributed far more than my fair share to our finances, but felt it wise to keep quiet.

Tom drummed his fingers on the table. 'After dinner, you and I need to sit down and talk about a few things.'

My heart sank. So, it was to be tonight.

'Tom, I think I'll have my shower first, if it's okay with you?' I felt any delay was preferable to the news I was about to hear.

'Go ahead. I'll read the paper.' Tom moved from the table, leaving his dirty dishes in situ.

As the hot water blissfully caressed my back, I wondered how I could survive without him. He was the one solid thing in my life. I know he only criticised me when it was necessary, and he obviously loved me or why else would he have supported my wish to have a baby? However, lately, there were times when I felt our relationship was more like that of a father and daughter, except in the sexual sense. At times it annoyed me that he was always the one in charge, always deciding what was right for us.

Tom was still reading the paper when I entered the lounge. My words escaped in a rushing torrent as soon as I sat down.

'Tom, I'm sorry I've talked so much lately about having a baby. I didn't mean to annoy you. I know I've gone on and on about it. It seems to have taken over my life and I know it's selfish. I'm going to change, I promise.'

His perplexed face looked over the top of the newspaper. He hesitated before speaking. 'What on earth are you talking about, sweetheart? My chickadee can be selfish, very selfish, but I don't think you're being selfish over your baby wish. It's what most women want, isn't it? So, tell your Tom, what exactly is this all about?'

'I thought perhaps that you're tired of me talking about babies all the time and I thought that because you already have a child you'd be fed up with—'

'Whoa! There's a lot of *thinking* going on in that sentence. What happened to discussion? Anyway, we've never spoken about my daughter. Have we?'

'No, not properly, but I thought that—'

'There you go again. Stop all this *thinking*.' He patted the empty seat beside him. 'Now, come and sit by me, and for goodness' sake, tell me what started all this.'

'I believe you've become bored with me and want to end our relationship.' I spoke the words with my head bowed, as I didn't dare look at his face.

'I could never be bored with you, but, if you want the truth, I am a little tired of playing second fiddle to a wannabe baby. But I'm about to do something about it, which is one of the things I've been wanting to tell you.'

I looked him full in the face and was met with his familiar hardened expression. It was one of the things I'd loved about him when we first met. It made me feel that he had everything sorted and would look after me.

He smiled as if something good was about to happen and even in that instant, I thought that good for him was likely to be bad for me.

'Kit, I know you want a baby, and I do understand. Before my ex-wife gave birth to Lucy, she spoke of nothing else. She drove me crazy.'

I didn't know what to say as Tom hardly ever spoke of his ex-wife.

'One of the things I want to talk to you about is my daughter, Lucy, but first I've something important to say.' Our eyes met. 'I do sympathise with your wish to give birth, believe me. I've been thinking about it a great deal lately. I've decided that perhaps you should seek another round of IVF, if that's what you want. If you wish to waste your savings on this and if it will make you feel happy, then go ahead. I give you my permission.'

My heart jumped between joy and mystery. Why on earth had Tom changed his mind?

'I thought you'd be pleased, chickadee.' He put his arm around my shoulder. 'Hasn't your Tom made a good decision?'

'Y-yes. I'm just a bit surprised, that's all. You were adamantly against it.'

'I know, but I've been thinking, why should I stop my lovely girl from using her own money to get pregnant if that makes her happy? I'm only thinking about your happiness, Kit. The other thing is that I think you should give up work while you're trying to conceive our baby. They say it's easier for a woman to conceive if she's relaxed and I can't believe that those awful women at work make you feel relaxed, do they?' Tom patted my hand. 'Your Tom will give you all the companionship you could possibly need.'

I put my arms around his neck and kissed his cheek. 'Thank you, Tom.'

'There's time for a better thank you later, chickadee. I've more good news for you. Now I want to talk about Lucy.'

I was once more taken aback. This was turning into a very strange evening.

'You remember I told you that when I divorced Gemma, I lost custody of Lucy. This was down to Gemma's lies at the time. I saw Lucy the other week and she's very unhappy living with her mother and I'm not at all surprised. My ex-wife is a selfish woman. Poor Lucy.' Tom shook his head. 'Anyway, she asked whether she could live with me instead. In fact, she pleaded. She's fifteen now, all grown up. I spoke to Gemma about this and she said she'd be glad to get rid of her. "Goodbye to bad rubbish" was how she put it. Lucy would make a great companion for you, Kit. And just think how helpful she'd be once you have your baby.'

Was I still breathing? My mind whirled and fear padded into my mind as sweat broke out onto my forehead. Every thought had been silenced by the words I'd just heard. I knew nothing of Tom meeting with his daughter or speaking to his ex. In fact, I'd no idea he knew where they lived.

The sound of Tom's voice broke into my trance. '… so, of course I said yes. I told Lucy you'd be thrilled and that you two would be friends, as she likes the same things as you. And who knows, Kit, if this IVF thing still doesn't work, then you have a ready-made daughter ready and waiting.' Tom squeezed my hand and the smile that beamed across his face transformed him from the domineering individual he could be into the man I loved.

'I can't take all this in.' I sought Tom's eyes for comfort. 'What if Lucy doesn't like me?'

'Like you? She'll love you. You're worrying over nothing.' Tom picked up the television remote. 'Let's watch the football, shall we?' He knew I'd no interest in football and would very likely find something else to do once he'd switched it on. 'Oh, I nearly forgot. I phoned your mother the other day.' 'Mother!'

Tom had never phoned my mother, not as far as I knew. Although given the information about contact with his ex and his daughter, I was unsure whether I could rely upon this belief. I didn't trust my legs to support me at that very moment, so I stayed perched on the edge of the sofa.

'Yes. Don't be surprised. She's quite a nice woman, if given a chance. Although I know you two have never got on. Anyway, I thought it was time that I did something about this.'

I didn't think I could take any more of Tom's announcements. What on earth was he about to reveal now?

'I told her that you were seeking IVF because we wanted a baby and d'you know what? She was very understanding. She said if there was anything she could do to help, we only had to ask. Wasn't that nice? She was so sympathetic. Have you ever wondered whether the cause of her drink problem might be you? You know how difficult you can be at times.'

I swallowed hard. I wanted to protest that Mother had always needed alcohol, even when I was a young child, but words failed me. In the last thirty minutes, I'd not only been told of the imminent arrival of Tom's daughter to live with us, but I'd also learned of his contact with his ex and my own mother. That wasn't even taking into account his go-ahead for IVF. My world had become absolutely crazy.

Telling Mother about IVF was something I'd never have done and I wished Tom hadn't said anything, as it only gave her more ammunition to criticise my failures.

My head was spinning as I made my way to the kitchen to clear up. What on earth was I to think? My mind whirled as I began to list all the problems that Tom's daughter living with us would cause. For a start, we didn't have a spare bed and where would she go to school? Perhaps more importantly, how would I get on with the girl? I'd never met Lucy in the flesh; only once seen an old picture of her as a petulant-looking twelve-year-old. Perhaps she wouldn't be happy about her dad having a younger girlfriend.

Robot-like, I dried the dishes and, as I did so, saw a reflection of myself in the glass window. I was smiling a little, a smile with a twist to it, rather like the smile of a child who was determined not to weep.

My stomach clenched with dread; it was as if I'd lost something I'd never be able to find again. There were no adequate words to describe my feelings, for it would be like describing a blank sheet of paper. I recognised in that instant that the bubble I'd believed to be love with Tom had broken; a new, grown-up me was emerging, and when the fragile chrysalis eventually broke free, I hoped that a different woman would be standing in my shoes – one who would be stronger and who would not be manipulated.

I looked at my watch for the umpteenth time as I sat in the reception area of the clinic, waiting for my name to be called. I'd been told that my initial appointment would be with a nurse who was obviously running late. Yet again, I pulled from my bag the copies of all the previous IVF test results that I'd been asked to bring. It was depressing reading. Failure. Failure. Failure. It was a relief when, at long last, I heard my name called.

'Do sit down, Kit. May I call you Kit or would you prefer Miss Langford?' The nurse gave me a tight-lipped smile as she indicated an expensive-looking armchair, which I soon realised sacrificed comfort for the sake of appearance. 'I'm Nurse Amber and we need to go through all the paperwork before you see the consultant. I apologise that we're running late today. It's unusual, I can assure you.' Another tight-lipped smile. 'Have you brought your photographic ID, etc.?'

Kit took the folder of paperwork from her bag. 'I'm not sure why you need my passport.'

'It's just a precaution. We don't want to transfer your embryo cultures to the wrong mummy, do we? A copy of your photograph will be attached to everything we hold about you. If you don't mind waiting just a minute, I'm going to photocopy all this paperwork in readiness for your appointment with the consultant.'

I studied the large Georgian fireplace; the carved centre block of intertwined ribbons and serpents somehow disturbed me. It wasn't helped by the huge Rubenesque figure of a woman that hung over it. She was cuddling a baby and surrounded by half a dozen angelic toddlers, all of whom were gazing at the woman with adoration. Opulence shouted from every part of the room and I could see why this private treatment was going to swallow up almost every penny of my savings.

By the time the nurse had marched back into the room, I'd decided that I didn't like her. Her condescending air seemed to match that of the room itself.

'Now then, here we are, Kit, a few forms for you to sign.' Nurse Amber smiled as she placed a pile of forms in front of me. 'I'll leave you for a few minutes as I expect you wish to peruse them, although most of our mummies give up halfway through. There's so many, you see.'

I'd signed the papers well before Nurse Amber returned to the room, as I'd joined the other 'mummies' by not reading every word. She gathered the papers together and put them in a folder. 'I'm now going to take you to the waiting room of your consultant, Mr Haugh. Once he's looked through your paperwork, he will call you.'

Mr Haugh's waiting room turned out to be even more opulent than the last room. I felt uncomfortable as I perched on the edge of the chaise lounge, wishing Tom had agreed to come with me to this first appointment.

'Do come in, Kit.' Mr Haugh's deep voice broke into my daydreaming.

He waited for me to seat myself in the chair on the opposite side of his desk before speaking. 'First of all, may I welcome you to our clinic. My name is Mr Haugh. I'm one of the gynaecologists and IVF specialists at this clinic. In choosing us, you've made a wise decision. We have over seventy per cent success rate and, as you're a relatively young woman, I believe we might soon be able to add you to the list.'

I felt this introductory speech had been said a million times before.

'I can see that you must have extensive experience and knowledge of IVF and how it works, so I won't labour you with more details. Why don't you ask me anything you'd like explained? We have thirty minutes, so plenty of time for me to reassure you or expand on anything.'

Throughout the entire procedure at the NHS Fertility Clinic, I'd only seen my consultant for less than ten minutes in total, so the thought of thirty minutes in the company of a fertility expert threw my mind into confusion. Before I'd arrived, dozens of important or, what I considered, intelligent questions had been racing through my mind. I wish I'd written them down as the overwhelming opulence of the building had spun my mind into a total blank, which resulted in Mr Haugh explaining procedures that I was familiar with. I sat, staring, smiling or nodding like a simpleton.

Thirty minutes later, as I stood outside the building, I studied a diagram that Mr Haugh had drawn for me. Its meaning had been crystal clear during the appointment, but now it didn't make an ounce of sense.

When I arrived home later that afternoon, I felt emotional and was surprised to see Tom sitting on the sofa. The sight of him released my inner voice.

'I thought you had a work appointment this afternoon and couldn't come with me to the clinic?' My tone was accusatory.

'I did, Kit. I did.' Tom rose and put his arm around my shoulder. 'It was cancelled and I didn't know where the clinic was, or I would have joined you.'

'Why didn't you text me?'

'Didn't think of it.' Tom shrugged and his hardened expression told me this was the end of the conversation.

I escaped to the bathroom where I stifled the ugly tears that threatened. When I returned to the lounge, Tom was in a genial mood and held a glass of red wine out to me even though he must know alcohol was off limits right now.

'Here you are, Kit. You deserve this.' He took a sip from his own glass and put my glass on the coffee table.

'Thank you.'

'Now, tell me, chickadee, when does your Tom have to go to the clinic to do his bit towards this baby of ours?'

A warm feeling overcame me and I thought he must care after all. 'I said you'd ring and make an appointment for the initial consultation.'

'That's fine. I'm not expecting any problems.' Tom grinned. 'You know me, I ooze healthy sperm. The last clinic told us that all my sperm parameters are normal. Why, fathering Lucy is total proof, isn't it?'

I quickly picked up my wine glass and made my way to the kitchen sink, where the offending liquid would be poured. Tom hadn't meant to hurt me, I felt sure, but nevertheless it had hurt and I hadn't known how to reply.

I was chopping cabbage for dinner when Tom put his head around the kitchen door. 'Kit, I've arranged for Lucy to come and live with us from next weekend.'

I knew he'd told me this so that I could organise the bedroom once the new bed arrived. I wanted to scream but gave Tom the only answer he expected. 'Yes, that's fine.'

'Good.' Tom smiled. 'You remember I told you the other day I'd phoned your mother? She rang today and wanted you to call her about the IVF. She seemed quite excited about the prospect of being a grandma. She wants to talk to you about it.'

I frowned. It'd been a strange day and it seemed set to continue. My mother telephoning didn't make sense. Mother never rang. Why had she done that? And then again her reaction to becoming a grandma, if indeed I could trust what Tom said.

I nodded and continued to chop the carrots. I decided I'd not call Mother; I'd enough on my plate as it was. Lucy would arrive within the week and my life with two was about to become three.

Something I did not relish.

Could I have handled the Lucy situation better? If so, I've no idea how. I only know that within a few weeks of Lucy moving in, my relationship with the girl reached deadlock. It didn't start well for on the very first night Tom told her that I was undergoing IVF so that he could have another child. 'And this time,' he sneered, 'we hope it's a boy.'

My cheeks turned strawberry red, knowing this was a complete lie. Lucy displayed a blank expression and I felt sorry for the girl. It seemed cruel to be told on the first night under her father's roof that he wished for another child and this time wanted a boy.

The quiet teenager that arrived that first night changed into a surly, confrontational individual as the weeks went by. I found it difficult to know how to handle this rebellious fifteen-year-old and started to read books on the subject, none of which helped. One of the hardest things to accept was that Tom always sided with his daughter when disputes arose, which they often did.

The Friday of the seventh week was the beginning of real problems. Tom had left for work by the time it was necessary to persuade Lucy to get up and get ready for school. Tom always missed the early morning fireworks and I sensed that he didn't want to know about it. If, later, I foolishly tried to tell him the problem, he always changed the subject as quickly as possible or alternatively he became angry.

'I'm not going to school today,' Lucy announced when I tried to encourage her out of bed that morning.

'You haven't a choice, Lucy, but it's the end of the week so you'll soon have the whole weekend free.'

'Free! Is that what you call living with you and Dad?'

'You chose to come and live with us.'

'Come and live with Dad, maybe. Not you.'

I bit my bottom lip to hold back my rising anger. 'Whether or not you want to live with me makes no difference. You still must go to school, so get up, get dressed and I'll give you a lift on my way to work.'

'No.'

The word sent a shiver down my spine. We'd had many spats during the past few weeks, but the defiant 'no' hadn't been used before. I was at a loss to know the next move, since I could hardly manhandle her out of bed and, in any case, Lucy would very probably win the tussle.

'No is a word that I do not accept. So, get up.'

'No.' Lucy stuck out her chin and glared at me. 'You can't make me. You've no right; you're not my mum.'

'I know I'm not your mum as you've told me this at least a dozen times since you moved in. But if you don't go to school, you'll never pass exams and then how will you get work?'

'Don't care.'

'What do you mean you "don't care"? It's important.'

'No, it's not.'

I sighed inwardly. 'Your dad said you want to be a hairdresser. You won't get onto a college course if you haven't any exams.'

'Will.'

'Of course you won't.'

'My friend Angel did, so what d'you know about it?'

I could feel a tic beginning in the corner of my eye and knew I had to leave before I became very angry. 'Lucy, I'm not going to stand here arguing with you. I must leave for work and either you come with me or you tell your dad tonight why you didn't. It's up to you.'

I turned and walked out of the bedroom, carefully stepping over the many clothes strewn over the floor. I was tired of picking up Lucy's dirty washing and a week ago had told her to put anything she wanted washed and ironed in the utility linen basket. None of Lucy's dirty clothes had yet appeared in the basket and I sensed another argument would soon be brewing with Tom about what he would consider my lack of motherly instincts.

I wondered whether to call Tom and let him know I'd left Lucy in bed. He'd be angry, probably more with me for being ineffective rather than with his rebellious daughter. No, I didn't need Tom's anger.

-o-

Work that day had gone well and I was sad to be leaving. My colleagues had clubbed together and bought me a pampering kit, beautifully presented in a stylish white gift box. There were lots of unexpected hugs, especially as I'd lost them their bonus payment for last year. It seemed all had been forgiven.

It was pouring with rain again as I walked to the bus stop at the end of that last working day. This English weather knew exactly how to spread misery. Perhaps Tom had been correct in saying that by not working I was more likely to be relaxed, and therefore more likely to get pregnant. Getting soaked in the rain was certainly not relaxing.

It wasn't until I popped into the local supermarket for a packet of sausages that the thought of Lucy surfaced once more. When I got home, I fully expected to see Lucy sprawled in front of the television or playing on her laptop, earphones protecting her from conversation. But when I opened the lounge door, there was no sign of her.

'Surely she isn't still in bed,' I mumbled as I made my way to the kitchen and started to prepare dinner.

I'd been home about five minutes when it struck me that perhaps I ought to make sure Lucy was in her bedroom. It would be of no use calling her as she was bound to ignore me, so I quietly crept to her bedroom and listened at the door. I could hear nothing, so tapped loudly. Still no response. I prepared myself for a confrontational Lucy as I turned the doorknob.

Pushing the door open against the tide of objects behind it, I looked at the mess before me. But where the hell was Lucy? There was no longer an inch of bedroom carpet visible, as piles of open books, some with pages torn out and strewn around, now joined the dirty knickers, sweaty T-shirts and jeans that had littered the floor earlier that day. The only clue that this chaos was made by a human being was the partially filled coffee cups littered about the floor, some of which lay on their side with the contents soaking into the carpet.

It wasn't until I'd tiptoed over the mess that I saw the empty gin bottle peeping out from under the bed. My hand flew to my mouth and it was then I heard the front door slam. I rushed back into the lounge, thinking I'd confront the wilful teenager before Tom got home. I could certainly do without his rage tonight, which could easily grow into a tornado as the blame was sure to be mine. I was surprised to see Tom open the lounge door.

'Hello, Kit. You look as though you've seen a ghost. It's only me, you know.'

I gulped. What on earth was I to say?

'What's the matter, chickadee?' He walked towards me, narrowing his eyes into the cold, hard stare that was so familiar.

My mouth was almost too dry to speak. 'It's Lucy. She's… she's not in her room. She should have been home from school hours ago.'

'Was she okay when you dropped her off at school this morning?'

My heart sank. 'I… I didn't drop her. She wouldn't get up so I had to leave her in bed.'

His bulging eyes glared at me. 'You left her here. Alone! Where's your common sense, you stupid woman? Why didn't you ring me?'

'I almost did.'

'Almost! Almost! Listen to yourself. You stupid cow.' His shout had become a roar.

I heard my shaky voice escape. 'Tom, I didn't mean to—'

His angry voice cut across mine. 'So, where is she? Did she leave a note?'

'I haven't searched yet.'

'Perhaps that's the first thing you should have done.' He strode towards Lucy's bedroom.

'What the hell's this! Look at her room.' Tom stood in the bedroom doorway, scowling at me. 'How the hell did you let it get like this?'

I shook my head. 'I've been telling her to clear it up, but she takes no notice of me.'

'I'm not surprised. Did you offer to help? Show her how to do it? I thought that was what a parent did.'

My voice could hardly be heard. 'But, Tom, I'm not her parent.'

'You ought to be acting like one when I'm not around. Who else does she have to guide her, if not you? Her own mother's a no-good waste of space.'

I studied the floor and gritted my teeth. Violence was already in the air and I knew Tom was far too angry to discuss things rationally. He frightened me and I hoped against hope that he didn't see the empty gin bottle.

He re-entered the bedroom and I heard him throwing things around, the uproar could have been heard next door. Then, abruptly, all was quiet.

He stood in the doorway, the empty bottle in his clenched fist. His eyes fixed on me with blind rage; it was though a fire had swept over him. He didn't raise his voice. At first he didn't move, but my fear of him increased as I looked at his tensed muscles and his face contorted with fury.

Normally I would try to soothe him, mother him and give him whatever would keep the peace, but something inside snapped. That his daughter was living with us wasn't my fault. Neither was the state of the bedroom. I didn't deserve to be on the receiving end of this.

'Tom, I don't think…' But no further words were allowed to escape.

I stumbled backwards when the impact from his clenched fist hit my face. I felt light-headed as my legs gave way and I crumpled to the ground. My vision blurred as tiny droplets of sweat ran down my forehead and joined the tiny river of blood that trickled from my nose.

The pain in my ribs from Tom's booted foot made me scream, which unleashed his tornado of anger. He pinned my arms to the floor and knelt on them painfully.

'You! You think you're so prim and proper, don't you? You can't even look after a fifteen-year-old properly.' His voice rose to crescendo. 'You don't deserve to have a baby of your own. You're a nothing. A waste of space.'

I was too frightened to cry as I looked up at his mottled crimson face and popping eyes, yet even in that instance the forced phlegm that he drew from the back of his throat and forcibly ejected over my face shocked me.

'You think you're better than my daughter, don't you? Don't you? You don't care where she is right now. You're a worthless piece of shit, and you'll never be any good.'

He snarled and clambered to his feet, drawing his foot back for a second attack.

'Tom. Tom. I…' but the words froze as his boot made contact with my ribs. I stifled a sob with the back of my hand.

'Get up. Get up! You lazy cow. Get this place cleaned up.' His gaze was unwavering as he glared down at me. There was no pity in his expression and I began to fear for my life.

It was then the phone rang, which seemed to awaken something in him, tampering his incandescent rage. He slammed the phone against the coffee table and immediately marched towards the front door.

I lay on the carpet for some time after the door slammed. My heart raced and my uncontrollably shaking limbs caused my teeth to chatter. He'd won this physical battle, but that'd been a foregone conclusion. However, I knew in the victory every ounce of love I thought I'd had for him vanished forever. I had to get away from him. And quickly.

Painfully, I moved to a crouching position. There wasn't a single area of my body that didn't hurt and I wondered whether I'd broken a rib as with each breath, hot knives pierced my chest.

I shuddered, remembering the terrible things Tom had threatened to do to me if I ever left him. Would he do these things to Lucy if he found her? Although we hadn't got on, she didn't deserve being permanently disfigured by her own father. I decided to search for any clue that might help me find Lucy before her father did.

Twenty minutes later, I found an address book in Lucy's room. One that the girl must have started many years before because the handwriting was spidery and uncontrolled. On the inside page was a scrawled address and providing 'Mum' hadn't moved, it seemed a good place to start.

When the concerned taxi driver pulled up outside the dilapidated house that might belong to Lucy's mum, his face dropped.

'Are you sure you want me to drop you here, Miss? If you take my advice, you'd be better off at A&E right now. The Great Northern is only just down the road. Let me take you there.'

'No. It's okay.' I handed him a £20 note and hoped it was enough, because barring a few small coins, it was all the money I had.

The house was in the middle of a terrace and looked as though it could do with a total refurbishment, as the windows were covered in a black-coloured fungus, which had rotted away much of the wooden frame. The door didn't look much better and I winced as I reached to press the bell.

I saw the curtains move in the front window. My heart dipped and, with it, a clammy glistening of cold sweat appeared on my forehead. Perhaps Tom was here. Why on earth hadn't that thought occurred to me before?

Whoever was peeping around that curtain obviously didn't want to open the door and I couldn't blame them. I'd be suspicious if an unknown woman with a swollen cheek and puffy lips caked in dried blood stood outside my front door.

I rang again, keeping the bell pressed for a long time. I hoped that whoever was inside would realise I'd no intention of going away.

The door inched open and hesitantly a thin woman peered around the half-open door. She frowned. 'Yes? What d'you want?'

'Are you Lucy's mum?'

'Who's asking?' Her voice was challenging.

'I'm Kit. Is Lucy here?'

'What's that to you?'

'She's been staying with Tom and me, but today she left. I'm looking for her as I'm worried.'

'You're that Kit, are you? Kit Langford?' I nodded. Where was this was leading?

'I did wonder. You look just as Tom described you. Small, thin and boring. I didn't know he'd made such a good job of beating you up, though.'

I didn't need this and struggled to remain civil. 'So is Lucy here? Is she okay?'

She stared at me with narrowed eyes.

'So, is she here?' My voice sounded stronger than I felt.

'Questions. Questions. The doorstep is hardly the place to discuss these things.'

The woman stood to one side and nodded to let me pass.

'Sit down.' It was a command rather than an invitation.

My eyes scanned the room. The sofa was placed against the far wall. The space was surprisingly clean and tidy with a huge television in the corner and a single armchair pulled in front of it.

The woman turned the armchair and sat facing me. 'How did you find this address? I bet you thought this was going to be a bit of a dive, didn't you? Tom said you like things to be posh. A bit hoity-toity is how he described you.'

'For crying out loud, who the hell are you?' My steely voice surprised me.

'I'd no idea that you'd a bit of spirit about you. Tom didn't mention that bit. I thought he'd have knocked that out of you by now.'

'How d'you know Tom?'

'I'm Gemma. Tom's my husband.'

'You mean ex-husband.'

Gemma's head jerked back and she laughed uproariously. 'Is that what he told you? He usually tells his women that I died tragically.'

A silence settled over the room and I felt my face crumple. I bit my lips together and the pain made me flinch. This must be a nightmare.

'I don't… I can't believe you.' The words dribbled out. 'How do I know you're telling me the truth?'

'I don't care whether you believe me or not, but no matter what he's told you, Tom and I are married. One hundred per cent married. We're not divorced and, as you can see, I'm one hundred per cent alive. You've been duped, but you're not the only woman he's deceived and you won't be the last either, if that makes you feel better.'

All thoughts were driven from my head. I had absolutely no idea what to say.

'I can see this is a shock for you.' Gemma hesitated a minute before continuing, 'I don't usually do this, but you seem a nice woman, a bit better than the kind he usually snares. I'm going to level with you. Since the early days of our marriage, Tom has wandered off now and then, usually for a few months at a time. He reports home occasionally and normally tells me all about his latest conquest. I'm not fond of these visits, mind you, because he usually beats me up. It's a warning, you see, not to get ideas of escape. Plus it's how he gets his kicks.' I shook my head.

'Tom said you were a bit of an innocent. Now I know what he means. Judging by your face, I can see Tom's been getting violent lately. That usually signals he has total control of the relationship. He's happy then. It means he can come and go or bash you about whenever he wants – that is, until he's fed up with you. He knows you'll be too scared to leave him. He'll make sure of that.'

'I don't know what to believe.'

'That's up to you. I'm in the same boat as you, so why should I lie?' She rolled up her sleeve and held out her arm. 'Look, this is one of the things he'll do if you try to leave him.'

I winced. Multiple circular cigarette scars covered her entire arm. 'Why don't you report him to the police?'

Gemma laughed. 'It isn't that easy. I've got to think of Lucy. He leaves her alone at the moment and I want it to remain that way until she's old enough to escape.'

'But there must be something you can do?'

'You try it and see what happens. He came here about an hour or so ago and he's gone to the pub right now. He told me you were a lazy slut and didn't clean things up. He also said you hadn't paid the rent, but as it's in your name, he isn't worried.'

'But only last week I gave him enough rent money for three months.'

Gemma shrugged. 'All I can say is more fool you then.'

'And Lucy, what about Lucy?'

'Lucy came home to me. She's upstairs right now.'

'I… I thought she didn't get on with you and wanted to be with Tom?'

'Well, that's Lucy for you. Blows hot and cold, just like her father.'

I shook my head, not knowing what to say. The realisation that I'd been totally deceived had yet to dip me into the depression and wariness of men that would last for a very long time.

I stared at Gemma. 'But don't you mind, mind that…' the words stumbled over one another.

'Are you trying to ask me whether I mind that he has other women?'

I nodded.

'No. Why should I? When he's gone, it's not me that's on the end of the violence. You know what a controlling man he is and if eventually his woman rebels, that's when the trouble starts. He broke the arm of one conquest.'

Had I just woken in an asylum? I couldn't have been any more confused. In the space of a few hours, I'd been plunged into madness. It was sinking in that Tom had never cared about me. It was never love; he'd never loved me. Yet his words had been spoken softly. Such beautiful lies. Lies I'd believed – I'd wanted to believe, needed to believe – but throughout it all, he had kept the keys of control firmly in his pocket. Could there be anything worse than deceitful love? Even Mother had never lied to me about a love she'd never felt for me.

Gemma stood. 'You'd better go. I don't want Tom to catch you here or we'll both be in trouble and you don't look as though you'd survive any more injuries today. I'd get home as quick as you can and make sure the flat is spic and span for when he returns. He won't be back for a couple of days and he's usually all sweetness and love when he returns after a beating, so you'll be okay at first.'

Before reaching the front door, Gemma paused and turned to me. 'Just a spot of advice, one woman to another.

I'm not sure how far down the fertility route you are right now, but if I were you, I'd ask that clinic of yours if they can undo any success they might have had.'

I felt my mouth drop open.

'He told me all about it. But it's not been as above board as you imagine and he's been laughing behind your back.' Gemma hesitated. 'You see, Tom had a vasectomy years ago.'

'But…'

'Yes, I know he's been playing the wannabe father game with you. He's done it before. I think it makes him feel all powerful, but he can't be a father again. It's not possible.'

'You're lying. What about the semen tests? He's plenty of sperm.'

'No, those aren't his. They belong to his brother.'

'Brother!'

'They're identical twins, so it's easy for his brother to attend the clinic on his behalf. They've done it before, thinking they're proper Jack the Lads. They're both bad 'uns. I sometimes wish somebody would kill them both.' She stared at me. 'This must all be a shock for you, but learn from it.' And with these words, she banged the front door, leaving me standing on the pavement.

The stunned silence was so thick you could've spread it on toast. My limbs moved slowly and my body slid down the closed door. My eyes flooded with tears as an incessant ringing started in my ears. I must have fainted, but I've no recollection of anything until I began to come round. I was in a moving vehicle, my teeth chattering and my body hurting in so many places that I couldn't start to describe the pain. Then, I became aware of worried eyes watching me from the driver's mirror. 'You okay, Miss?'

I nodded slowly. How on earth did I come to be in the back of a car? Then, I realised it wasn't a car, it was a taxi – the same taxi I'd hailed to get to Gemma's house.

I screwed up my eyes and attempted speech. 'How? Where?'

'Don't worry, Miss. You're okay. D'you remember me? I drove you to that hovel – I can't describe it as a house.'

I swallowed hard, hoping the moisture would restore the power of speech. 'I thought you'd gone.'

'Well, Miss. I saw you go in the house, but I didn't like the look of the woman who let you in. What with her and the house itself,
I was a bit concerned, so I thought I'd wait for a bit.'

'Where are we g…' my voice petered out.

'Where we should have gone in the first place. A&E.'

'But—'

'No buts. You need medical attention and that's where I'm going to take you.'

I sank back in the seat, too weary to argue.

'I'm going to personally escort you to the emergency department, and I will wait for you and drive you home afterwards. Unless they keep you in, of course.'

'That's very kind, but I can't pay you.'

'That's alright, Miss. I don't want money. Think of it as my good deed for the day. I have a daughter about your age and I'd like to think that someone would help her if they found her in a similar position.'

-o-

I was in the hospital for quite some time that evening. They suspected physical abuse and encouraged me to report the assault to the police, but fear of Tom made me deny their suspicions.

Bandaged and bruised, the taxi driver carefully helped me into the back of his car and drove me home. The good thing was Tom hadn't broken my ribs, although when my good Samaritan gave me a gentle hug before he left, I pressed my lips together to swallow the pain.

'Here's my card.' He held out a small, white card. 'They're handmade – nothing posh, I'm afraid – but I'm a one-man band and, well, you know what it's like.'

'You've been so kind. I can't thank you enough.'

'Just use my taxi whenever you want to travel and, more importantly, get rid of the bloke who did this to you.'

I smiled weakly. Supporting his taxi would be easy. Getting rid of Tom would be a totally different matter.

My hand shook as I attempted to put my key in the front door and despite Gemma telling me Tom wouldn't be home for a few days, I couldn't help feeling he might be inside. An audible sigh of relief filled the lounge when I realised I was alone. I poured myself a brandy and headed for bed. Tonight, I needed sleep; tomorrow, I would plan my escape.

Next morning, I awoke from the nirvana of escape that painkillers and alcohol had induced. I became aware of the day stretching out before me; I was rudderless and felt acutely alone. Gemma's words were the first to hit my conscious mind and pasting a tight-lipped smile on my face I made my way to the bathroom. With the smile firmly fixed, I broke the expensive small phials of fertility drugs and allowed the liquid to drain away down the sink. A sudden involuntary intake of breath filled the silent room as the unused injection needles and syringes joined the broken glass in the bin. I avoided looking in the mirror as I had no wish to be reminded of my swelling cheek, which I knew would be glistening with falling tears. Was I crying for my unborn baby, the money I'd wasted or myself? I didn't know.

The exertion of crying brought on a nasty sharp jabbing pain in my chest and I hugged my body tenderly, willing the pain to go away. This was no good; I had to get myself together and plan.

An hour later, my packed suitcase stood in the hallway, waiting. I'd no wish to take anything that would remind me of Tom, so the case was going to be a light burden to carry. The problem was: where could I go?

I didn't have enough money to rent a different flat. I shook my head, knowing that the fertility treatment had cost me dearly. I no longer had any close friends – Tom had seen to that. My brother was unlikely to welcome me with open arms and, in fact, I was no longer sure where he lived. The idea of returning to Mother appalled me. Could I endure the jibes and comments about yet another failure? Though living with an increasingly dominant and now extremely violent partner was unbearable, too.

I stood inert. What the hell could I do? I kept replaying in my head different scenarios that had taken place between myself and Lucy; maybe if I'd approached things differently, been able to talk with the girl instead of always arguing with her, perhaps then it would have been different.

Time was passing and I knew the time for dithering was over. I'd already swallowed way over the recommended dose of paracetamol and if I didn't move soon, my head would be too fuzzy to take command of my limbs.

My shaking hand dialled the number.

That I'd no option but to flee to Mother's house shows the desperation of my situation. However, she was about to surprise me in ways I could never have imagined and at long last I'd catch a glimpse of the woman who gave birth to me.

Mother's expression matched the straight-laced woman stood on the doorstep and my heart sank. She seemed about to speak, but then swallowed whatever words she was about to say and instead reached out and cradled me in her arms. Could this possibly be Mother? I don't remember her ever hugging me before. I'd no idea what to think.

I wiped my shoes on the doormat and slunk past Mother, not looking left nor right. When I'd phoned earlier, it was as though she'd been expecting the call and her voice had been friendly. Now, with this greeting, I felt uncomfortable. Everything was weird.

I stood in the hallway, clutching my bag. 'I'm sorry I had to come. I'd nowhere else to go. I won't stay long, just until I can get on my feet. I promise.' The garbled words streamed out.

'Don't worry, Kit. You can stay as long as you want. I've been expecting you since Tom's recent visits and his call last night, but he certainly underestimated the extent of your injuries. That cheek of yours looks very painful. Have you seen a doctor?'

That Mother used the plural of 'visit' wasn't lost on me. I'd no idea he'd even visited once. And as for the 'extent of my injuries', what on earth could Tom have said? My heart plunged. Could there be more lies to uncover? I wasn't sure I could take more.

'I've bought spaghetti bolognese at the supermarket to microwave for our dinner tonight. I don't do home-cooking much – you'll remember I was always rubbish at it.' Mother smiled, although 'smile' wasn't quite the right description. There was a faint curve to her lips, but there was no movement of the cheeks and no crease below the eyes. I thought that on anyone else it might be regarded as a grimace, at best, but on Mother it was a sign of happiness. 'Shall we eat at about seven?'

'Yes, that's fine.' Was this conversation happening? 'I think I'll unpack now, if that's okay with you?'

'I'll show you your room.' Another grimace smile appeared. 'Shall we watch TV together before dinner tonight? That is, if you want, Kit. Not if you don't.'

I was glad to escape to the bedroom, as I was beginning to feel I'd walked from one crazy situation into another. What on earth was Mother up to? I'd never known her to behave like this.

It was sometime later, when we were sat awkwardly in the lounge, that I realised Mother hadn't reached for the alcohol since I'd arrived. I had to say something, I couldn't help myself.

'Mother, you're not drinking. Not even a glass of wine.'

'You're right, Kit. My drinking days are behind me. It was out of hand for a very long time. I had to do something about it. My entire adult life, I let alcohol be my crutch.'

'So, what happened. Why now?'

'Live or die. It was as simple as that. I couldn't stop my body violently shaking and then I started vomiting blood. The doctors said I'll always tremble now, but it's nothing compared to how bad it was before. After the hospital tests, the consultant told me that I have cirrhosis and my liver is significantly scarred.'

'So will giving up alcohol reverse the damage?'

'No, it can never be reversed, but if I don't drink, it'll slow its progression. So that's a positive move. I joined AA last year. Best thing I ever did.'

An awkward silence returned and then we both spoke at once. 'Kit, do you see anything of J—'

'You've made this room very ni... Oh, sorry, you go first.'

'I was only going to ask whether you'd seen anything of Jess lately?'

'Haven't seen him for ages.'

Mother's voice took on a sharp edge. 'He came here a couple of months ago. He told me that your father's doing well with his new woman. Apparently, she's half his age. He said that the pair of them are living in style. Your father's bought a place in Spain and they spend the winter there. It's okay for some, isn't it?'

'But you're okay here, aren't you, Mother? This is a cosy little place and I've never seen you looking so well.'

'Yes, I'm okay here. I've got everything I need and it's your father I need to thank for that. He still supports me financially, albeit a pittance. I suppose I should be more generous in my judgement.'

'Is Jess doing well?'

'When did Jess ever not do well? He manipulates people to give him exactly what he wants. He's fine. Still working in London doing something important, of course. Or so he tells me.'

'What about Lily?'

'She's still around. He says she's okay. Anyway, she's a sharp one. When they do eventually break up, she'll have squirrelled away enough money to do more than just survive.'

'I think he met his match with Lily.'

'It's amazing she puts up with his affairs, but then maybe she has affairs of her own. And I can talk! I turned a blind eye to your father's women for years.'

'Did Jess visit for anything in particular? Social visiting seems out of character somehow, especially after the way you…' My voice trailed away.

'The way I treated you both. Go on, Kit, say it. It's true and it's not something I'm proud of. Alcohol ruled my life. It was more important to me than my children.'

'I'm sorry, I shouldn't have started that sentence.'

'It's okay. Nowadays, I accept myself for what I am, but I can't expect forgiveness from others.' Mother smiled, weakly. 'You're right, social visiting doesn't sit well on Jess's shoulders. To be honest, I think he visited to make sure I wasn't dead. He had a bit of a shock, I can tell you. I'm sure he thought I'd be staggering about the floor in a drunken stupor.' I laughed and Mother joined in.

'No, honestly, you should have seen his face when I told him I attend Alcoholics Anonymous every week. It was a picture. He didn't stay long. I'm not the parent with the money, so I'm not important to him. It's Father he sucks up to; he's got to keep in with him.'

'I imagine Jess might be worried about Father's women. What if he marries one of them? Then there'd be no inheritance money coming his way.'

'That's true and what if there was a baby? Ooh, I can see sparks flying then.' She looked me straight in the eye. 'How would you feel if that happened, Kit? Would you mind if there wasn't any money for you?'

I shrugged. 'I haven't thought much about it. Money isn't something I chase. I like to live comfortably, doesn't everyone? But masses of wealth. No. It's not me.'

'I should never have married your father. You know that, don't you? We were never suited, not really, but it was a case of needs must.' Mother sighed. 'It's amazing how you fool yourself when young.'

I frowned and thought of Tom, but immediately tried to dismiss him from my mind. The memory was too raw.

'I messed up all our lives, didn't I?'

I took her hand and momentarily squeezed it. 'We all have our paths to make. As adults, Jess and I had choices. You had nothing to do with those.'

'No, but had I given you both a better start, you might have chosen differently. Anyway, I want to make up for it now. I have ideas, Kit. Ideas to help you.'

The paracetamol I'd taken earlier was wearing off and I winced as the pain in my cheek came pounding back.

'Oh, Kit, you poor thing. Perhaps it'd be best to have an early night. I can tell you my ideas tomorrow.' She patted my hand. 'You look tired and you can't possibly have got over the shock of the attack yet, let alone everything else. That cheek of yours looks so swollen and painful.'

'Attack?' What had Tom told her?

'Tom told me, but said you'd rather put it behind you.'

'It was a shock, I admit. I didn't expect it.'

'Well, who does expect to be attacked, especially in broad daylight? Were there any witnesses?'

'Witnesses?' I was now sure that whatever Tom had said was nowhere near the truth. 'Mother, I was beaten up at home. It was Tom that did it.'

She sat down and shook her head as though my words were incomprehensible. 'Tom?'

'Yes. Tom.'

'But why?'

'His controlling personality has been getting worse. I will tell you all about it, but not tonight.'

'I'm so sorry, Kit. I'd no idea.'

'I'm not surprised – Tom's an expert liar. Should he phone, don't let him know I'm here, no matter what he says.'

'I'm not afraid of him, Kit.' Her voice raised a notch. 'Just let him try anything and he won't know what's hit him.'

'I need to find a way to leave him and it's best he doesn't know where I am until I've figured it out.'

'I don't understand. You're not married or anything. You can go wherever you want.'

'He's threatened to kill me if I walk out. I've seen the cigarette burns on his wife's arms and she told me that he broke the arm of another woman who tried to leave him.'

'Oh my God! The man's a sadist.'

'Yes, he is. Trouble is, he's saddled me with debts as well.' I felt my lip tremble. 'I don't know where to turn, to be honest, and I'm scared.'

Mother pulled herself up tall. 'Well, I know where to turn and I know who can sort him out. Your father has many contacts – contacts that Tom will not like. Don't you worry; once some of your father's men have visited Tom, he won't be bothering you again. Mark my words. And as for debts, they'll be paid, and if Tom can't pay them with money, he'll be forced to pay in other ways. He's going to be very sorry for the way he's treated you.'

She shakily reached for my hand and this movement gave me the courage to think that maybe there could be a future after all. We embraced, holding each other tightly, and it was the moment when love between mother and daughter finally arrived.

MOTHER

Although it had been wonderful spending time with Kit, I wished the circumstances could have been different. I was shocked when she rang, asking if she could stay a few days, and when I saw the state of her face, I had to hold back tears of pity. And as her terrible story unfolded, I felt my gut clench with anger against Tom and with myself for not having been there to help her.

Next morning, when she entered the kitchen, I noticed a tinge of pink had returned to the unbandaged side of her face and she looked a little brighter. I had buttered a small pile of crumpets and placed them in the middle of the table, alongside the toast and jams. But she said she only wanted coffee as she didn't eat breakfast, which reinforced how little I knew about my grown-up daughter. We sat opposite sides of the small kitchen table awkwardly, half-smiling if we caught the other's eye.

Eventually, she broke the silence. 'Let's go out. Let's celebrate.'

'Celebrate what?'

'Us.'

'D'you feel up to it? What about your face?'

'To be honest, my ribs hurt far more than my face this morning. But I'm not advocating a hike to the top of Everest, just a leisurely stroll to the park and maybe a little lunch in some quiet little restaurant.'

'I haven't done anything like that for years.'

And so it was that we spent the day together. We didn't do anything particularly exciting. It was a simple day where two people enjoyed each other's company for the first time ever. Neither of us probed the past and the issue of present problems was left buried for now. In fact, it wasn't until much later that evening, after the television had been switched off, that any remotely difficult conversation was resumed. I made mugs of hot chocolate and brought them into the lounge.

I plunged into the subject on my mind. 'You remember I said I had ideas, Kit? I know it's early days, but d'you think it might be wise to have a conversation about the baby?'

Her eyes widened. 'The baby?'

'Yes. I hate to mention his name, wicked man, but Tom told me all about the IVF, and I'm so pleased for you. I was only too sorry that I couldn't give you any more money towards it. I hope the little I gave helped a bit. At least Tom managed to get the remainder together in the end, so that was good.' I gave her a huge smile. 'It seems to me that congratulations are in order.'

She frowned. 'I'm not sure about that.'

'Kit, bringing a baby into this world is an amazing thing, believe me. And now Tom's no longer around to help you, I will, if you'll let me. It'll be wonderful to help with what will be my first grandchild.'

'But Mother—'

'No, don't say anything. Not yet. I want to tell you something. Giving birth is one of the most amazing things in the world; he or she will always be yours, no matter what happens. There'll be a bond that will be impossible for anyone to break.'

'But—'

'Shush, Kit. Let me finish. This is difficult. What I'm trying to say is that a long time ago, before you were born, I lost a baby.'

'Oh, Mother, I'd no idea. I'm so sorry.'

'It's a long time back and I stopped crying about it many years ago. There's nothing that can be done. It's life. It happens. But as a mother, you never forget, even as an alcoholic mother. Sometimes, in bleak moments, I've felt my memories impossible to bear and I'm sure it coloured the way I behaved with you and Jess. Even now, I think of the child that I might have held.

Thoughts of the baby I lost don't go away, they never will.' She looked at me as though I was mad.

I continued, 'So, I say to you, Kit, don't get rid of this baby just because Tom's no longer around to help you. You'll regret it forever.'

'Mother, I have to say—'

I held up the palm of my hand. 'Stop, Kit. Stop. I know we haven't had a great relationship so far, but please don't judge me by what I did years ago. I was a bad mother, but I've learned and I'm a different person now, surely you can see that. Let me help you. Please.'

A quietness descended.

She looked me in the eye. 'I don't know what Tom's told you, but the truth is I'm not pregnant.'

'Not pregnant.' My voice was barely audible.

'No. I've never been pregnant. I finished two programmes of IVF with the NHS, neither of which was successful, and I'd been looking into a private programme – in fact, I had the first appointment. However, yesterday I threw away all the fertility drugs they gave me. I no longer want to be pregnant. I paid for the treatment with my own money; Tom didn't give me a penny towards it.' I could feel hot tears welling up in my eyes. 'I'm sorry to say, Tom is not the man I thought, as I believe you're beginning to see. He's handsome all right, but inside he's vile.' My tears suddenly burst like a dam.

'Kit. I'd no idea. Don't cry. Don't cry. No man's worth it.'

'I'm not… I'm not… crying… over Tom,' her hiccupy voice sputtered. 'I'm crying for me. I've been a complete idiot.'

We hugged until her tears subsided and then I made my way to the kitchen, returning with two large glasses of brandy, plus the bottle.

'Here, drink this. You need it.'

Her shocked face drove away the remaining tears. 'But you're not supposed to drink alcohol.'

'No – however, this is an emergency, Kit. Your brother left this bottle just in case I ever needed it. And today, I think we both do.' I could feel tears gathering and sat on the sofa besides Kit, so she could only see a profile of my face. I'm not sure how long we sat there in the semi-darkness, but I know our physical closeness brought some kind of peace, and after we'd consumed another glass of brandy, I felt it was time to confess everything as I realised I'd misled Kit earlier, just as I had done all her life. It was time to come clean. I looked ahead, not wishing to see her reaction to my confession.

'Kit, I've something I need to tell you, something I'm not proud of, but it goes a long way to explain why I treated you as I did when you were a child. Earlier, I told you I'd lost a baby, and that is true, but I lost it in a way you might not imagine. She didn't die. My daughter was conceived before I married and she doesn't share the same father as you and Jess. She's your half-sister, which, of course, means you're not my eldest child. I was selfish and tricked your father into believing the baby was his. All went well at first, but then my baby's biological father threatened to tell Henry unless I gave him money. I didn't have the amount of money he wanted and decided the only thing I could do was confess everything to Henry. Your father was livid and told me either I gave up the child for adoption or he'd divorce me. I didn't want to lose my baby; I loved her and agonised about my choices, but in the end I felt I'd no choice.

'A few days later, your father suddenly took my baby out of her crib, just after I'd breastfed her. I had no opportunity to say goodbye and I've never seen her since. I'm afraid when you came along a few years later, I resented you. It was as if you'd replaced my first baby and I hated you for it. As you know, I took to alcohol and it was a downward spiral from then on. You have no idea how heartbroken I am about this now, but there are no excuses. I behaved badly. I didn't love you as I should. I wish I could go back, start again; this time I'd make up for everything. You were a sad child and, no thanks to me, you've become such a wonderful adult.
I don't expect you to forgive me, Kit. I've been too wicked for that, but could you see it in your heart to let us start over? I swear I'll be different this time around.'

My shoulders dropped and I felt tears threaten as I turned to Kit. She was slumped back on the sofa, head resting against the pillow, mouth slightly open and eyes closed. She was fast asleep.

A surge of sorrow welled up inside. I'd missed my opportunity to come clean and I didn't think I'd ever be brave enough to say those words again. Now she'd never know.

KIT

The connection between dreaming and reality was very thin and as my mind re-entered the present, confusion covered me like a blanket. Patterns of the sea no longer shimmered on the wall of my balcony as cloud had hidden the sunshine in a menacing darkness.

The television I'd switched on to hear the news still filled the room, but now the image was of someone dancing. I rubbed my eyes and turned to the desk. The small box was still there – its brown paper as pristine as the day it had been handed to me. This was reality. This was now. I only wish I could return to the past and change the course of things, but, of course, it was too late.

Planning on a quiet afternoon with a book, I requested sandwiches be delivered to my room. I hadn't planned on red wine, but I saw the opened bottle on the side and it beckoned to me. So much for plans, because an hour later, my book closed on the bed beside me, I was drifting in and out of sleep. A noise in the corridor outside my room brought me back to the present and then I heard a loud bang on the door.

'I'm sorry,' a frazzled woman cried as I opened it. She immediately pointed to a toddler, who was screaming as he manhandled a large green toy tractor along the corridor. 'He needs L-plates; he's bumping into walls and doors everywhere. Sorry to have disturbed you.'

I nodded and quietly closed the door, realising that dusk was falling and, judging by my fuzzy head, I'd drunk too much wine. It was time to walk around the ship and clear my head.

I was tempted to listen to the serene piano music when I arrived on deck eight, but the thought of bumping into Jess made me seek a quieter area. I took the lift to the upper deck and, in the everincreasing blackness of the night, made my way to the floodlit starboard rail. For some inexplicable reason, I found the smell of the ocean comforting, akin to summer holidays spent on the beach back home.

It was then I spied the figure nestled in a deckchair. How on earth could fate have engineered our paths to cross yet again?

'Hi, Lou. We meet again.'

'Kit, this is amazing. I can't believe we keep bumping into each other. Anyone would think we were on a small ferry, not a giant ship.'

'Where are your friends?'

'Can't you guess?' Lou smiled. 'They're on a manhunt. They started in the champagne bar and they were drinking shots when I left them.'

'I must admit I've been drinking wine. I've had a little too much, to be honest, although it could be that I haven't had much to eat all day.'

Lou gave a cheeky wink. 'Sometimes too much wine is good for a person, eh? In my book, there are times when it's necessary. It's a bit expensive to buy on board, though. I've been sticking to drinking beer.'

I'd forgotten that I enjoyed a privileged lifestyle on board and felt a little shamefaced. I hoped Lou didn't think I was showing off.

I changed the subject. 'I love the smell of the sea, don't you? It reminds me of summer holidays.'

'Oh, yes. Sand between your toes, fish and chips, seagulls and all that stuff. It seems such a long time ago that I went on a beach holiday.'

'Me, too, come to think of it.'

She waved her hand towards the invisible distance. 'It's so quiet on deck at this time of night. I love it. This ocean seems to have gone to sleep. I can hardly hear the movement of the sea.'

'Long may it last.'

'Is this a holiday for you, Kit? Or are you on some important mission, James Bond-style?' The laughter in Lou's voice was obvious.

'Definitely the 007 variety.'

We both laughed.

'Kit, that was nosey of me. Didn't mean to pry.'

'It's okay. I've nothing to hide. I'm quite a boring person.'

'You do yourself down.' She shook her head. 'I don't think you're at all boring.'

'It's kind of you to say that.'

'Not kind. True. The youngsters I'm with can be boring at times, but I put that down to their age. We're going to New York as a celebration.'

'Celebration?'

'Yes. That's not quite the right description. Amy was jilted, you see. Let down at the altar.'

My face obviously registered shock.

'Yes. At the altar. The bastard! He let her stand there, dressed in her beautiful white bridal dress. Just didn't turn up. Can you imagine how that must feel?'

'Poor Amy.'

'That's what we all say. So this little holiday is a celebration. A celebration to be rid of him. He was never any good, we always knew that, but you can't exactly say it to her, can you? Especially when she thought he was wonderful and that they were in love.'

I nodded and my thoughts were forced back to a similar man that once viewed large in my own life. 'Is she over him now?'

'Who knows, but she realises it's time to move on. Honestly, we're not a man-hunting group, it's just a bit of fun. We're trying to give Amy a new perspective on life.' Lou sucked air between her teeth before continuing. 'Although, this boat… ship… liner… whatever you want to call it… hasn't quite the abundance of available young men we thought it might have. It seems to bemostly couples or groups. I know the ship's crew are supposed to look after single women, dance with them, you know, all that stuff, but, hey, Amy's young. She needs a little flirting; a young man to let her hair down with; someone who'll tell her she's attractive.' I knew exactly what Lou meant.

'Do you have anyone special in your life, Kit?' Lou's hand fled to her mouth. 'Oh, there I go again. Prying. I'm sorry. I should learn to keep my big mouth shut.'

'No, it's okay. I used to have someone, but it turned out he was like Amy's man. Not to be trusted.'

'Men. Eh! They're great if you find the right one, but it seems to me there aren't enough of those to go around.'

'You're right.'

She sighed. 'If you haven't had much to eat, are you hungry? I haven't had dinner yet. We could eat together.'

'Why not? The restaurants are still open; we might as well get our money's worth.' I hadn't been particularly hungry, but I enjoyed Lou's company, and once I read a menu I felt sure there'd be something I'd fancy.

The something I fancied turned out to be lobster thermidor. As the waiter placed a creamy mixture of lobster meat stuffed into a lobster shell in front of me, I turned to Lou. 'I'll never get through all this. It's enormous.'

'Don't worry. The ship's cat will be pleased. Anyway, look at mine, have you ever seen such a huge beef Wellington? They like to build meat on your bones in this restaurant.'

There was a festive atmosphere, caused mainly by several parties who were obviously celebrating birthdays or anniversaries. The chatter and laughter that surrounded us, not forgetting our shared bottle of Cabernet Sauvignon, lulled us both into a state of happiness.

'Let's go mad and do something outrageous tonight.' Lou's eyes sparkled.

'Like what? A manhunt?'

Our joint laughter matched that of the celebration tables.

'Why not? Not just any man, though. I fancy one with a little sophistication. He doesn't have to have drop-dead gorgeous looks, just rugged with the kind of face that can stop you in your tracks.'

'You mean someone who resembles ET then?'

Our raucous giggling caused the lone man on the next table to stare at us. Lou jerked her thumb in his direction. 'How about Mr Friendly over there? He looks a right misery.'

'I think I'll give him a miss.'

'Your turn, Kit. What's your Romeo going to look like?

'He's got to have tousled, thick brown hair – that's a must. He can have a few flecks of silver, though, that'll be okay.'

'Ah, a George Clooney lookalike.'

'No, not a lookalike. The real thing.' My high-pitched laughter exploded with a squeal and I couldn't stop once I saw the tears of laughter coursing down Lou's face.

'Lou, we'd best go. That man is glaring at us and I reckon he'll complain soon. Mind you, he'd not be bad-looking himself if only he smiled a bit.'

Lou pretended to take off non-existent glasses. 'Here, borrow my glasses, you're imagining things. He's just a crabby misery. I bet he doesn't know how to smile.'

I gripped the table to stand. 'I think I've drunk too much.'

'A little walk will sober you up. Come on, let's head for the bar and discuss our night of debauchery.'

The bar was empty when we arrived and, for once, finding a seat wasn't going to be a problem. I'd forgotten my wish to avoid seeing Jess, but it fleetingly returned when Lou voiced a similar feeling about seeing her little party. 'I hope I don't bump into my crowd tonight. I'm fed up with playing the chaperone role.'

I chuckled. 'We'd best avoid the bars then.'

We chose seats near the window and, as soon as we sat down, Lou voiced the obvious question. 'So, what shall we do tonight then?'

'I don't know. I don't fancy the theatre nor the roulette tables, nor the cinema – and save me from the dancing. That's not for me.'

'I'll ask the waiter where it's at for two young things like us, shall I?'

'Young things? Let's hope he's in need of glasses. I don't think these wrinkles will pass mustard.'

Lou smiled coquettishly at the young bartender. His cheeks coloured and he seemed embarrassed by the question. 'Uh, there's a good film starting soon.'

'No. No. No. We want to have fun.' Lou had no idea that she'd raised her voice. 'Fun with a capital F.'

'Samuel will be back on duty soon. I'll ask him.' The fresh-faced bartender scurried away as quickly as possible.

I smiled. 'Poor lamb, I think he's afraid of us.'

'He doesn't look old enough to serve in a bar, does he? But, wow, just look at the hunk of masculinity that's just walked in.' Lou indicated with her eyes towards the bar.

'He must be Samuel.'

'Well, if he is, then all I can say is that Samuel is my George Clooney.'

It didn't take long for the new member of staff to settle things behind the bar before approaching our table with a tray containing two cocktail glasses plus a dish of peanuts.

'I don't like to see you two beautiful ladies sitting in my bar without a drink, so I thought you might wish to try our popular pink G&T – it's raspberry, lavender and juniper, plus ice, of course.' His smile reached from one ear to the other. 'Naturally, if you want me to add gin, you need only say.'

Lou grinned at him with the sophistication of a seventeen-yearold. 'Are you Samuel?'

'I am. My colleague said that you wish to find fun tonight. Perhaps I can help you?'

I was in no doubt that the double entendre was intended.

Lou's eyes sparkled. 'My friend and I wish to do something different. Something that would appeal to sophisticated young ladies. What would you suggest?'

Samuel's white teeth flashed in Lou's direction. 'One moment, ladies. I must return to the bar. New customers.' He nodded in the direction of a couple who'd just arrived. 'I will return once I've checked a few things.'

As soon as he was out of earshot, Lou chuckled. 'I think I've had too much to drink. I'm flirting like a teenager. Looking after my little group must be having an effect.'

'You're obviously having an effect on Samuel. He likes you.'

'He's good-looking, though, isn't he? He probably flirts with all the women.'

'Maybe, but a little flirting is nice now and then, don't you think? It makes you feel attractive and that can't be a bad thing.'

We watched Samuel as he served the customers and then spent an inordinate amount of time on the phone.

'I think he's gone off us,' Lou said as she sipped her drink.

'I don't believe he's gone off you. He'll be back, just you wait and see.'

When Samuel did eventually return, he was bearing a printed invitation that he had signed. 'I've consulted with colleagues and we all agree that this is what you need. It'll get you into the most exclusive party of the night. It's by invitation only and it'll perfectly suit two attractive ladies.'

I was intrigued. 'What is it?'

'It's the midnight Flash Mob Party. Organised by the staff.'

Lou fingered the invitation. 'What on earth is a Flash Mob Party?'

'It's great fun. The music's great and our entertainment team will encourage everyone to take part in the choreographed dancing. Later, when the disco starts, the ice will have been well and truly broken and then everyone lets their hair down pretty quickly.'

'It sounds insane.'

'It can be. Last time I went, the evening ended with the "Kissing Tag" game.'

Lou laughed. 'What on earth is that?'

'It's similar to regular tag, only when you catch someone, you have to kiss them.'

'What if you don't want to be kissed by the person catching you?'

'To be honest, by that time of the morning, most people have chosen who they want and who they're willing to be kissed by, but if they don't fall into that category, then they're usually game to kiss anyone.'

Lou stroked her chin. 'So, who goes to these Flash Mob events? I haven't seen it advertised on the daily activities sheet.'

'No, it's by invitation only. Staff can give an invitation to two or three passengers.'

'Sounds crazy.' Lou shook her head. 'You could end up with a room full of people who don't join in any of the activities, or maybe passengers don't turn up and the room will be half empty.'

Samuel looked doubtful. 'We could, but we know the type of passengers we're looking for and each member of staff has strict instructions on whom they can invite.'

'And what was your criteria for tonight?'

'Maximum of three. Female. Looking for fun.'

Lou looked at Samuel. 'Apart from the entertainment team, do other staff go?'

'Yes. Not all staff, naturally. Some staff have no wish to take part, but those that do put their name in a ballot. There's only one Flash Mob event per voyage and it depends upon what duties you might have on that night. Sometimes you can't be released from work in any case. It's very popular, as this is our one and only opportunity to spend an evening with passengers without being on duty.'

Samuel noticed more new customers stood at the bar. 'Ladies, I must leave you. If you decide you'd like to go, meet me at midnight outside the Carnival Room on the fourth deck. Don't be late because only the first two hundred passengers will be admitted. I'll be there as quickly as I can once my shift has ended and I'll be looking for you. Very much hope to see you both later. Yes?'

Lou's eyes widened and I knew that the 'Perhaps' she threw at Samuel was a given *'Wild horses won't keep me away'*. Samuel also read this message accurately and he bent to kiss Lou's hand, then winked slowly at her before heading for the bar.

For my part, the thought of kissing some stranger certainly didn't appeal and I desperately searched my befuddled mind as to how to get out of this problem, but I didn't think quick enough.

'Isn't this great, Kit? I'm looking forward to it already. Reckon we're going to have a bit of fun tonight, don't you?' She looked at me expectantly.

What could I say? I didn't want to be a spoilsport, so I smiled and nodded. 'Yes, it'll be good.'

When we entered the Carnival Room, it was obvious that the party was already in full swing even though we'd arrived early. The entertainment team were stood by the door and shouted their welcome above the noise of the music and a racket I could only describe as a pack of howling wolves.

A glass of cava was thrust into my hand, and I glanced at Lou, who took a big gulp from her glass and winked at me. Her broad grin was reflected in the many mirrors and sparkling lights that adorned every wall.

The room was divided into two areas. To the right was a dance floor where the crowd were bunched up like sardines in a can, which obviously had a life of its own. Their vibrant clothes shone beneath the dry-ice smoke that swirled an array of blues, acid greens and golds. It reminded me of pictures I'd seen of the Northern Lights. The loud music throbbed over the dance floor as if it had fused with the hot, sweating bodies, and the fight for the most dominant perfume hit the back of my throat.

The smaller area to the left wouldn't have been out of place in a Las Vegas casino. There was a huge roulette table in the corner and a green felted blackjack table nearby. Gold painted artificial columns held up a false shimmering ceiling of netting, and luminescent dice cubes suspended from ornate poles reflected the colours of the rainbow. One or two men were walking around the area, but for the most part it was empty. The loudness of the music would have made it impossible to hear a croupier in any case.

I spied an enormous net of balloons plus dozens of giant inflatable pigs and beach balls anchored in huge buckets. My heart sank; playing mindless grown-up games always filled me with dread and it looked as though lots more than choreographed dancing had been planned. My initial reaction was one of apprehension, but then I caught sight of Lou, who was happily grinning from ear to ear. I chided myself and decided it was time for a new policy – one that embraced life rather than shying away from it.

Lou winked at me as she placed her already empty cava glass back on a tray and reached for a second. 'I reckon this is going to be a great night, don't you? Just look at all these people; there must be a couple of nice men here for us. Don't you think?'

It was at that moment I glanced behind and saw Samuel by the door. He was in deep discussion with one of the entertainment team.

'I thought you were making a play for Samuel.'

'Yes, but it might not work out. Who knows, he might have his sights set on a pretty young señorita that someone else invites. He certainly knows how to flirt. In fact, I imagine he certainly knows how to do everything.' Lou's laugh was loud and raucous.

I smiled. 'I see they've got a roulette table over there.'

'I don't have much money on my cruise card, which is probably just as well as I've never had a gambler's lucky streak. What about you?'

'I've never played.'

'You're kidding. You must have led a very sheltered life.'

'I suppose I've never been anywhere where there was a roulette table. Is it easy to play?'

'Very easy. I'll show you later if they open that area. Come on, let's have a walk about before the real music starts.'

'What do you call real music? This sounds fine.'

'Well, that's good.' She grabbed my free arm and led me through the crowds. 'But let's take a walk and see who we fancy.' It wasn't long before I heard a familiar voice behind us.

'Hello, ladies.' Samuel's voice was raised a notch or two to be heard above the noise. 'I'm glad you both came.' He politely kissed us both on the cheek before ushering forward the man that stood
behind him. 'This is Alexander. Alex for short.'

My eyes drank in the tall man opposite me. Oh my God, it was him. The exercise fanatic. I fought the rising alarm as panic crept up my spine.

The gauche figure raised the ghost of a smile. He shook my hand limply as his head bobbed up and down for no apparent reason. It was difficult to look away from his face, the skin of which appeared shrunken, making every feature exaggerated.

'I see you've got a drink already. That's good.' Samuel's smile was only for Lou. 'Alex works on board, don't you, Alex?'

The tall man nodded, smiling slightly, but he remained silent. My scalp prickled and I thought his decayed smile would have brought despair to the most optimistic dentist. But I felt sorry for him. He was obviously ill at ease and uncomfortable, and I knew exactly how that felt.
I swallowed my misgivings. 'Where exactly do you work, Alex?'

It was clearly the right question as a grin crossed his face before his high-pitched voice yelled at me, 'My work is in the engineering section. I'm the ship's Master Craftsman First Engineer and I'm in charge of not only the operation of all the engine room plant, but all the staff in that section, too.

Being the only Master Craftsman First Engineer on board is an important job. I have many people working for me. I also oversee the fuel and oil bunkering and potable water production on board. It is very interesting, you know.'

I doubted that but remained polite. 'Is it a job you've done for a long time?'

'Oh, yes. I've always been passionate about inventing, designing and analysing machinery, even when I was a little boy. At school I was able to demonstrate numerical and scientific abilities, and with my problem-solving skills, it all seemed to come naturally. The careers advisor thought a job in engineering would be perfect for me, and he was right.'

I stared at the gap in front of his mouth where a tooth should have been and wondered how he'd managed to talk for so long without a pause for breath.

He coughed loudly as if about to give a speech and then, to my dismay, quickly continued. The odd thing was that all the time he was speaking, his dark hollow eyes never looked at me. His gaze was fixed somewhere over my shoulder, which was disconcerting.

'Without proper maintenance of the main propulsion machinery on board, then our engines would stop, so I'm sure you can understand the importance of my work. Not many people think about how the propulsion engine works. Have you thought about it?'

It was not a question because his voice resumed the monologue instantly. I felt the need to hold my breath to reduce the effect of his vaporous breath. To say that it smelled of garlic fumes was an understatement.

'Of course, many older cruise ships use diesel engines to generate power for propulsion, but this ocean liner... in fact, all modern cruise ships are powered by electricity nowadays. Marvellous, isn't it?'

Relief came in the form of a tap on Alex's shoulder. 'You two seem to be getting along well, so Lou and I are going to mingle for a bit. We may see you later, but if not I hope you both have a good night.'

Lou winked at me. 'If I don't see you later, my stateroom number is 2022. Keep in touch.'

My heart sank as Samuel led Lou by the hand onto the crowded dance floor. Before they were out of sight, Alex's voice filled the air. 'Now, where was I?'

In desperation, I grabbed a ship's coaster from the nearby table. 'Alex, have you seen these lovely coasters? I've spotted them all over the ship; they're lovely. I'm tempted to take one home with me as a souvenir.'

Alex surveyed the cardboard drinks coaster as though it was something contagious. 'It's just a picture of an anchor.'

'Yes, but it would be a reminder of the time I crossed the Atlantic, wouldn't it?'

'Yes. If that's the kind of thing you like. As for me, I'd rather an image of the main propulsion machinery. Speaking personally, that is.'

My heart sank and all words deserted me.

His voice broke the short silence. 'Do you know how interesting the history of Atlantic crossings are? It's quite fascinating. Take the liner *Mauretania*, way back in 1907. It was able to cross—'

I held up my upward palm towards him. 'I'm sorry, Alex, fascinating as this is, I can't stay here in all this noise. I've such a headache and I'm going to return to my stateroom.'

'Oh, I'm sorry, Kay.'

'Kit. It's Kit.'

'You must let me walk you to your room. It's easy to get lost in all the corridors.'

'No, it's fine, honestly. I can find my way.'

'But I insist.'

'No, I wouldn't hear of it. Bye, Alex, it was nice to meet you.' And with these words, I quickly turned and rushed for the exit.

The entertainment team member standing by the door grinned as I passed. 'You off already?'

'Headache.' I called over my shoulder, but not before I'd noticed the lopsided smirk on his lips. Had he been watching me with Alex? If so, I decided he must have got a kick out of my distress.

My heart was pounding as I moved away from the Carnival Room and the dull ache that'd been in my head since dinner had now developed into a throbbing sensation. However, despite the discomfort, I was proud of myself. I'd walked away from a situation I didn't want and I knew my younger self would never have had the confidence to do that.

I made my way past the open doors of the empty theatre and thought it looked gloomy with all the lights off. Here and there, one or two people were still around, mostly in the bars or by the elevators, but most passengers had now retired to their staterooms.

When I reached the seventh floor, I noticed a man seated near the elevator doors, reading a book. I looked at my watch: it was gone two in the morning. Why on earth wasn't he doing this in his room at such a late hour? People are odd.

It was about this time I saw the shadow of a person out of the corner of my eye. The shadow was still there as I entered the long, empty corridor where my stateroom was situated. I stopped in front of a picture on the wall to give myself the opportunity of peeking behind. Sure enough, the shadow materialised into a real person. An involuntary sound caught in my throat and every muscle in my body tightened. No. Surely not. It couldn't be.

The tall, thin man had stopped walking and immediately turned his body towards one of the stateroom doors, holding out his hand as though he was about to insert a plastic key card. I jerked my head to the front and quickly walked on.

There was a smaller corridor leading off to the left where the staff kept clean laundry and cleaning products in locked rooms. This was also a shortcut through to an identical long, parallel corridor on the port side of the ship. I quickly turned left and immediately broke into a run.

With heart racing, I slowed from a run to a jog and checked over my shoulder. In the grip of silent panic, I saw the figure turn into my corridor. I swallowed a guttural cry and once more broke into a run. At least I was now heading back towards the elevator area where I'd earlier spotted the man reading a book. *Please be there. Please be there* was the mantra that went round and round my head as I saw the corridor opening out towards its end.

Sweat was pouring down my face as I crashed into the man, who dropped his book to the floor in astonishment. He looked at me with an open mouth.

I panted and pointed down the corridor. 'Please help me. A man is following me. He's down there.'

It took a second or two for my information to sink in, but then the man stood and looked down the long, straight corridor. 'I can't see anyone. You sit here, I'll go and have a look.'

'No. No. Please don't leave me on my own. I'll come with you.'

With shaking legs, I followed the man, letting my eyes peek from behind the safety of his body. He ran the entire length of the corridor and then paused at the end, before returning to explore the turnings off and eventually the entire parallel starboard corridor.

'There's nobody here,' the man eventually said and then added soothingly, 'at least not now.'

I shivered and my eyes felt as though they were frozen wide open in an expression of stunned shock.

'Don't worry. We'll report this. I'll come with you to reception right away. Do you have any relatives or friends on board? We'll get reception to ring them for you.'

'A brother.' I noticed the kindness in the stranger's eyes and for the first time thought there was something familiar about him.

'Well, there you go. We'll get him to come and take care of you and see you safely back to your stateroom.'

My legs turned to concrete and refused to move. It was as though my shoes were glued to the carpet. I started to shiver. 'I'm sorry.' My words dribbled quietly out.

'Don't be sorry. You've had a shock, but it'll be all right. Don't worry.' The man took the jacket from his shoulders and draped it around me. 'Would you rather sit here and I'll go to reception for you?'

I shook my head, fear of seeing Alex uppermost in my mind. Silent sobs shook my entire body. It was then that everything became a blur, a blur that swirled out of existence. I took one step forward and crumpled like a puppet suddenly released of its strings. Time seemed to slow and in the nanoseconds it took me to reach the ground, the only thing I saw was the kindly eyes of the stranger creating waves on my vision.

I knew even in that instant that something magical had just happened and an emotional door that I'd kept firmly shut had eased open a crack. My heart beat out a silent joy and I lost consciousness.

DAVID

This voyage was turning into the cruise from hell. When I boarded the liner, I had been hoping for a few days of quiet relaxation to help put into context the months of fighting with Carly. I needed to decide just how much I was willing to sacrifice to be part of my daughter's life and, perhaps more to the point, whether Sophie even wanted a dad in her life after all these years. I was halfway through the cruise and no nearer an answer.

Things hadn't started well. On arrival, I discovered they'd double-booked my cabin – masses of apologies, of course, but the offered replacement was nowhere near as nice as the one I'd booked. In fact, it didn't even have a balcony. After tough words, I was upgraded to one of the upmarket staterooms on the seventh floor, but by the time this happened I'd developed a sore throat and couldn't stop sneezing. I was now getting over what had turned into a slight cold, but it hadn't been the best of starts.

The thing I hadn't expected about this liner was the noise. You could be quietly relaxing on deck when some bright entertainment guy would come along and whip up an audience for bingo, shuffleboard or whatever. You'd be surprised the clamour this produced among the passengers. The decibels of support would rival a football crowd any day.

There also seemed to be an enormous number of women in need of company on board, as no sooner had I sat at a bar than I was accosted and asked whether the seat next to me was free, despite many other empty seats around. Then, of course, there was the bored male passenger who wanted to share man talk about football (I had no interest) or cars (again, providing they were half decent and didn't break down, I was not that bothered). I was beginning to sound a right gripe, I realised, but I didn't mean to. It was just that this was supposed to be a precious quiet time to sort my life out.

Last night was a case in point. I'd opted for a late dinner as I had found it quieter dining later — but not last night. Oh no. It started when two women were shown to the table opposite me; they'd obviously had quite a bit to drink as their raucous voices and riotous laughter started almost as soon as they arrived. And it didn't stop. Throughout dinner, their shrieks must have been heard at the other end of the restaurant. I looked at them sternly but it had no effect. It was lucky they left when they did because I saw one of the waiters pointing at them and discussing the situation with the maître d'.

The oddest thing of all was that, hours later, I saw one of the women again, only this time in very different circumstances. I was reading my book while sitting in one of the lounge chairs on deck seven. I preferred to read there in the early hours; it wasn't as claustrophobic as my cabin, and after midnight there was usually nobody around so it was perfectly quiet. I saw her run out of the corridor on my right. She was trembling as she gripped my arms, shaking them with an urgency that matched her crazed eyes and white face.

'Help me,' she cried. I recognised her at once and wondered whether she was drunk, but something in her manner made me think that she was genuinely fearful. She pointed to the corridor and said there was man following her.

She insisted on coming with me to look even though I would have been quicker on my own, but we didn't find anyone despite searching all the corridors around the area.

She said she had a brother on board and I was about to get hold of him when she fainted right in front of me. That gave me a shock, I can tell you.

Everything moved in slow motion for a while. I willed someone, anyone, to come along, but they didn't, so I ran back to my cabin, which luckily wasn't far away, and rang for help, after which I dashed back to her as quickly as possible.

She was sitting up, leaning against the leg of the chair when the first-aid man arrived. It was a relief to me that I could hand her over to someone who knew what they were doing.

On reflection, my inadequacy over the collapsed woman matched my failings over Sophie. I didn't seem to be much good at anything.

KIT

Next morning, the ringing phone broke into my dream and, for a fleeting moment, I didn't know where I was.

'Hello.' My husky voice was still captured by sleep.

'Kit, are you all right this morning?' Jess's voice boomed.

Rapidly, the events of the previous night hit centre stage.

'Oh, Jess, it's you. Yes, I'm okay.'

'Good. You had us all concerned.'

I had no words of reply. It was too early to think.

'Kit?'

'I'm here, but I've only just woken up.'

'Look, give me a ring when you've come to. I'm having breakfast in my stateroom, so I'll be here for a while.'

'Okay.' My head slumped back on the pillow. I failed miserably to recapture the world of slumber and drowsily glanced around my stateroom. I pondered that there must be an area on board stocked with every imaginable flower, otherwise how did Juan manage to change my flowers every day? The yellow funnel-shaped freesia petals caught in the bright sunshine peeping through the curtains; to describe them as 'pretty' didn't do them justice. It was then I noticed a jacket draped over the chair behind them. A light blue jacket that didn't belong to me.

A picture of the kind eyes of a stranger leapt to mind and immediately the memory of the embarrassing events of last night took over. I quickly got out of bed and examined the jacket. It was a single-breasted classic suit coat in twill. I hesitated before searching the pockets. It didn't seem right to do so, but how on earth would I be able to return the jacket to its owner if I didn't?

I plunged my hand deep into the breast pocket, causing a shiver to run down my spine. The aroma of a cologne I'd learned to fear rose to greet me.

Acqua di Parma was the eau de cologne that Tom insisted I bought him one Christmas. When I gave him the travel size because it was all I could afford, he'd thrown it across the room and raised his fist to me, although on that occasion he'd only harangued me verbally not physically.

My unease lingered as I showered and dressed, but by the time I called Jess, it was virtually buried. That was until the perfume returned as I carried the jacket over my arm in the enclosed space of the elevator.

Jess was waiting for me at the reception area and took me to one side before we approached the desk. 'I suppose you've checked the jacket for the owner's details. You never know, he might want to give you a reward.'

'Jess, for goodness' sake, it was *he* who did the favour and, in answer to your question, the pockets are empty.'

'All right. Keep your hair on. I only thought I'd mention it.' He changed the subject quickly. 'Last night, the man you said followed you, was that really as it happened? I mean, you didn't invite him back and change your mind or anything?'

'Why would I do that?'

'Maybe he came on a bit strong even before you'd reached your stateroom or something.'

I glared at Jess. 'You're talking rot. There was a point when I believed the shadow was a boring man I'd met at the Flash Mob event. Today, I'm not so sure. Maybe it was my imagination.'

'Flash Mob event? What the hell's that?'

'Don't ask. It wasn't great and, in any case, I left before it got going.'

'Perhaps we should tell the receptionist anyway. They might know of this man, whoever he is. He might prey on unaccompanied women.'

'I might be totally wrong, Jess. And he would get into big trouble if I accused him, as he works in the engine room on this liner.'

'I still think that you should say something.'

'No, Jess, I've got other plans.'

With these words, I gave him no chance for further interrogation and walked to the reception desk. I filled in a lost property form, leaving out the description of owner if known. I could hardly write 'kind eyes' because that was all I could remember. As I handed over the jacket, a tinge of sadness overcame me. It was doubtful I'd ever see him again and he had seemed such a nice person.

Jess interrupted my thoughts. 'Have you heard from the captain yet?'

'No. Have you?'

'Not yet, but I imagine he'll be in touch soon.'

'Yes, I suppose so. It's not that much longer until we reach New York.'

'Talking of New York; when we arrive, I'll probably leave the liner with Allegra. We thought we'd stay at The Peter Hotel. Allegra tells me it's the best in New York. It's exclusive and in the perfect location, right next to Central Park. In all honesty, it doesn't seem your kind of hotel. You don't mind, do you?'

I knew this wasn't a question Jess wanted answered. 'It sounds expensive.'

'It most certainly is, but once we land, Allegra is about to put some very lucrative work my way. I need to keep up appearances.' Jess momentarily gazed out of the window. 'I'll probably not travel back to the UK with you; I might stay in the States for a while.

Allegra tells me it'll be easy to get the necessary visa.'

I nodded, not really knowing what to say. I speculated as to whether the Lady Allegra would be paying for herself at this posh New York hotel, but felt it best to keep quiet on the matter.

'Allegra and I have decided not to dine at Le Blanc Hibiscus restaurant tonight.' I knew Jess well enough to know that the beaming smile he gave was false. 'Although, come to think of it, I haven't seen you there since that first night. You must be dining at a different time.'

'Yes. I must.' I was not going to give Jess the satisfaction of knowing my dining arrangements, such as they were.

'I only mention this so that you aren't looking for us tonight, Kit.'

'I wouldn't have been. No worries. We'll get in touch when we receive the captain's information. Yes?'

'Yes. You've still got the package safely stowed somewhere, haven't you?'

I glared at him and sighed noisily. Then I abruptly turned tail and walked away.

I knew this was not the compliant sister that Jess was used to, but, in all honesty, I was wearying of trying to keep everyone happy.

I passed the rest of the morning strolling around various public decks of the liner, all the time instinctively knowing Jess was hiding something, but I didn't know what. Unfortunately, I had no idea of the questions I needed to ask to get to the bottom of the mystery.

I decided to return to my room and change into my bikini before heading up to the lido deck for something to eat and a spot of sunbathing. Maybe lounging on a sunbed by the pool would plant the right questions in my mind. I preferred the public pool to the exclusive one my expensive stateroom offered. Sharing a pool area with passengers who'd booked penthouse suites and wore £500 swimwear that didn't get wet filled me with dread.

I was ready to leave and choosing which book to read when I heard a knock on the door. I was surprised to see the immaculate figure of my butler.

'Ma'am.' Juan politely nodded his head. 'I've been asked to give you this letter and wait for a reply. Also, Ma'am, this beautiful red rose was left outside your cabin. I think you must have a secret admirer.'

I bent my head to inhale the sweet fragrance. 'I've no idea who left this. Did you see anyone in the corridor?'

'Sorry, Ma'am, no.'

'Never mind. It's a beautiful rose. Come in, Juan.' I waved my arms expansively, but Juan stepped just inside and held the door ajar.

'Is this letter from the captain?'

'I don't know, Ma'am. However, if you wish to write a reply right now, paper and envelopes are in your desk.' Juan pointed towards the antique rosewood writing desk, the surface of which displayed my small brown package in splendid isolation.

'Alternatively, I can take a message.'

I expected it to be from the captain, but I was wrong. It was from a member of the reception team who explained that a request had been made to give my stateroom extension number to a Mr David Stephens, who wished to thank me personally for the return of his jacket. I skimmed the last paragraph of the letter because my heart flipped, causing my mouth to break into a huge grin.

'It looks as though the contents has pleased you, Ma'am.'

'It has, Juan, it most certainly has. I can't quite believe it.'

'What would you wish me to do, Ma'am? Will you write?'

'No, Juan. Will you tell Jo Bulman, the Passenger Services Representative, that I give my permission.'

'Certainly, Ma'am. I'll do it right away. Is there anything else you would like me to do for you?'

'I don't think so, but thank you.'

After Juan had quietly closed the door, I roamed aimlessly around the room, fingering objects and stroking furniture with an absence of purpose. My head whirled and I felt I was floating on air. Catching sight of the rose laying on the bed brought a huge beam to my face. It was David. It must have been David who left it by my door. I hugged myself in pleasure at the thought.

'You're mad,' I admonished myself out loud. 'Calm down. You're behaving like a lovesick teenager.' But it was no use. It took two cups of coffee and half an hour of gazing at the passing sea before I reached anywhere near my normal equilibrium.

My quiet voice addressed the balcony terrace. 'Listen, Kit Langford, you promised yourself you'd be wary of all men after last time. You know nothing about David. He could be a serial killer, a womaniser or a bully, for all you know. He might even be married.'

It was the last sentence that caused my bubble to finally burst. I wondered why I hadn't thought of it before. My smile disappeared and it was in that moment I realised the rose could not have been left by David, for he had no idea of my stateroom number.

So, who? I rubbed my lower lip with my forefinger and then, unexpectedly, panic as thin as cellophane entered my consciousness. The memory of his decayed smile and obnoxious breath cut my stomach as if I'd swallowed shards of glass.

'Oh no.' I reached for the rose and crushed its beautiful petals in my fisted hand before tossing it in the bin. In that instant, all I could think of was escape. With jittery fingers, I grabbed my already prepared holdall and ran out of the room.

-o-

I pushed the lunchtime salad around with the fork. There was nothing wrong with it, but my appetite had disappeared along with the rose petals in the bin. Two minutes later, I drifted into the pool deck bar and decided I might as well pull a sunbed under the glass windshield of its open deck. It might be sunny, but the Atlantic wind chill certainly kept the temperatures down. In fact, the afternoon warmth was now as deflated as my mood.

I tried to read, but there was a non-stop loop of unwanted images floating through my head. It didn't help that the book I'd chosen was boring. Perhaps a dip in the heated pool would raise my spirits. It didn't. The only difference was that I now felt wet when I returned to the sunbed.

No sooner had I sat down than one of the entertainment team rushed up to me. 'Come and join in. It's going to be fun and you might just win the big prize.'

'No, thank you.' I studied my toes.

'Oh, come on. You only live once. You can lie on this sunbed afterwards and enjoy your free cocktail. Every contestant gets a cocktail of their choosing. Give it a go. Pretty girl like you; you're bound to have the audience on your side.'

I thought madness must've taken over my brain when I heard myself ask what I'd have to do. This was something I'd never have done in the past. Perhaps, at long last, I was overcoming the legacy of Tom's control.

'That's the ticket.' The man took my question for willingness and held out his hand. 'Let me help you up.'

I climbed the steps to the small stage overhanging the swimming pool; an excessively made-up female shook my hand and placed a microphone under my chin. 'Welcome. Welcome to "Sing That Tune". I'm Trixie, your friendly entertainment lass. What's your name?'

'Kit.'

'Big round of applause for Kit, everybody. The last of our brave contestants to stand up here and sing for you this afternoon.' 'I've got a terrible voice,' I whispered.

Trixie covered the microphone with her free hand. 'Don't worry, love, with your looks they'll love you even if you sound like a cracked bell. Pretty girls always go down well.'

That was twice within five minutes someone had said I was pretty. *These entertainment people sure know how to flatter*, I thought and moved to stand alongside the other four contestants. It was a relief when I was told I'd be the last to sing. At least I'd get time to watch the others and work out what I was supposed to do.

'Right, folks, these lovely people up here are going to choose from a list of well-known songs,' Trixie boomed. She didn't need a microphone. 'They'll start to sing with the music, but we're going to stop it at some point and they must keep going. Who do you think will be on cue when the music restarts? We're about to find out, but whatever happens, don't forget to cheer as though your life depended upon it. Come on, let's see how loud you can do it before our first contestant steps forward.'

The crowd went wild. Anyone would think Kanye West or Lady Gaga was about to entertain them.

I listened to the other contestants with a sinking feeling and the nearer it came to my turn, the sweatier my palms felt and the fluttery nervous butterflies in my stomach increased.

The young man before me was going to be a very hard act to follow and not only did he rejoin the song at the right point, he had a lovely voice. The audience gave him rapturous applause and he deserved it.

'Now, ladies and gentlemen, boys and girls, we come to our last contestant. The lovely Kit.' Trixie signalled me to come to the front. 'Are you ready, Kit?'

'I have to warn you, I've a terrible voice.' I heard the quiet echo of my words boom over the loudspeakers.

'Ha. Don't worry, Kit. We're all on your side. Aren't we, everybody?' Trixie raised her arm to the crowd and a huge cheer broke out. I looked at my stomach, shining with suntan oil and felt overexposed. I so wished I'd wrapped my sarong on top of the bikini before coming onto this stage.

'Good luck. Here she is everyone, the lovely Kit.' My hand shook as I took the microphone from Trixie.

The music started and I instantly gave thanks to Jess for playing this song over and over back in the 90s. At least I knew the beginning, even if I wasn't sure of the words all the way through. I sang along with the opening bars, hiding behind the voices of Robson and Jerome, but I knew crunch time was coming and, sure enough, the music stopped at the part I wasn't too sure about.

My voice carried on alone, but at times my memory failed me and I needed to resort to inserting a 'la la la' or two simply to keep going. It was a nightmare. Relief flooded through me as Robson and Jerome rejoined and covered my inadequate warbling. By an absolute miracle, I was at exactly the right point in the song. My legs were now shaking as I managed to sing along with them to the end of the song, and as the last bars faded, I wondered how on earth I'd had the nerve to stand in front of this crowd and sing.

'Wasn't she wonderful, ladies and gentlemen? Come on, a big round of applause for your last contestant, the beautiful Kit. Come on. Come on. Louder. Louder applause needed!' Trixie played the crowd and whipped up the noise.

Eventually, she waved her hands downwards, waiting for the expected hush. 'Now comes crunch time, everyone. The winner will depend upon your participation. Each and every one of these wonderful people have given up their time and done their best to entertain you this afternoon. But I'm sorry to say only two people managed to rejoin their song with the correct words at the precise moment the music started again – and they were Dave and Kit. Who could forget the wonderful dulcet tones of Dave or the "la la la la" genius of Kit, eh?'

I felt this part of the entertainment went on forever as I stood, arms across my stomach, at the back of the stage. Trixie shook hands with those contestants leaving the stage and gave them a certificate and a bar token. I breathed deeply, knowing the ordeal was almost behind me. In a funny kind of way, I felt pleased with myself; never in a million years did I think I'd have the nerve to do such a thing. Now the worst was behind me, I felt brave enough to glance around the crowd. People were waving flags; some waving at the stage while others whistled or cheered madly. Then, at the front of the crowd, I saw him. It was him. I was sure.

Panic began like a cluster of spark plugs in my abdomen and I felt as though someone had turned out the switch to my brain. My face must have shown the tension I felt.

His eyes captured mine and I found it impossible to look away as they had a mesmeric effect. His gap-toothed smile stretched from one ear to the other. It was with uncomfortable horror I watched him frantically rub his crutch through his shorts and then point to me. Then, I felt disgust as he made a blow-job sign using his pointed thumb towards his right cheek as he puffed out the left. Memories of Tom immediately came flooding back. Memories I preferred to forget. Surely someone in the crowd must have observed his lewd behaviour. Had he no shame? How could he do this with so many little children around?

He cupped his hand to the side of his face, holding his thumb to his ear and his little finger to his mouth, then once more outstretched his pointing finger to me. I closed my eyes before I could witness more. Panic hit me. Surely, he didn't know my extension number. He couldn't phone me. Could he? I prayed to God that he was bluffing. Knowing my extension meant he definitely knew my stateroom number.

Trixie's voice broke into my wild thoughts. 'And so, ladies and gentlemen, boys and girls, we have our two finalists.' She put her arms around both Dave and I and pulled us to the front of the stage. 'My goodness, gentlemen, you've no idea how cold our little Kit is. She has goosebumps even on this red-hot afternoon. Come on, guys, blow her some kisses, warm her up a little.'

Trixie was certainly good at whipping up the crowd as the men cheered loudly, clapped, blew kisses and shouted bawdy comments at me, although, if truth be told, I was only half listening. My head was elsewhere and my eyes had already noticed the space in the front row where Alex had been standing.

'And so we come to the crunch,' Trixie continued. 'Whoever gets the loudest claps and most noise will be our "Sing That Tune" winner for today, and he or she will become the lucky owner of our coveted Winner Medal. Now, everybody, who will you clap loudest for? Will you clap for the lovely Kit, or for the dulcet tones of Dave? Ladies first, yes?'

Trixie grinned at us both and then whispered, 'Are you two guys ready? It's going to be noisy.'

She was right. The noise that followed even seeped through the barrier of fear I'd erected. I'd no idea who won and didn't care. It was a long cacophony of deafening noise that seemed to go on forever.

It was a relief when Trixie pulled Dave to the front and raised his arm aloft, rather like that of a boxing champion. 'I give you your winner. Obviously that deep romantic voice has won you over, but before you go wild for Dave, a big hand is needed for our beautiful, sporting Kit. Please give it up right now.'

I left the stage, bar token and paper certificate in hand, my ears registering the many invitations from the men I passed, most of whom seemed to think that they could *warm me up*.

My heart was racing, along with my mind, as I returned to my sunbed. My eyes darted in all directions, fearing I'd see the man that had caused these trembles. It was quite some time before my hands stopped shaking and my mind allowed a slither of normality to return, but the circle of worry continued. What if Alex knew my stateroom number? What if he'd been stalking me? I then countered this with the opposite view: perhaps he'd been passing and had simply seen me on stage; perhaps he'd pretended that he knew my room number; or maybe I'd totally misunderstood his message.

An hour later, I was no further ahead with these deliberations. The only thing I felt sure about was that it was Alex and I wondered why he was on the passenger deck. Staff were not allowed to be in passenger areas unless they were working.

Overriding every thought, every worry and every concern that had darted around my head constantly since I walked off that stage was one big question that returned over and over. What should I do about it? And as I packed the suntan cream back into my bag, I was no closer to answering that question than I was when I'd first thought it.

-o-

I tapped the extension Juan had left for me and looked at the pristine brown package on the desk. I felt as though it was watching me. Judging me. But I knew that was silly.

Nevertheless, I turned my back on it when I heard a voice answer the phone. 'Good afternoon. This is the butler's extension. How may I help you?' The female voice caused confusion as I expected to hear Juan.

'Um. Can I speak to Juan, please?'

'Can I ask you to confirm your stateroom number, please, Ma'am?'

'7109.'

'If you wouldn't mind holding the line just one second, Miss Langford, I will connect you with your butler immediately.'

Juan's soothing voice crooned down the line. 'Miss Langford, Ma'am, how may I help you?'

'Juan?' I hesitated. I'd formulated the words I wished to say, but somehow the rehearsal hadn't helped.

'Yes, Ma'am, I'm listening.'

'Juan, this is going to sound silly, but I wanted to ask you about the rules and regulations around staff on this ship.'

'It's not silly at all. Would you prefer to discuss this in your room? I can bring Ms Kopf, our senior Human Resources manager, who will probably be better able to answer any questions you may have.' Juan paused, briefly. 'I do hope that you have found my services satisfactory, Ma'am. You need only say if there is anything else I can do for you.'

'No, it has nothing to do with you, Juan. It's just a simple question. I wonder whether I'm correct in thinking that members of the staff are not allowed in guest areas on board unless they happen to be working in that area?'

'That is quite correct, Ma'am, but has something happened? Is there something that concerns you?'

'I've probably got things totally wrong, so no problem. I just wanted to know, that's all.'

'Ma'am, if there is anything that concerns you even in the slightest, then I am here to help you.'

'I know, Juan. Just one more question. How can I find out the names of employees on board?'

'I do not think that this sensitive type of information is ever divulged, Ma'am. The Data Protection Act covers everyone nowadays.'

'Yes, of course. Perhaps you may be able to answer a different question then. Is there such a job as Master Craftsman First Engineer?' I was now glad that Alex had insisted on lauding the work title he believed to be so important when we'd met.

'I am no expert in this field. So I will determine the correct answer to your question and come back to you. Does that meet with your approval, Ma'am?'

'Yes, that's fine.'

'Is this query urgent, Ma'am?'

'No. Not urgent. I'd just wish to know, that's all.'

'Certainly. I will make sure you have the information.'

My headache was on the verge of turning me into a migraine prisoner. I took a bottle of chilled water from the fridge and escaped to the terrace with a packet of ibuprofen in hand. Relying on painkillers was becoming far more regular than I wished.

Thirty minutes later, with my headache receding, I furtively scanned the corridor outside my room before cautiously making my way to Samuel's bar. He was the one person I knew who had any connection to Alex and perhaps he might be able to throw some light on this mysterious man.

The only person in the bar when I arrived was the young, fresh-faced bartender who'd been on duty the previous night. It was too early for the pre-dinner crowd and the bartender was cleaning the shelves behind the bar before restocking them with bottles of spirits.

'Is Samuel on duty?' I asked when he eventually looked my way.

'No.' The young man looked at his watch. 'He'll be on duty in an hour.' Embarrassment reddened his cheeks, and he quickly turned away to continue his task.

I coughed to attract his attention once more. 'Excuse me.'

'Yes. Oh, sorry. Did you want a drink?'

'No, thank you, but I wanted to ask you whether you know someone called Alex. He works in the engineering section on board this ship. I believe he's Samuel's friend.'

'Samuel's friend?'

'Yes.'

'It's unlikely I'll know him then. Samuel and I don't see much of each other unless we're working in this bar together.'

I could well imagine that. 'Okay, well, thanks anyway. Will you tell Samuel that I'll pop back to see him this evening? I'm presuming he's on duty all evening?'

The young man looked at his watch once more as though Samuel's working timetable would be printed there. 'Yes, he'll be here until we close.'

'Which is what time?'

'When the last customer leaves, usually around one o'clock in the morning if we're lucky.'

The bartender returned to stocking the shelves and I doubted he even heard me say thank you. My next plan was to ring Lou. After all, she and Samuel had been very close last night. Maybe Alex had been mentioned, although I felt this was a long shot since talking about Alex wouldn't have been very high on the agenda of either of them.

I felt on edge as I made my way back to my stateroom and this was coupled with an anger that this man could impose this ridiculous fear.

Lou's chirpy voice was the panacea I needed.

'Hi, Lou. It's Kit.'

'No need to tell me who you are; how could I possibly not recognise that lovely melodic voice of yours?'

I laughed. 'Melodic, eh? Well, thank you very much.'

'Now tell me how you got on last night with, what's his name, Alistair?'

'Alex.'

'Sorry. Alex.'

'Not great. I left almost immediately after you and Samuel disappeared onto the dance floor. How about you, did you have a good time?'

'Sort of.'

'Sort of? What does that mean?'

'It was okay. Samuel was fun and we had a laugh, but without copious amounts of alcohol I don't think it would have been so great. He's great with the compliments and making you feel special, as you know. But he's a bit too in love with himself. A real Casanova eyeing up the next conquest, even when he's talking to you.'

'But you had fun?'

'Yeah, it was all right for one night. So, what happened with Alex?'

'He was so boring. He talked non-stop about his work and he had this weird way of gazing over my shoulder as he talked. I don't think he ever looked at my face.'

'Oh dear. I didn't think he was particularly good-looking, but I hoped his personality might have made up for that.'

'No chance. To be honest, it's about Alex that I'm ringing you. I wondered whether Samuel told you anything about him?'

'No. In fact, he didn't mention him at all once we'd left you both. Why? Is there something wrong?'

'I'm not sure. I might be overreacting and at times I think I'm imagining the whole thing, but I've an idea that he's been following me.'

'Following you!'

I told Lou the whole story, including details of the embarrassing stage performance. When all words were spent, the line fell silent for what felt like minutes although, in fact, it would have been only seconds.

'I don't know what to say, Kit. It certainly doesn't sound right.
Are you sure it was him?'

'That's what I keep asking myself. From the stage, I was sure I spied that gap in the front of his teeth, but even now I question myself about it.'

'Have you reported it?'

'Who to? My brother knows some of it and I've tried to see Samuel, but he's not on duty yet. I plan to go back to his bar tonight.'

'I'll go with you. That is, if you want?'

'Yes, of course. Between us, we're more likely to think of the right questions to ask.' It was as I spoke that I heard a knock on the door, which made me jump. 'There's someone

knocking at the door, Lou. I'll have to go. I'll see you at the bar around eight.
Okay?'

I stood behind the door momentarily, as though my very presence there would drive away Alex – if indeed it was Alex waiting the other side of the heavy wooden door. Another knock. Another jump on my part.

'Who's there?' The volume of my voice was no match for the thickness of the wood. I slowly released the lock, but as I did the phone rang, which had the effect of making me totally inert as I stood in the partly opened doorway.

It was Juan's voice that broke my trance. 'Ma'am, I have the information you requested, but would you prefer to answer your phone while I wait outside?'

I nodded and moved towards the ringing. 'H-hello.'

'Hello. This is David Stephens. Am I speaking to Miss Langford? The passenger services representative gave me this number.'

The soothing softness of his voice caused my shoulders to immediately relax. 'Yes, I'm Kit Langford.'

'I wanted to thank you, Miss Langford, for returning my jacket.'

'It's I that should be thanking you. I'm embarrassed at being so silly and causing you all that trouble. It was stupid of me.'

'Not stupid at all. It was obvious that you were very upset and I was glad to have been of help. How are you today?'

'Fine. I shouldn't have caused all the fuss. I'm sorry.'

'Please don't be sorry. Thank you again for returning my jacket.'

The phone was silent with neither of us wishing to end the conversation. It was David who eventually spoke. 'I don't suppose you'd let me thank you personally? Perhaps I could buy you a cocktail or something before dinner this evening?'

I heard the involuntary catch in my throat, which was obviously heard on the other end of the line. 'I'm sorry if I've spoken out of turn, Miss Langford. You probably have other plans.'

'No, it's okay. I was just a little surprised, that's all.' My heart raced. 'It would be nice to meet you for a pre-dinner drink.'

'Good. Shall we say the cocktail bar, 7.30?'

'Fine.'

'My friends call me David, by the way.'

'I'm Kit.'

'Well, Kit, I shall look forward to meeting you properly.'

He could not see the huge smile that had spread over my face. Neither did he see the little dance as I shimmied around the room. I glanced at the neatly wrapped brown paper; perhaps it wasn't such a dreadful thing to be forced to travel on this ship, after all.

I suddenly remembered Juan outside the door and, hot on the heels of this memory, my appointment with Lou sprang to mind. *Still*, I thought, as I opened the door to a very patient Juan, *nothing is insurmountable*.

I couldn't make up my mind what to wear that night. Everything was tried on, paraded in front of the mirror and, in the end, discarded. Of course, that meant that jewellery and shoes were also changed. When I eventually left the room, it looked as though a chaotic teenager had just emptied her wardrobe all over the floor.

I made my way to the bar with all the nerves of an adolescent on her first date and when I caught sight of my reflection decided that my flushed cheeks and wide eyes fitted the category well. I escaped into a nearby washroom to check for the umpteenth time that my lipstick was intact and hair in place.

The male silhouette stood outside the cocktail bar could be the man from the previous evening, but in essence it was only his eyes I could clearly recall, so I wasn't sure this was David. As I drew nearer, the man turned my way and, in an instant, I recognised those familiar kind eyes. A smile flashed across his face. 'Hello. I'm David and I know you're Kit.' I nodded, sensible words having left me.

'Where would you like to sit? There's plenty of choice.'

'I don't mind.' He gently put his hand in the small of my back and guided me towards the first empty table.

'You certainly look much better today, Kit.'

'I am and, once again, I'm sorry about last night. It was foolish of me.'

'Not foolish at all as I said on the phone. Anyway, you rescued my jacket so we're even.'

I nodded yet again. 'Oh, I meant to ask—'

'So, Kit—'

Our voices clashed, bringing a smile to both of our faces.

'You first, Kit.'

'I was going to ask whether you know anything about a rose outside my cabin door earlier today. It was beautiful.'

David looked puzzled. 'It wasn't me, although I wish it had been. You must have a secret admirer.'

'I can't think who it could possibly be.' I shuddered, praying it wasn't from the only man I could think of. 'Your turn; what were you about to say?'

'Only to ask whether you were enjoying the cruise?'

'Yes and I'm looking forward to seeing The Big Apple.'

'Is it your first visit?'

'Mm.'

'This is my first visit as a tourist and I especially want to climb up the Statue of Liberty. There's never time to do that sort of thing when you're in New York on business.'

'Can you climb right up to the very top?'

'I think so. I should've booked a ticket before we set sail, but I ran out of time. It's the first thing I'm going to do when I reach the hotel. Have you plans to see anything, Kit?'

I dragged my memory to recall anything about New York attractions. I so wished I'd taken an interest in my destination instead of just seeing it as the end of an ordeal. 'It would be great to stroll through Central Park and see where John Lennon lived.'

'That's a nice idea. I hadn't thought of going to his memorial park.' David's smile radiated his entire face.

'Did you choose this ship for any particular reason or was it just a way to get to New York?' As I said the words, I thought they sounded banal.

'To be honest, I've never been on a liner before and everyone said this is the very best cruise liner. I've also wanted to see New York as a tourist for a long time, so it seemed a good way to combine both things.'

'It's a lovely ship… sorry, liner.'

David laughed. 'You, too. I keep making that mistake. It's confusing, isn't it? I believe it's something to do with the size.' David bent forward and whispered, 'There are some people on this ship who seem to think it's vital to apply the correct description, and don't they just love to tell you if you get it wrong. It must make them think they're important.'

David made me feel at ease and I managed to ignore a warning bell in my head that tried to remind me I'd also felt this way about Tom all those years ago, and just look what a bastard he turned out to be.

Our conversation flowed naturally and it was only when our cocktail glasses were almost empty that I remembered Lou. I glanced at my watch.

'David, I'm sorry I must go. I have to meet someone and I'm already late.'

His face folded and he looked genuinely disappointed. He smiled, but I could see it was forced and felt I should explain.

'It's a lady I met on board the first night. I've promised to meet her tonight.'

I wasn't quite sure how to say goodbye, but I needn't have worried for David guided the conversation.

'Kit, I've enjoyed talking tonight. Maybe we could meet again tomorrow?'

My face probably gave away my answer, but nevertheless I nodded.

'Shall I ring your room in the morning or would you rather we decided now?' David held my eyes as he spoke. 'We could meet after lunch. There's a music quiz by the main pool tomorrow afternoon, if you fancy your chances. It's for fun, no serious questions — at least that's what the advert says.'

'Okay.'

'Perfect. Shall we say two o'clock by the pool?'

'Two o'clock, it is. Whoever's first should save two sunbeds in the shade.'

'In the shade, it will be.' David held his right hand towards me in a gesture of goodbye, but his face came so close there was hardly a breath of air between us.

The smell of David's Acqua di Parma aftershave floated over me like a bubble of memories about to burst. It was a smell that instantly took me back and not one that I wished to be reminded of, but it was too late. Tom's image forced its way in.

I turned, quickly ignoring David's outstretched hand, and rushed from the bar, which must have left a perplexed David watching my hasty exit.

-o-

Lou was talking to the fresh-faced bartender when I arrived, rushing in as though wild horses were pursuing me.

'Whoa, girl, where's the fire?' Lou looked at me with wide eyes.

'I'm sorry I'm late. I didn't realise the time.'

'It doesn't matter. You're here now. I've been chatting to our friendly young bartender.' Lou rolled her eyes.

The young bartender had turned away by this point and hadn't thought to ask whether I wanted a drink.

'Are you drinking, Kit, or do you want to go straight for dinner?'

'Let's eat, shall we?'

'Fine and you can tell me what the big mystery is. You sounded quite excited when you put back the time of our meeting.'

By the time the coffee was in front of us, I'd finished telling Lou about David, at least the little I knew, though the entire story had been darkened by the black cloud that was Tom. Once resurrected, it was always difficult to eradicate him.

'David sounds very nice.'

'Mm.'

'But you don't really like him?'

I bit my lip. 'No. It's not that. It's… well… it's…'

'Come on, Kit. What on earth is it? Does he have two heads or something?'

I smiled. 'It's just that he reminds me of someone I knew a long time ago, at least his cologne does. Someone I lived with for a while until I found out what he was really like.'

'Oh, that sort of man. All nice at the beginning, but once you live with them, the true bastard slips out. Still, you can't judge David by his cologne.' Lou pursed her lips together. 'Although, sometimes I think we're better off being single. Play the field, have a bit of fun and move on – that's my motto nowadays.'

'It sounds like you've had a bad relationship too, Lou.'

'Relationship? Oh no, I went the full hog and married him. Fool that I was. Three months' bliss and three years of hell. I've got the scars to prove it. His forte was to punch me if he thought I was out of line. Mind you, he always chose somewhere where the bruises would be hidden. At least it didn't happen every day, but who needs it even if it's not very often?'

'Jeez! That's awful.'

Lou nodded, wistfully. 'What's awful is that I put up with it for so long. He always managed to persuade me that I deserved it. And to think I believed him, the controlling bastard. Outsiders only see a fraction of any relationship don't they?'

'I'm so sorry, Lou. Tom didn't punch me at the beginning of our relationship; everything started well, but he gradually took control of my life and in time I lost my self-confidence and all my friends. My money somehow became his, although not much of his came my way. Towards the end, he would pinch or punch me when he became angry and throughout our relationship he liked forceful sex, which was sometimes painful. And to think I put up with that, too.'

Lou nodded, sadly. 'Do you know my man even tried to say the bruises were self-inflicted when I sought help? Said I was the crazy one.'

I placed my hand over Lou's. 'Looks like we've both been through it and look at us now, putting ourselves through it all over again. Come on, Lou, they're not worth it. We're on this lovely liner and we should try and enjoy ourselves.'

'You're right. What on earth are we doing dragging up these lowlife men? Let's go and find Samuel and sort out Mr Lowlife Alex, shall we?'

It was a silent walk to Samuel's bar; we were obviously both locked in our thoughts and it wasn't until we stepped out of the lift on the fourth floor that Lou broke the silence.

'What exactly are you planning to ask Samuel?'

'Just the truth. Who is Alex and how does he know him?'

'He might close ranks to protect him.'

'Protect him from what? I'm not about to tell him the whole story, just a slightly different version.'

'Aha, I sense there's a bit of an actor in you.'

'Well, if there is, then it's only just been given wings.'

The bar was busy and both bartenders were flat out serving the crowd of after-dinner customers. It was a little while before Samuel saw us and when he did, he waved cheerily, flashing Lou a smile at the same time, but it was another ten minutes before he managed to make his way across to us.

'Ladies, what a pleasure to see you both again.' Samuel lifted Lou's hand to his lips and kissed it gently, gazing into her eyes at the same time. 'Kit, I'm so glad you've joined Lou this evening. Now, what delightful drink can I get my favourite females?'

'Glass of red for me, Samuel. What about you, Kit?'

'I think I've had enough alcohol tonight. Just an orange juice will be fine. Thanks.'

Samuel scurried away, returning quite quickly with our drinks and a huge dish of peanuts – his treat, he told us, as he majestically laid the dish on the table.

'Samuel, I wanted to ask you about Alex. Have you time to join us for a few minutes?'

'Oh, Kit, my dear, it's more than my job's worth to sit with a customer when the bar is so busy. Maybe if you wait an hour or so, things will quieten down; alternatively, if you see a couple of bar seats become free, then grab them quickly. We could have a conversation there, even though it might become a little disjointed.'

It was the bar seats that appeared first and Samuel noticed our move immediately as we perched on the seats at one end of the bar.

'The nibbles you requested, ladies.' He winked and placed a dish of green olives before us. 'Shall I refresh your drinks?'

Lou smiled and gave him her plastic stateroom card. 'Please put both drinks on my card, bartender.'

Samuel chuckled as he took the card. 'Thank you, Ma'am. I hope you're having a pleasant cruise.'

'It's been wonderful so far.'

'That pleases me, Ma'am. I hope the rest of your cruise is as pleasurable,' and with another wink, he hurried away to dispense our drinks. I noticed that Samuel didn't activate any payment on Lou's card, he just went through the motions. When he returned it, his fingers lingered briefly on top of hers, pressing a small piece of paper into her hand as he did so.

Lou scanned the paper and grinned. 'He's inviting me for a drink later.'

'Will you go?'

'Probably not. One night with Romeo is enough.'

It was ages before Samuel returned to our end of the bar. He nodded at me and then smiled at Lou. 'Now, how can I help you?'

I coughed unnecessarily. 'It's Alex; I lost touch with him last night before we exchanged phone details and would like to meet him again.'

Samuel looked genuinely surprised, but before he could reply, he was called to the other end of the bar.

A few minutes later, he returned. 'I don't know him that well, Kit. I'm not sure if I can help.'

'He said he was the Master Craftsman First Engineer on this ship, but when I asked my butler he told me there was no such job title. Perhaps I misheard him, but somehow I don't think so because he repeated it several times.'

'Butler! You have a butler?' Lou noisily interrupted, her voice taking on an edge of indignation.

It was only then I realised the words I'd spoken and wished I could take them back. 'It's not important, Lou. Just a detail.'

Our conversation was interrupted yet again, as Samuel was needed at the other end of the bar.

'You must be in one of the really posh cabins to have a butler.' 'I didn't choose it. It was all down to my brother.'

'But still, why didn't you say? I thought you were ordinary like us.' Her annoyance lingered around every word.

'I am. The people in the posh areas of this liner are full of their own self-importance and I'd far rather stay in my room than mix with them. I'm far happier with you and the girls. Honestly, Lou.' Unspeaking, she gave me a belligerent stare.

Samuel returned at this point and I sensed a change in him. 'Kit, I don't think I'm going to be able to help you. Data Protection and all that. I'm sure you understand.'

'No, I don't understand. Is Alex your friend or not? You introduced him as your friend last night.'

'Well, yes, but not a close friend. I see him rarely.'

'But you see him, so you must know a little about him. For a start, does he work in the engineering department of this liner?'

'I don't know. As I said, I don't know him that well.'

'I'm sorry, Samuel, that's not good enough. You introduced us.
You must have known how to get a hold of him in the first place.'

Samuel's eyes widened. 'Look, I'd help you if I was able, but I can't.'

'Okay, have it like that. I'll go to reception to see someone in a position to sort this out for me. Don't worry yourself about it,
Samuel.'

Samuel and Lou stared at me in disbelief.

'Kit. Kit. Stop,' Samuel called to my retreating back. 'Look, if you can wait until I'm off duty, I'll sit down with you and explain everything.'

'What time are you off duty?'

'Difficult to say. The last customer usually leaves before two o'clock.'

'Two o'clock is far too late for me. When are you free in the morning?'

Samuel looked genuinely bewildered. 'Mornings? That's my sleeping time. I could meet you before I start work. Say, one o'clock.'

'No. I'll meet you here at ten o'clock prompt. I have things to do at one o'clock. It's that or I'll see whether I can find out more by other means.'

Samuel put a hand across his mouth and rubbed upwards. The flesh of his cheek bunched up around his dark eyes. 'Okay. Okay. Ten o'clock. But I can't guarantee that I'll be wide awake.'

'I'll see you prompt at ten. Don't be late. Oh and, by the way, you've an irate customer waiting at the other end of this bar. I think he's been waiting for a long time.'

As I marched out of the bar, Lou ran to catch me up. 'Hold on, Kit. Hold on.'

I turned, hoping that a petty disagreement wasn't brewing. I felt too exhausted for another battle. Five minutes ago, someone with far more confidence had taken over my body. Now I knew that person was vacating and I felt vulnerable.

'Kit. I just wanted to say that I'm sorry if I came on a bit heavy back there.' Lou's sad smile weighed heavy on her lips. 'It's just it was a shock that you have a butler. I'd no idea you had money.'

'Money! Huh. Tell me about it. Look, Lou, I've enjoyed our time together; it's been good having you as a friend on this liner. It would be nice to continue our friendship for the rest of the cruise, but if you'd rather not hang around with someone who has a butler, then I'll understand.' I heard the words I'd spoken as though a bystander.

Lou's gently put her hand on my arm. 'Let's continue to be friends. Shall we? I'd like that. I promise I'll never refer to the matter of money or a butler again.'

'It's okay, Lou. I'll tell you all about it sometime, but not tonight. I'm weary and all I want to do is climb into bed.'

'Shall I see you tomorrow?'

I nodded. 'I've got your extension number. I'll ring you.'

Tiredness temporarily drove all thoughts of Alex and stalking from my mind as I trudged back to my stateroom. I realised I'd unlocked an inner voice that evening and it was liberating. It'd also been exhausting and I wondered whether standing one's ground was always like this. If it was, I didn't think I could keep it up.

When I opened my door, I noticed a creased piece of paper that must have been forced under the door. I looked at the crude drawing of a naked woman and immediately I felt a catch in my throat. The name *Kit* was written in almost childlike writing beside the enormous boobs and there was an arrow pointing to the crotch with the message 'Soon Darling' scrawled beside it. Sweat broke out on my forehead and my hand flew to cover my mouth.

A loud bang on the door made me jump. Frozen to the spot, I could hear my heart pounding as the hair on my arms stood to attention. Eventually, I heard my own quiet voice call, 'Who is it?' I knew as I asked that there was no chance of anyone hearing me through the thick door, but my voice had at least roused me from inertia.

The thought that this man could frighten me roused my anger and, as it mounted to fury, I threw caution to the wind and took a step towards the door, ferociously jerking it open.

There was silence. Nothing. But then I saw him leaning against a wall at the end of the corridor. He waved. He leered inanely and pointed at me and then to his crotch, before slowly turning and walking away. At that moment, my resolve melted and I realised I was gripping my hands so tightly that one of my fingernails had drawn blood. I rushed inside, locking the door with shaking hands.

I sat on the bed and it was some time before I became aware of the faint hum of the liner's engine once more. I picked up the creased paper and the crude picture seemed to jump out at me. Crumpling it into a ball, I angrily tossed it across the room, realising

I'd been naïve to open the door. Reaching for the brandy decanter, I downed a glass in one, then followed it with a second accompanied by two paracetamol tablets. I craved oblivion – that and the power to stop my limbs shaking.

I lay on the bed, waiting for the alcohol to work. I didn't want to think about it. Not right then. In fact, I didn't want to think about anything. Tomorrow would be time enough. Slowly, my breathing became heavy as my body relaxed into the stupor I craved.

The chemicals worked until three the next morning, when I awoke with a start. Images of Tom and Alex merged into a blur that seemed to float aimlessly around the pool of my thoughts. For a moment, I felt frantic in the darkness, but the bedside light brought relief and I struggled to bring my mind to the present time as I reached for the glass of water on the bedside cabinet.

My thoughts were slow and cumbersome, one frightening stillframe after another. Closing my eyes, I made a pact with myself. Nobody should be able to frighten me like that ever again. Nobody. I knew I had to attack the fear of Alex head on.

Gradually, the ticking clock brought a numbness and I turned over and fell back to sleep.

Next day, the early morning sunshine determinedly made its way into my room, its brightness dragging my brain from the land of sleep. No sooner had I opened my eyes than a chilling image of Alex leering at me took centre stage. What on earth was I going to do? The confidence that alcohol had instilled now evaporated.

I noticed a white envelope on the bedside table, placed beside the neat little tray of canapés that Juan must have left for me last night. I guessed from the neat writing of my name in blue fountain pen that it was from the captain.

My tired eyes scanned the page. The words 'precise coordinates' stood out but the words 'eleven o'clock tomorrow evening' eclipsed them.

I glanced at the little brown parcel sitting safely on the desk. So, finally it was to be opened. I didn't know whether to feel sad or happy. Relieved might be a better description, but as my eyes closed, feelings of any sort were whisked away into the morning sky. I'd deal with emotions later; right now, I simply needed to sleep again.

On waking a second time, my mind turned to thoughts of Mother. She had been in my mind such a lot these past few months and always conjured up a different memory – some good, others the very opposite. Today's memory was of a happy time after I'd left Tom and she was doing her best to support me, which had brought us closer together. She'd become a teetotaller by then and I wished I'd asked why she'd felt driven to alcohol in the first place, but I hadn't been able to voice the question. *Are other daughters as cowardly?* I wondered.

Out of the corner of my eye, I saw the white envelope again and remembered that this was to be the day. The day this whole trip was about. I hoped that at least I'd be able to move on, for, in truth, I was sick of it all. The shock. The overwhelming helplessness. The uncertainty. It will all soon be over and I so longed for a normal life again.

I phoned Jess and we arranged to meet in the café on the shuffleboard deck. I was already drinking my coffee by the time he arrived.

'Hi, Sis. How's things?'

I smiled and wondered whether I should tell him about Alex, but knowing Jess of old, I didn't think he'd be much help. 'I'm fine. How about you?'

'Oh, you know, life on board is much the same. All this fine dining is splendid, but I'm beginning to long for something simple such as a boiled egg.' Jess patted his stomach. 'And too much of a good thing doesn't do much for my waistline.'

'They'd boil you an egg if you ask and there's always the gym.'

'I get enough exercise with Allegra, thank you very much. That woman is a coiled spring ready to pounce! She's the most demanding woman I've ever been with.'

'Why do you stay with her then?'

Jess sighed. 'Oh my innocent little sister, why do you think? She has contacts. She has money and we're on our way to *her* country.
She's going to be the one to give me smooth entry into the world I'm seeking.'

'Well, if I were you, and if she isn't making your life happy, I wouldn't bother.'

'Aah, but you've never had any interest in making a name for yourself, have you? The knowledge of money and what it can bring seems to have passed you by.'

'As long as I've enough to get by, that'll do me.' I glanced at my watch. 'Anyway, I've got to meet someone at ten, so this is just a quick meeting to see if you're happy with the captain's instructions. I don't mind the deck he's suggested. Do you?'

'No. The quicker we can get it over, the better.'

'The captain said to phone any particular requirements. Have you done this?'

'No. Not yet.' Jess shrugged. 'I thought something simple and low-key would do. Is that okay with you?'

'Yes, that's fine. Will you let the captain know?'

'I'll ring him when I get back. Do you think we'll have to do anything?'

'I imagine the captain will guide us, but I can't imagine we'll need to sign anything or assist him in any way. I suppose a few words might be nice, if they're sincere.'

'Of course, if I'm asked to speak, my words will be sincere. Why shouldn't they be?'

I could think of a thousand reasons but kept quiet and stood to leave. 'You're not thinking of bringing Allegra, are you?'

Jess raised an eyebrow. 'Of course not. I keep her well out of the private side of my life. Anyway, you enjoy your ten o'clock rendezvous, big Sis.' He threw me a dazzling smile. 'You're a real dark horse, you are!'

'See you tonight at eleven then and don't be late.' I flung the last remark over my shoulder as I walked away.

My arranged meeting with Samuel, for some inexplicable reason, reminded me of the meeting I'd arranged with David for later today. It seemed a miracle that David had entered my world. The joy I felt just thinking about him transferred itself to a huge grin, which must have filled my face, although I was unaware of this until I realised strangers were returning my permanent smile.

As I approached the bar, I prayed that my assertive side would return, though I wasn't confident I could summon it on demand. I needn't have worried because, as I glanced around the empty bar, stirrings of anger churned in my stomach. My watch showed one minute to ten and I instinctively knew I'd give Samuel one minute to arrive. At ten o'clock precisely, I'd make my way to the reception area.

The one minute that I stood alone in the room gave me the time needed to stoke my fury and as an apologetic Samuel rushed in with only a few seconds to go, I glared at him, my anger having buried the permanent smile I wore only a few minutes ago.

I looked at my watch. 'Cutting it fine, aren't you?'

'I'm so sorry, Kit. I've no excuses, but I'm here now and it's only just ten o'clock.' He bent to kiss my hand, but I snatched it away before his lips could even brush the surface. An embarrassed cough left his lips. 'Shall we sit down, Kit?'

I chose two chairs that were facing each other and sat on the one in the window alcove, figuring that Samuel's face would be in full sunshine and it would be more difficult for him to hide any discomfort. 'Right, Samuel. I want to know all about Alex and please don't tell me lies.'

Samuel practised one of his disarming smiles, which bounced off my stony face. 'I wouldn't lie to you, Kit.'

'You tried to last night. This is your second and last chance to explain things and this time I expect honesty.'

Samuel sighed. 'I'm truly sorry that Alex didn't leave you contact details, but I'm telling you the truth when I say I'm unable to get in touch with him.'

'That be as it may, but I'm telling you that unless you wish me to report to reception what happened last night, then your memory had better improve.'

Samuel studied the rings on his hand and groaned. 'Kit, why won't you believe me?'

'Because it's not the whole story, is it? Perhaps you don't know Alex's phone extension, but there's more to this than you're letting on. So, I'm waiting… it's best you tell me what you know.'

'Look, I hardly knew Alex.' Samuel's voice was almost a whisper. 'He's been visiting the bar every night since we set sail. He told me he fancied you.'

'But I didn't know him until you introduced us last night.'

'However, he's been watching you ever since we set sail.'

'Good God, didn't it ever cross your mind that that was odd?'

'Well, no. Lots of men see a woman they fancy. I've done it myself.'

I rolled my eyes. Words escaped me.

'Alex asked me whether I could arrange a meeting. At first, I said it wasn't possible and you have to believe me this is completely true. But he was insistent and then he offered me money.'

'Money!'

Samuel studied the rings once more. 'Yes. Money. I'm sorry to say I took it. I need it. I've got quite a few financial problems.'

'How much?'

Samuel gulped. 'This sounds awful. It was two hundred American dollars.'

'Two hundred!'

'I'm not proud of this and if it ever got out, I'd lose my job, but I am being honest with you.'

'So all that baloney about Flash Mob night wasn't true?'

'No, Flash Mob night is the one occasion each sailing when we're able to invite passengers to a party. The only thing is Alex was invited as my guest, along with Lou and yourself. He's not employed on the ship. I lied about that.'

I sat back in the chair, my brain struggling to comprehend. 'For crying out loud, didn't it ever occur to you that was wrong?' He looked over my shoulder at the sea and shrugged.

'Another thing, why did Alex pretend he worked on the ship?'

'He seemed to think you'd find him more attractive if he had an important job.'

'I don't know what to say. You flirted with Lou, used her kind nature just so that you could invite me to this party. And at the bottom of it all was the knowledge you'd pocket two hundred dollars if you introduced me to Alex.'

'I'm sorry if it's upset you, Kit. Truly I am.'

The silence that filled the room had a frozen quality to it and I used the time to consider my next step. Samuel shifted and gripped the arms of his chair as though to stand, but I hadn't finished yet.

'Samuel, I think you owe me something.'

'Anything.'

'First of all, the money you were given by Alex should go to charity. You decide which charity and I'll organise it.' His face remained expressionless.

'Secondly, what time does Alex usually visit the bar?'

'He's either very early or very late.'

'I'll visit the bar tonight at six thirty. If he comes in before that time, you must keep him talking until I get here. It's impossible for me to come in late tonight, so I'll think again if I don't see him at six thirty. Okay?'

'Yes, Kit, that's fine, but please don't cause trouble in the bar tonight. And above all, I'm begging you don't talk about this to anyone else.'

I looked him straight in the eye. 'Let's see how it goes from here, shall we? I'll expect two hundred American dollars in a plain envelope this evening. Don't forget.' I stood and walked towards the exit, making it obvious that he'd been dismissed, but it didn't make me feel any better. In fact, I wondered whether I'd ever wake from this nightmare.

I pushed the salad around my plate with no thought of raising any of its parts to my lips. I felt guilty about the amount of food I'd wasted since boarding this liner and studied my handbag as though it was the receptacle for guilty thoughts.

A few minutes later, as I climbed the stairs to meet David, my excitement was mounting. I knew I was behaving like a lovesick teenager and wondered whether I was being foolish again. Suddenly, I saw a figure lurking in the shadow near the top of the stairs. I helplessly watched as it slowly moved towards the top stair. The sound of blood pumping in my ears blocked out all other sounds and I steadied myself against the wall as a sensation of nausea travelled from my gut to my throat. My first thought was escape and I prayed for someone to appear as I was unsure my legs were capable of running down the stairs.

'Are you all right? You look as though you've seen a ghost.' A stranger's voice broke through my fear and I looked at him with unseeing eyes. It wasn't Alex. It wasn't him. Thank God. My relief was slow to catch up with my racing heart.

The stranger was kind, leading me to an empty chair near the bottom of the stairs. He insisted on fetching a glass of water, which my trembling hand had difficulty holding.

'Do you have a friend on board? Somebody I could try and find for you?'

I shook my head and sat quietly next to the man who only a few minutes ago had caused my limbs to shake. Slowly, the girdle of fear loosened as my body regained normality. Now embarrassment replaced panic.

'You look much better now the colour's returned to your cheeks.' The man's voice sounded concerned. 'Are you sure there's no one on board I can contact for you before I leave?' It was a kindness I was grateful for, but nevertheless declined.

I had no idea how long I sat alone watching people walk past, but eventually thoughts of David drove Alex from my mind and courage returned. Gradually, I mounted the stairs once more, purposely averting my eyes from the area where I'd previously thought Alex had been hidden.

I felt uneasy as I searched the crowds on the main pool deck. With each footstep, a warning caution nagged me to remember Tom, but it was counterbalanced by my heart singing loudly as my eyes scanned the deck for David. As soon as I caught sight of him, I knew the heart had won.

David stood when he saw me approach. 'Are these two sunbeds okay?' He waved his arms expansively around the two neatly towelled beds.

'Yes. They're perfect. You've chosen a nice spot.'

'Good.'

I spent the first few minutes deciding where to place the various bits and pieces I'd unpacked from my holdall and when at last the suntan cream, Kindle, bottled water and all the other paraphernalia were in place I realised that nerves were causing all this unnecessary action. Nerves and the recent encounter on the stairs.

We exchanged smiles before an embarrassed silence settled over us. I reached for my Kindle.

'Is it a good book?' David asked as he settled back onto his sunbed.

'It's okay.' I wriggled my nose. 'I preferred her last one. She seems to have reinvented the same plot in this one.'

'Some authors do that, don't they? And television is as bad. Just because there were huge audience figures for the first programme, it doesn't mean we want the formula repeated ad infinitum. I immediately switch over nowadays when any cookery programme comes on and I used to love them.'

From this point onwards, our conversation flowed naturally from TV programmes to films, travel and, of course, cruising.

Throughout it all, I knew I was burying the personal subjects I longed to discuss.

We both gave the entertainment woman a withering look when she interrupted with the quiz leaflet. David glanced at the paper she'd thrust into his hands and looked at me. 'Do you want to do this? It looks as though there's twenty questions to answer.'

I'm not normally keen on quizzes, but the interruption had upset the glue of our conversation. 'If you want to, I don't mind. I suppose as we're sitting here, we're going to be forced to hear all the questions in any case.'

David smiled. 'Okay then, Miss Brain of Britain, we're in. Your first job is to think of a team name.'

'What about "The Young Sea Dogs"?'

David clapped his hands. 'Perfect first time.'

The next hour dissolved into itself. It felt as though seconds had passed before the winning team was on the stage being presented with their cocktail vouchers.

'Doesn't seem fair,' I quipped as I looked at the party on the stage. 'There are six of them and only two of us.'

'Never mind. We did okay. Fifteen out of twenty isn't bad.' David's eyes twinkled. 'Although I know that it was I who provided most of the answers.'

I pretended to hit him with my towel and we laughed, relaxing back into the softness of our sun loungers. David reached for my hand. 'Kit, I've enjoyed our afternoon together. I'd love to learn more about you as we've hardly talked about ourselves. I hope we might meet again on this cruise?'

Until he'd uttered these words, I hadn't realised quite how much I'd hoped to hear them. 'I'd love to spend more time with you, too, David, but there's plenty of time left this afternoon. Let's start now. Tell me about yourself.'

David smiled. 'What would you like to know?'

'Start with the basics. You know: hobbies, where you were born, your family, work – that kind of thing.'

'Okay. It's pretty boring, mind you.' He grimaced. 'Get ready to fall asleep. My hobbies? I suppose I only have one that's serious. I enjoy martial arts.'

'I don't know much about martial arts. My mind conjures up kicking and punching, just as you see in video games.'

David laughed. 'Well, there's a bit more to it than that. It's more about defence and self-discipline. I joined my club to get fit, then I got hooked.'

'Oh, I thought you meant you watched martial arts, not took part in it.'

He gave a lopsided grin. 'Next question?'

'Where were you born?'

'A little town called Almaraz in Spain, but I don't remember anything about it because my parents moved back to the UK when I was a baby. We lived in Somerset because my dad got a job at Hinkley Point Nuclear Power Station.' David paused and rubbed his chin. 'I'm the eldest and I've two sisters, both bossy as hell. What else do you want to know?'

'Your work. And how about your personal life. What do you like doing? Have you been in a serious relationship etc.?' I threw in the last question very quickly, feeling self-conscious as I did so.

'My work is often considered dull, but I love it. I'm a software engineer. Get ready, here's the boring description bit – I promise it won't be scintillating. In a nutshell, I determine operational feasibility by evaluating analysis, problem definition and, at the end, hopefully, come up with development and solutions.'

I was immediately reminded of Alex and wondered whether David might have a solution to this problem.

'My likes: dining out in nice restaurants, listening to music and as well as practising karate, I do enjoy travelling. So whenever I get the chance of a holiday, I grab it with both hands. Your question about relationships.' He paused. 'I don't want to lie to you. They haven't been great.'

I realise I'm holding my breath.

'I married when I was nineteen. At the time I thought it was love, but I was too young to know the difference between love and lust. It wasn't to last and it was over a long time ago.' He shrugged. 'And here's the sad bit about it all… I wouldn't accept the situation. From the moment my wife said it was over, I refused to believe her and tried to find solutions to our problems. I experienced panic, rage, numbness – you say it, I felt it.'

'David, you don't have to tell me any more. Honestly. I shouldn't have asked.'

He shook his head. 'No. I want to tell you everything. Make a clean slate. Otherwise, we have no foundation.'

He closed his eyes for a few seconds. Then, at last, with hands held before him and the tips of his fingers touching, he spoke again.

'When my wife told me she was filing for divorce, I thought if I found another woman, she'd come to her senses. She'd be jealous and realise she loved me. I met Carly in a pub, spent lots of money on her over several weeks and it developed from there. I want you to know that I'm not proud of this, Kit.'

I was unable to speak. There seemed to be no words to say.

'Unfortunately, Carly didn't make my wife jealous. In fact, my wife seemed pleased that I'd found someone else. And do you know the worst thing of all?' I shook my head.

'The baby.'

'A baby. Your child?'

David's sigh was resigned and weary. 'Yes, my child. She's called Sophie.'

My eyes remained fixed on David's face. It was as if my brain needed time to process what had been said.

'She's fourteen years old now. Lives with her mother in London.'

'Are you close with her?'

'Sophie or her mother?'

'Sophie.'

'I'd like to be, she's all I have. She's part of me. But I see her twice a year, around Christmas and her birthday. That's all. Because Carly and I did not marry, it's difficult gaining access to see my daughter.'

'Difficult?'

'Carly didn't put my name on the birth certificate as the father, so I've no legal rights or access to Sophie. I do give

Carly money to help with the costs of bringing up my child, but she insisted from the outset that the money had to be in cash placed in an envelope and handed to her at a local park or some other public place. We exchange no words at these meetings.' David grimaced. 'In fact, it's a bit like a scene from a James Bond movie. Espionage has nothing compared to the way we behave.'

'That's awful. Can't you request a DNA test so you can prove you're Sophie's father?'

'I've tried. But without Carly's agreement, it can't happen, and she's refused to sign anything.'

'There must be something you can do. What if you stopped giving her the money? Maybe that would force her into signing.'

'That doesn't seem right. I would be depriving my child of support and I don't want to do that.'

'You've got a big problem.'

'There is a possibility I could request a DNA test be completed by an order of the court, but even that isn't straightforward or easy. In any case, I believe it's too late. Sophie will soon be fifteen and I doubt she'd welcome a dad in her life now.' David's eyes caught mine. 'Carly and I were together for less than a year and you'd never call our relationship meaningful. I now speak to her once a year on the phone to discuss maintenance payments. That's it, really.'

'Is Sophie your only child?' It was such a personal question and totally outside my comfort zone, but if David and I were to have any kind of relationship, there must be no secrets from the start. 'If you mean, did my wife and I have children, the answer is no. Sophie is my only child.'

'Well, Kit. That's it. My life. My messy life. You know it all now, there are no other secrets to reveal.'

'I'm glad you've told me all of this and I promise nothing will be repeated.'

'So, dare I believe you still feel favourably towards our friendship?'

I smiled. 'Yes, I do and thank you for trusting me by sharing your past. D'you know what someone once told me?' David shook his head.

'That the thing that helps most when you have troubles is to talk about them.'

'I've certainly done that. I've never told anyone all this before. I've even surprised myself. Now it's time for you to tell all.'

I gave him a potted version of my life. It felt right to tell him about Tom and my dream of becoming a Mum. I skirted round my relationship with Mother and tried to talk positively about Jess – he was my brother, after all.

When all words had been spoken, we laid back on our sunbeds and when David reached for my hand, I clasped it eagerly. I suppose anyone glancing at us that afternoon would have presumed we were partners. The safeness I felt being with him told me it was time to let my guard down and let go of the past. Perhaps this was the turning point in my life.

DAVID

The quietness of my cabin allowed my feelings of guilt to overpower. How stupid could a man be? I leant against the wall, shoulders rigid, my feet refusing to move from the spot. *Why did you lie?* I wanted to shout the words, but I swallowed them instead. I'd locked too many memories behind a door, but Kit had forced me to glimpse the sliver of light underneath and yet still Id refused to come clean and unlock the door.

I walked in a fog of regret towards the terrace and collapsed into one of the recliners. I should have told Kit the truth today. But I hadn't. Despite well-laid plans and rehearsed words, those bright, honest eyes studying mine had made truth impossible. Had I revealed everything, all my selfish baggage, I'm sure she'd have walked away there and then, and that would have been the end of our relationship, such as it is.

I reached for my wallet and took out a picture of Sophie standing with her mother, their hands shielding their eyes from the bright seaside sunshine. It's the only photo I have – I stole it from Carly's mantlepiece a year or so back, but I wished it was just a photo of my daughter as I've no wish to be reminded of Carly.

Thoughts of Carly always reminded me of her words after one hell-rooster of a fight we'd endured; the air was blue as Carly's temper increased and then she spat out the sentence she knew would hurt me the most, 'Abortion is a sin, you know, and you instigated it.' I wish I'd never told Carly that particular secret on the intimate, wine-soaked night we'd once enjoyed, but then again I deserved her barbs, for I was as guilty as my wife.

My face, unseen by anyone on that windy terrace, crumpled as I looked at my daughter's beautiful face. To think I might have had two children had I behaved differently.

It was some time before I carefully returned the picture to my wallet and, when I did, it felt as though my heart was being crushed slowly in a vice. I lowered my face into my hands and let out an audible shaky sigh. Today, I'd wasted a precious opportunity to tell the woman who already meant so much to me the truth about my past – maybe I'd never be strong enough to do so. However, if I didn't tell her, I knew the secret would eventually stifle the dim chance we had that love might develop.

I stood and reached for the whisky bottle. I needed to escape these thoughts, escape this situation and obliterate all thoughts of Kit from my mind. I must stop reality from entering my consciousness. At least for now. Tonight, I would meet Kit again and I needed to act with some normality. Oh, why was life so difficult?

KIT

As I made my way to Samuel's bar later that afternoon, I concluded that regardless of how things turned out, meeting David on this liner was an important turning point in my life. Almost as important as the time I'd stayed with Mother and been given the chance to get to know her better. The pity was that there'd only been that one chance, for Mother's guilt and painful memories returned far too soon and then, once more, she couldn't bear to be sober. For my entire life, I'd feared I might follow in her footsteps. There was always a feeling of failure in my life, like a heavy blanket I'd been unable to shake off. But the late arrival of maturity and a blossoming confidence was, at last, making me realise that I was no different to everyone else. Yes, I was as okay as the next woman.

I wasn't foolish enough to believe that everything would always be happy and positive, but I knew I'd never again let my life bob up and down, out of control in the deep sea. I'd well and truly ditched self-evaluation based on other people's opinions, as Samuel was once more about to find out.

Samuel rushed from behind the bar to greet me as I entered the room.

'He's not been in tonight, Kit,' he whispered as he gently touched my elbow and guided me towards a quieter area of the room. 'He did pop in at lunchtime, though, which is unusual.'

My cold stare instantly told Samuel that I was taking no prisoners and the hard edge to my voice made him wince. 'And didn't you think to encourage Alex to pop in around this time of day or at least find out what time he might call again?'

'Wait. Kit. Listen to what I've got to say.' He fidgeted with the bar coasters on the table. 'Alex came in to ask whether I knew where you were as he hadn't seen you around and he wanted to talk with you. He said he has very deep feelings for you.'

I sucked in sharply, not trusting myself to speak.

Samuel frowned. 'Kit, I'm in total confusion here. You've never told me why you want to see him. I think you owe me that information. Do you, by any chance, like him?' My face proclaimed the answer.

'Mm. I thought it would be unlikely. He's a bit of a strange man.'

'A bit?'

'I think he means well, but he's very nervous around people, especially females. Do you mind if I ask whether he's done something wrong? Did he behave improperly on Flash Mob night? That is, if it's okay to ask you this, Kit.'

I wondered whether to trust Samuel, but decided he just might have some idea of the next move. 'Samuel, I'm going to tell you something in confidence and it's going to sound a little odd.' I hesitated. 'I believe Alex is stalking me.'

'No, I can't believe that.'

'I'm absolutely sure it's him.' I told Samuel of the various encounters and his face told me he was uncomfortable hearing the words.

'So,' I concluded, 'I want to talk to him, face to face, in a busy public area.'

'Do you have a plan of what you want to say?'

'Basically, leave me alone.'

'Do you think that'll do anything?'

'It's better than doing nothing, isn't it? Do you have any other suggestions?'

Samuel made a noisy intake of breath. 'It seems to me that we need something on him – you know, incriminating proof that he's done something wrong.'

'He has. He's been stalking me, but I'm not sure how I'm going to get proof. People could say it was my imagination.'

'We'll fabricate proof. Make something up. Look, will you leave it with me, Kit? Let me think about it. Can you pop in later?'

I looked at my watch. 'There's not much free time, to be honest, as I'm meeting someone for dinner.'

'Tell you what, just for you, I'll be in the bar in the morning at, say, twelve o'clock? I should be asleep, mind you.'

'Thank you, Samuel. I appreciate it.'

'I take it that the two hundred dollars might be overlooked now?'

'Let's just see what happens, shall we? But at this moment in time, I think charity needs it more than you.' a

I rushed back to my cabin, trying to bury the thought that Alex might be around the next corner. I was aware that I had very little time to prepare myself mentally for the evening ahead. After all, this was what the entire trip had been about.

I picked up the box, its brown paper still pristine. Tonight, Jess and I would face the ordeal of opening it together. I sighed. At least the waiting would be over and that could only be good. Carefully placing the box back on the desk, I scuttled towards the bathroom. I was well aware that within the hour I'd be in David's company and in three hours I'd be with Jess and the captain.

This was going to be a very peculiar evening and confusion ruled my mind as I endeavoured to sort out my feelings. The shower water, for some inexplicable reason, brought memories of Mother to the fore, and my uncontrollable tears joined the water spray. I'd never thought of grief as a physical thing, but at times my limbs felt so heavy that to move them took effort. This hadn't happened before the depressing days, when I'd sorted through Mother's belongings. I could only think there was a relationship between the two.

I'd taken many bags of clothing to charity shops, driving miles out of my way as I'd no wish to see Mother's belongings in a charity shop near home. Jess, of course, had been nowhere to be seen throughout this difficult period and did nothing. He once visited Mother's house early after her death, but I believed this was because he thought valuable jewellery might be around. I was glad in some ways that Mother had sold anything valuable years before, although sadly the money it made had been spent on alcohol rather than other comforts.

Mr Jones-Regal, Mother's solicitor, had guided me through the abundant paperwork that a death demands, and when I'd reached the point of having nothing left to do, I tried to carry on with some semblance of normal life. Although, from that time onwards, hardly a day had passed when I hadn't thought about Mother and wished I'd known her better.

I dressed quickly in readiness for meeting David but had difficultly losing those morbid thoughts. After all, I told myself, I was going to meet a man I liked. A man who was special. Surely sadness could wait for later. I made my way to one of the big plush chairs in the library and flicked through a magazine that was neatly arranged on the coffee table. At last, anticipation drove reminisces of sadness away.

'Am I late?' David looked worried as he entered the library. 'I'm sorry.'

'No, you're not late. I was a little early, that's all.'

'Thank goodness. Have you thought about which restaurant you'd like to visit tonight?'

'I don't mind. Do you have any preference?'

'I was wondering whether Le Blanc Hibiscus might be a good choice.'

'You know only certain passengers are allowed to use that restaurant?'

He cocked his head to one side and smiled. 'So? Come on, let's see if the maître d' has one of those lumière tables free tonight.' We walked silently towards the restaurant. When we entered the ornate glass doors, I hoped for once that Jess and Allegra were there. I would enjoy seeing their faces when they saw David and I hand in hand. David looked very handsome in his navy suit; he could turn the heads of many of the fashionable women in this restaurant.

A smiling waiter seated us in the centre of the restaurant and proceeded to hand us the evening menu.

David looked at the waiter. 'All the waiters look especially smart tonight; your red jackets add something special to the evening.'

The waiter self-consciously brushed down the front of his jacket. 'This is my classic jacket. I only wear it when a special occasion calls for all banquet servers to be traditionally dressed as befits the function.'

'What is the special celebration this evening?'

'It's not a celebration, Sir. We're remembering and honouring those who lost their lives on the *Titanic* during a transatlantic crossing.'

We stared transfixed at the waiter.

'We dress to pay our respects. There's a short service and wreath laying tonight when we pass over the spot that the *Titanic* sank. You've probably seen the notices around the ship, plus information would have been left in your cabin by your butler.' 'A service, you say. Where?' My voice sounded weak.

'On the upper deck, Ma'am. It will be on the starboard side, somewhere near the main swimming pool. Everyone is welcome.'

'Thank you.'

David took my hand in his. 'Is everything all right?'

I nodded and reached for the menu, hoping to hide my discomfort.

When, a little later, orders had been placed, we sat quietly staring at the dining table. I absentmindedly repositioned my cutlery by a few centimetres and then put everything back to its original place. 'Kit, whatever's the matter? Don't you want to eat in this restaurant? You should have said before.'

'No, I don't mind eating here and there is nothing wrong.'

'But there so obviously is. What on earth is it? Have I said something to upset you?'

'David, you've been wonderful company and a perfect companion.' I shrugged. 'It's just me.'

'Well, are you going to tell me what it is, or do I have to sit in this strange atmosphere all night?'

'I'm sorry, David. Really, I am.'

'Right. Apologies over.' He placed his hand on top of mine and smiled. 'Last night I told you my problems, now it's your turn. I'm listening.'

Later, I could remember very little of that evening. I've no idea what I ate or whether I saw Jess. In fact, my biggest memory is that of unburdening a lifetime of sorrow about my relationship with Mother. I decided that there was something about the finality of death that allowed memories to surface. The wonder of it all was that David seemed to understand. He really did. This man lit up my heart and made me feel safe. I thought I was falling in love and this time there'd be no sorrow. It was going to be for good.

The time I'd dreaded had almost arrived. I left David waiting at the end of the corridor while I returned to my room to collect the treasured parcel, but it didn't seem long before I heard a gentle knock on the door.

'Are you okay? You've been gone quite a while.'

'Oh, I'm sorry, David. I've been lost in my thoughts. Come in for a second.'

As soon as I'd closed the door, there was another knock. This time it was a ship's officer dressed in a pristine white suit. 'Ma'am, my name is Mathew Rowberry and I'm the First Officer on board. The captain has asked me to accompany you to the lower stern deck.'

'I'd no idea that anyone would escort me.'

'I'll wait outside, Ma'am, until you're ready.'

David put his arm around my shoulders. 'This is it, Kit. It's not going to be easy, but remember it's what your mother wanted.' I nodded, as I couldn't trust words to leave my throat.

'Ready?'

I smiled weakly and held the box like it had the fragility of a rainbow as we descended the stairs down to the lower deck. Jess stared at me curiously when he saw I was holding the arm of David, a man he'd never met.

The captain and the waiting officers bowed their heads as we approached and when everyone seemed ready, Captain Hurley addressed Jess and I directly.

'We are gathered here for a very sad occasion. To scatter the ashes of a parent is never pleasant, but to scatter the ashes of both parents must be very difficult for you both. However, this evening, we're making a fitting tribute to two loved ones, who, during their long lifetimes, adored sailing and life aboard their many different sailing vessels.' The captain's face was sombre as he glanced around our little group. 'I have discussed this ceremony with both Kit and Jess and they have decided they wish this service to be a quiet, low-key affair, as their parents would have wished. In a few minutes, we will scatter the ashes of Mr and Mrs Langford at the position the *Titanic* went down, but first Jess wishes to say a few words.'

Jess removed a single piece of paper from his pocket and glanced at it before taking a step forwards. 'Our father lived a long life and was a good man. He loved his family and he loved his boats. In fact, his favourite pastime was to get away for a weekend of sailing. Once they married, Mother soon adopted a love of sailing that matched that of Father.' Jess cleared his throat. 'Father was a serious and disciplined man, who single-handedly built a business empire. His knowledge, mental toughness and forward-thinking made Global International Pulses the largest distributor of pulses in the world. He was a great man and a wonderful father.'

I shifted from one foot to another. This was not the father I remembered and I wondered when Mother was going to be mentioned.

Jess glanced at his notes. 'And now to our mother. A beautiful, charismatic woman in her younger days, or so I've been told, but by the time I was an adult and old enough to know her properly, illness had entered her life and coloured her existence. Nevertheless, we want to thank you, Mother, for everything you've given us. And Father, thank you for the warmth we shared during your precious time on earth. God bless you. Always.'

That Jess had said so little about Mother angered me and, out of the blue, I heard myself ask the captain if I could say a few words.

The captain smiled 'Of course you may, Kit. Perhaps you would like to do so now.'

I looked nervously around at the small party. 'I hadn't planned to speak tonight but have decided I wish to say a few words after all. I've not made any notes, so I'm afraid my words will not be as polished as those of my brother, but they are coming from the heart.'

I swallowed hard. 'I didn't know Father well. He was often away on business when I was a child and when our parents divorced, I was still very young. I saw even less of him after the divorce, so I think there's very little I can add to Jess's words. Our mother, on the other hand, I got to know a little better, especially when, as an adult, my own life developed its problems. She was there for me then, she welcomed me to her home and looked after me. She comforted me and, for the first time in our lives, we actually had meaningful conversations. In fact, it was then that we became close. I came to realise that the illness, as Jess described it, was her way of coping. She would rather not have been ill, but seemed powerless to escape from it. I haven't much more to say except to thank them both for the gift of life and to say I shall miss my mother and dearly wish we had enjoyed a more meaningful time together.'

I looked at the captain before continuing, 'I've copied a poem that I thought you might read before the ashes are scattered. It seemed so appropriate.'

'Kit, may I suggest that perhaps you and your brother read the poem together as I scatter the ashes?' The captain unwrapped the paper and took out the box that I'd so carefully looked after. He undid the clasp of the plastic bag inside and moved to the ship's rail, smiling remorsefully as he nodded at Jess and me.

'This poem was written by Val Hughes and is called "White Horses".' From some mysterious place, my voice became strong as Jess's voice joined mine.

> *White horses crest the waves*
> *Riding the tides as must we yet*
> *Holding fast to the life you lived*
> *Memories made.*
>
> *Go gently into the spirit winds*
> *That drift across the ocean plains*
> *Ride those horses, travel on*
> *While we take comfort from*
> *The sea of life you used to be.*

I'm not going to cry, I thought savagely, as I watched the last of the ashes drift down to the sea. Captain Hurley allowed silence to cloak our little crowd for a few minutes so that each person had time to reflect upon their feelings.

Eventually, he spoke, 'The final wishes of Jess and Kit's parents have been honoured here this evening. This ceremony is what they wanted, but I think this is a good time to remind everyone that death is only the end of a chapter. Mourn not the passing of a life, but celebrate its existence. Count the times your souls smiled together and as their spirits watch over you, accept them into your heart and remember them with love.'

He smiled directly at Jess and me. 'Unfortunately, I'm unable to stay with you longer this evening as I'm needed on pool deck where a small service is being undertaken to honour those who tragically lost their lives when the *Titanic* sank. However, I have arranged for a drink and a few canapes to be available in one of the private rooms. Mathew, my First Officer, together with Robert and Gavin, two of my senior officers, will escort you there if this is something you wish, but if you prefer to be alone, you need only say.'

Captain Hurley inclined his head, 'May I say on a personal note that I'm very sorry for your loss, and I hope our little gathering this evening has gone some way to easing the pain you must be feeling.'

With these words, he shook hands with Jess and I before departing. -o-

It was over. The time to say goodbye had passed and I remember nothing of the hour that followed. It wasn't until I'd returned to my cabin in the early hours of the following morning that I allowed myself to grieve and the tears I'd fought throughout the ceremony finally won. The finality of it all passed through me like a hurricane and I let out a long, doleful moan, identical to that of an injured animal. The floodgates opened then and tears burst forth like water from a dam.

I was grateful that David hadn't allowed me to stay alone and as I sank from the sofa to my knees, my world turned into a blur. David lowered himself beside me and gathered me to his chest. He instinctively seemed to know there was no point in making empty platitudes. I needed this release.

It was some time before my stomach relaxed and the raw emptiness I felt inside began to subside. I knew that the ferocity of my tears would never bring Mother back and grief would undo nothing, but this was of little consequence. I wept until there were no tears left and then David and I simply sat there, hand in hand.

Eventually, I turned to him. 'I'm sorry. I...' Words faltered as he gently wiped my face with tissues.

'There's no need to be sorry, Kit. You've had quite a week one way or another and you've been very brave.'

'But Mother might still be here if only she'd given up the alcohol. It took everything from her.' A sob escaped.

'I know, Kit. I know. But she's at peace. She's free now. Didn't that lovely poem you chose say just that?'

'But now I'll have no chance of getting to know her.'

'You're her only daughter and I believe you've already got to know her far more than you realise. Those months you lived together seem to me to be her swan song especially for you. A final gesture to show you that she wished to make up for everything that had gone before. She loved you, Kit. That's obvious from what you've told me. You've got to be brave. Live your life to the full. For her sake.'

'I'm so tired, David. So tired.'

'I know. Time for bed.'

'David, would you stay? Just this one night. It would be comforting to have another person in the room tonight.'

'Of course I'll stay, if it helps.' He smiled tenderly. 'You've got a huge sofa.'

Ten minutes later, I climbed into my own gigantic bed and in those brief minutes between waking and sleeping, when reality begins to warp, I heard David's soothing voice and felt him kiss my forehead.

Within seconds, I was lost to the world.

The first thing I saw next morning was a slip of paper on the bedside table.

> *Hope you're okay. I left quietly this morning.*
> *Didn't want to wake you. Thought you needed your sleep.*
> *Returned to my stateroom.*
> *Ring me when/where to meet.*
>
> *David x*

The words brought it all back and embarrassment flooded over me. What must he think? A grown woman needing another adult in the room while they slept. The next memory that uncomfortably marched into my head was that of Alex. I shivered. Yesterday, I'd said goodbye to my parents. Today, I hoped against hope I'd be saying goodbye and good riddance to Alex.

My eyes took in the rays of sunshine and I knew I'd slept too long. I glanced at the clock. Ten o'clock! My limbs flexed in shock. I was supposed to visit Captain Hurley at ten o'clock. Good grief.

In the grip of silent panic, I rushed to the bathroom and then turned around and immediately headed back to the phone.

'Hello. Hello. Can I speak to Captain Hurley?'

'I am sorry, Ma'am. Captain Hurley doesn't take calls from passengers unless it's been previously arranged.'

'But I'm supposed to be seeing him right now.'

'I'm sorry, Ma'am. I'll connect you to one of his officers. Perhaps they'll be able to help you.'

'But…' It was of no use, only clicks and whirls could be heard on the other end of the line. I tapped my fingers on the table. 'Come on. Come on.'

A minute passed, but it felt like an hour. I banged the phone down and instantly picked it up again. This time, my call was answered quickly.

'One minute I'll put you through.'

'Juan. It's Kit Langford, stateroom 7109. Can you help me, please?'

'Of course, Ma'am. What can I do for you?' Juan's voice was soothing, but it did not stop the agitation that was taking place in my brain.

As soon as I'd explained the situation, Juan assured me that Captain Hurley would know immediately, and he promised to call me if the captain wished to make alternative arrangements.

The phone rang just as I was about to step into the shower. 'It's Juan, Ma'am. Captain Hurley said not to worry. He's talking to your brother at the moment, but if you are able to join them before eleven o'clock, he would be pleased to see you. I can escort you to his office by the bridge if you wish, Ma'am.'

'Thank you, Juan. Yes, please. I'll be ready in ten minutes. Maybe even five.'

'I'll wait in the corridor outside your stateroom. Join me when you're ready, Ma'am.'

I was ready in five minutes. I threw clothes on, made a one sentence call to David and rushed out of the door. It wasn't until I caught sight of myself in the lift mirror that I realised I was wearing odd sandals. *Oh well*, I thought, *I doubt anyone will notice.*

Jess's voice attacked my ears when Captain Hurley opened his office door. 'Where on earth have you been, Kit? We've been waiting ages for you.'

'Never mind.' Captain Hurley smiled at me and gestured that I sit in the chair next to Jess. 'You're here now, that's all that matters. It was quite a day for you yesterday. Quite a day for you both. Your brother and I have had an interesting conversation about cricket, so no worries.'

'I was here on time.' Jess looked directly at me, his annoyance obvious.

The captain diverted the conversation. 'Ah, but we're men. Our ladies are a little more fragile in these situations. Don't you think?' Jess nodded begrudgingly and the captain made his way to his side of the desk. He unlocked the middle drawer and took out two envelopes.

'Let's begin, shall we? As you know, Mr Jones-Regal, the Bristol solicitor who represented your parents, charged me with the responsibility of overseeing the scattering of the ashes.' Both Jess and I nodded solemnly.

'I contacted Mr Jones-Regal first thing this morning. The time difference between the UK and our present position is in our favour, so he replied immediately, confirming that I should now hand you the envelopes left in my care.'

Captain Hurley pulled a small form from the same drawer. 'Please could you both sign here and then here to confirm that I've given you a sealed envelope. This is just a formality and one of these copies will be returned to Mr Jones-Regal for his records.'

I recognised Mother's handwriting on the envelope as it was handed to me. Whether Jess recognised the writing would never be known for as soon as the envelope was in his hand, he instantly tore it open. His nostrils flared and his mouth was frozen wide open as he scanned the one-page contents of his envelope.

'What the…' Jess's booming voice angrily filled the room. 'This isn't the will!'

'I'm sorry I have no idea of the contents of these envelopes. I was tasked with the duty of handing them to you at the appropriate time.' Captain Hurley stood and slowly made his way to the door. 'I do not need this office for a while so I will leave you both here to talk things over. If you decide you wish to call Mr Jones-Regal, then it can be arranged. Perhaps you will let the Officer in the room outside know if this is the case.'

'Captain Hurley.' My voice was almost a whisper. 'I just wanted to say thank you from both of us. You've been very kind and helpful throughout this difficult time.'

'It's my pleasure, Kit.' He smiled warmly. 'I hope that things proceed smoothly from now on.'

As soon as the door closed, I turned to Jess. 'That was rude, Jess. You didn't even say thank you.'

'So what? I heard you say it for me. That'll do, won't it?' I pursed my lips together. Sometimes, I despair of my brother.

Jess frantically waved his piece of paper in front of me. 'See this. What's our mother playing at? I thought we were going to get a copy of the will today, didn't you?'

'I didn't think about it, to be honest. Since we boarded this liner, my mind's been on scattering the ashes most of the time.'

'Well, we've been well and truly stitched up by Mother. It seems we have to wait until we get to New York to officially find out the contents of the will.'

I fingered my sealed envelope.

'Don't bother to open it. It's going to be the same as mine. Apparently, when we land in New York, we have to contact Messrs Selby and Cromwell, who specialise in wills and probate. Our mother informs us that they have been working with dear Mr Jones-Regal, back in Bristol. What next? How many more hoops do we have to jump through? I bet they'll have us clean the Statue of Liberty, which, of course, will be closely monitored before we learn the contents of the will.'

'Jess, why are you so angry about this? There's only the two of us and odds on they've decided to divide the estate in half. Don't you think?'

Jess shot me a strange look and grunted as he made his way to the door. 'It's all this time wasting. Mr Jones-Regal could have simply read the will to us when we were in Bristol instead of all this messing around.'

'No, he couldn't. He had to honour Mother and Father's wishes.'

I thrust the unopened envelope into my bag. I was aware that time was fast running away and I needed to meet David. There'd be no time to explain about Alex before meeting Samuel now. A potted version would have to do.

-o-

There was a concerned expression on David's face as I drew near a few minutes later.

'Are you all right, Kit?'

'Yes. I'm getting there. I've just come from the captain's office. I'll tell you all about that later.'

'Do you have any plans for this morning? We could have a late brunch, if you haven't eaten.'

'I haven't had time to eat yet, but I must tell you something before we see Samuel. Perhaps we can eat afterwards.'

'Samuel?'

'It's a long story and I'll tell you the full story later, but for now an outline will have to do.'

David's eyes grew larger as I gave him a summarised version of things. 'So, this Flash Mob night was the evening we first met?' David asked when I'd eventually finished.

I nodded.

'And this man called Alex was who you thought was following you that night?'

'I wasn't sure it was Alex at the time, but now I am.'

'What are you hoping for from this meeting with Samuel?'

'I'm not sure. It depends on what he tells me. Would you to come with me? You don't need to say a word unless you want to. Just be by my side.'

David reached for my hand and gave it a gentle squeeze. 'Of course I'll come. There's no need to ask.'

-o-

Samuel stared when he saw us walk into the bar. 'Kit, I thought this was going to be a meeting between just the two of us.'

'I didn't say that, Samuel. This is my friend, David. David meet Samuel.'

Samuel shifted weight from one foot to another as he shook hands with David. 'I'm unsure about discussing anything in front of another person.'

'David knows about everything, including the two hundred dollars you were paid. You've nothing to fear. Or hide.' I sat in the nearest chair. 'Samuel, I've had a difficult morning already, so before you begin, do you think we could all have a glass of iced water and sit here like civilised people discussing things rationally and honestly?'

'I'm afraid there are no peanuts or anything – it's all locked away,' Samuel announced as he put down the tray with three glasses of iced water.

'Peanuts aren't important. Now, have you seen Alex since we last spoke?'

'Yes. He propped up the bar last night. He stayed hours and drove me mad saying how much he loved you. He's moved on from simply saying that he had deep feelings for you.'

I noticed David had clenched his fists together and was obviously uncomfortable, a fact made even more obvious by his tight-lipped smile.

'He said that he just has to see you again. Or he'll go crazy.' 'He'll go crazy. What about me?' I pointed to my chest.

'I don't think his thoughts wander much outside of himself, to be quite honest.'

'Right. Tell me then, what have you arranged?'

'He's given me his room number and I've promised to phone him next time you come into the bar.'

I rubbed my forehead roughly and a brief silence descended on all three of us.

'You said yesterday about fabricating something on him. Have you come up with any ideas?'

Before Samuel could reply, David butted in, 'I don't think that's a very good idea. It wouldn't be honest. There must be some other way.'

Something flashed beneath the surface of Samuel's calm outward demeanour. 'And just what do you suggest, David?'

'I haven't had time to think about it yet.'

'That's not much help then, is it?'

I let out a slow, controlled breath, hoping to diffuse the rising tension. 'This is getting us nowhere. Let's try to put ourselves in Alex's position. He's been stalking me, but that would be hard to prove. He's lied by telling me he's a First Engineer on board. He's been vulgar and lewd to me in front of an audience.' 'Lewd!' David spat the word out.

'Yes, I was on the stage as a contestant in some silly singing competition, and he was in the audience frantically rubbing his crotch and making blow-job signs at me. It was disgusting.'

'It's more than disgusting, Kit. It's revolting. Surely that's sexual harassment? Did anybody see it?'

'They must have, but I was too embarrassed to take much notice of anyone's reaction.'

'But can't you see, Kit? That's it. We meet him and accuse him of sexual harassment. We can say that we're going to tell the authorities on board.'

'I haven't any witnesses.'

'Alex doesn't know that.' David grinned. 'I could say I witnessed it.'

Samuel's face fell. 'You were telling me that my idea to fabricate something was dishonest. Now you're suggesting that we do just that.'

'This is different, though. Alex actually was lewd. It's not being made-up – no fabrication whatsoever. He did it and moreover he did it when surrounded by passengers. The only false bit of information is that I say that I saw it.'

'I don't think it will work.'

'Samuel, it will work, believe me, and if he's sceptical, we can always throw in the stalking. He knows he's guilty. He'll cave in.

Believe me—'

I interrupted. 'David, I think you might have something. It's worth a try.'

Samuel grimaced. 'What do you two geniuses want me to say to Alex then?'

'I want to get it over with as soon as possible. Perhaps I should visit him in his cabin this afternoon?'

'His cabin!' David's voice exploded with a sudden force.

'Yes. It needs to be a quiet place and he's bound to be welcoming to me. I'll explain to him that I've been approached by someone who witnessed his behaviour by the pool and I want him to stop following me, otherwise I'll allow the witness to take things further.'

'You're playing a dangerous game, Kit. I don't think this is a good idea.'

'Can't you see it's best I go alone? If you stand in the corridor outside, I'll have backup just in case. I've got to face Alex and put this fear behind me. I'm going to turn into a quivering mess otherwise.'

'I do understand.' David smiled at me. 'But you've no idea what he might do. He'll be much stronger than you and I won't be able to get through a closed door to help. Let's go together.'

'No, David. I don't think he'll let us both in and then we've blown our cover. At least he doesn't know about you at the moment.'

David shook his head. 'Well, I don't like it. It's dangerous.'

'I've decided. I'll get inside his cabin and make sure that he doesn't put the lock down on the door. Then, if you hear me shout, you can rush in.' My voice sounded far more confident than the inner churning of my gut proclaimed.

'Samuel, ring him and tell him I'll be knocking on his cabin door at three o'clock this afternoon. Don't tell him anything else. And remember, I haven't decided yet what I'm going to do about the money you've been paid.'

'Are you sure about this? David might have something -'

'Three o'clock, Samuel.'

'I'll arrange it, but that's my part over, Kit. I'm doing no more.' David and I walked hand in hand away from the bar, leaving Samuel to do his bit.

'Are you sure about this, Kit?'

'I've got to get it over with as soon as possible and at least my brave side is in control at the moment. Anyway, I think I've got one of those panic whistles in my luggage somewhere. I'll fish it out. I bought it for New York, never dreaming I might need it on the liner.'

David stopped walking and shook his head. 'I wish you wouldn't do this, Kit.'

'I'm going to do it. With or without your help. I believe Alex isn't a nasty person deep down. Just a bit sad. That's all. He probably needs help or at least someone to care about him.'

David sighed. 'I'll be right outside the door, so you just make sure that lock isn't on.'

'I will, don't worry. Thank you for supporting me and, while I'm saying thank you, I'm sorry that I made you sleep on the sofa in my room last night. A grown woman needing another adult in the room while they sleep, it doesn't bear thinking about.'

'Don't be silly. You've had quite a journey and yesterday was the culmination of everything. I understood how you felt and I was glad that I was able to help.'

'I've been so lucky to meet you on this voyage. I'm not sure what I'd have done without you. You've been such a good friend to me.'

Our eyes momentarily met, then David leaned in a little closer and our foreheads touched. We both knew it was coming. He put his arm around my waist and pulled my body closer. Our lips met. It was slow, soft and comforting in ways that words could never be.

The kiss obliterated every thought in my head and, for the first time in forever, my mind was locked into the present.

DAVID

This cruise had turned into something I could never in my wildest dreams have imagined. I kissed her today; I couldn't help it. I was falling more and more in love with this woman and I believed she felt something for me, too. But I couldn't let it happen; it was something I must fight. If she knew about the way I'd behaved, the lies I'd told her, the abortion I'd insisted upon, she wouldn't give me a second thought. I'd never be able to tell her the truth and there was no way I wanted to hurt her. When this liner docked at New York, I'd make my farewells. It was better that way.

Fancy having to scatter the ashes of your parents at sea. Poor Kit. I felt so inadequate the other night. There was nothing I could do to help, and when she said afterwards that she'd 'never have a chance to get to know her Mother now', I could have wept with her.

I watched Kit when the captain was speaking and her face showed one of the saddest expressions I have ever seen on a fellow human being. Her puffy eyes were testament to the suffering she has been going through this week. Not so her brother – he seemed a hard case. I don't like to use the word arrogant, but it was what I felt when he read the elegy to his parents. I don't think he missed them one little bit, but look at me. I've absolutely no right to say that.

I was touched when Kit asked me to stay in her cabin that night. When I brushed her forehead with a kiss, I longed to tell her I loved her and would look after her if she'd let me, but I managed to stifle the words. It would have been a false promise.

On top of everything else, I learned today of Kit's problem with a stalker. 'Problem' doesn't seem to be an adequate description of what this man has been putting her through. How much more was this unfortunate woman going to be put through? I wished I could beat the living daylights out of him for all the worry he's caused. Kit thinks he's simply a sad person in need of help, but she sees good in everyone.

I'm afraid of what might happen this afternoon. What if she doesn't manage to leave the door unlocked? Then I won't be able to hear what's going on inside or be able to open the door. She would be in a room with a man who could be violent or physically abusive, and there was no way I'd be able to help.

Yet no matter what I said, she wouldn't change her mind about this plan. I feared she was being naïve, but she wouldn't listen to me. I had a very bad feeling about this.

KIT

It was a relief to put the meeting with Samuel behind me and I was glad that David had been there to support me. We were spending the next couple of hours by the pool. David thought going for a swim would distract us from what lay ahead. I wasn't sure he was right.

My bikini was as dry as the moment I lay on this sunbed – swimming had no appeal. In all honesty, nothing appealed at the moment. David ordered sandwiches and double coffee, but I'd no appetite for either. All I could think was that I'd soon be confronting Alex. I had felt quite brave about it earlier, but now doubt was setting in.

Look at David, poor man. I didn't think he had got much sleep on my sofa last night and the copious amount of coffee didn't seem to have worked. I knew I should rehearse the words I'd say to Alex, but each time I started, my thoughts ran wild and I relived his lewd behaviour.

It was no use; I needed distraction and it would be unkind to wake David. Gathering up my sarong and purse, I decided I'd see what was going on around the ship. Any action had to be better than frightening myself to death on this sunbed.

The thumping music from the gym caught my attention when I reached the upper deck. I watched the beautiful fit bodies stretching their designer Lycra and thought it was just as well I never got round to going. The fencing classes held little interest, but when I reached the ballroom I watched the tango dancers for a while. It all seemed vaguely lustful. The women were mostly looking into the eyes of their partners or sensuously tucking their heads into their partners' necks. I thought it would be great to learn this dance with David as my partner – too late for this voyage, but perhaps it was something we could do in the future. It struck me that I was thinking of a future with David. Why was I so positive about this man? I'd promised myself to never get involved with any man again. Less heartache that way, but I couldn't stop thinking about him. He was different and I was growing closer to him. The music was making me sentimental. Time to move on.

I strolled through the designer shops in the Tamara Shopping Arcade with no intention of buying anything at their prices. It was then I spotted Jess with Allegra by his side. They were looking at Cartier jewellery and Allegra seemed engrossed in trying on rings. Feeling more confident around my brother than I'd ever been, I decided to interrupt. Painting a false smile, I touched his arm.

'Hello, Jess, how are you today?' I turned to Allegra as though in surprise. 'Oh hello, Allegra. I didn't see you there.'

Jess's face was a puzzle and I could see he couldn't quite work out the new me. He paused before speaking. 'Hello, Kit. I'm good.
All well with you after yesterday?'

'Yes, of course,' I lied.

I could tell this was not the answer Jess had expected and for once he had no reply.

'So, what are you two going to buy today?'

Allegra beamed and kissed Jess's cheek. 'Your brother is about to buy me a ring. I thought about this gorgeous Panthère. Just look at those brilliant diamonds sitting so prettily in the gold band. Do you like it, darling?'

'Isn't it a wedding ring?'

'It could be, but nowadays it really doesn't matter. Most brides would want something a little more opulent than this, don't you think?'

'No, to be honest. I don't agree, Allegra. That most definitely appears to be a wedding ring to me, and with a price tag of almost four thousand dollars, it would certainly be good enough for most brides, unless, of course, they possess delusions of grandeur.'

'Kit!' The word spluttered from Jess's lips but before he could continue, I interrupted.

'Anyway, I must be going. I'll leave my brother to squander his money. Goodbye to you both.' And with these words, I turned sharply and walked away, imagining the daggers of cold stares on my back.

My heart was pounding in tune with my footsteps as I marched down the main avenue of the huge shopping area. My mouth was dry and my fingers were slightly trembling, but I felt proud of myself. This was the first time in my life that I'd said exactly what
I felt.

I glanced at my watch. It was time to head back to David, but then I heard a familiar, high-pitched voice that sent my heart racing. I stood, fixed to the floor, goosebumps prickling my skin.

'Hello, Kit. I didn't expect you for at least another twenty minutes. You're eager. That's wonderful.'

I flinched as I turned to face him. 'Hello, Alex.'

'I was surprised when Samuel said you wanted to meet in my cabin. But it's fine, Kit. It's perfect, in fact.'

I fought the rising panic. 'I… I need to go and collect my things, Alex. I've left them on the upper deck.'

'No matter, Kit. No matter. You look absolutely gorgeous in that colourful wrap and I can see you're wearing such a cute little bikini underneath. It's picture-perfect.'

'But I must—'

'My dear Kit, I can see you're nervous. Don't worry. Your Alexander is here. We've both been waiting for this moment, haven't we?' Alex put his arm tightly around my waist and quickly bundled me towards the exit corridor.

'My cabin's just along here.'

I feared I might throw up when Alex's cabin door loomed large. 'Alex, I should rescue my things. Someone might take them.'

'My darling Kit, don't worry. We'll collect them together afterwards.'

I winced out of distress rather than pain as his arm tightened around my waist. Now there was no way I could escape. I silently sent distress messages to David.

'Kit, my darling. Welcome to my cabin.' Immediately the door swung open, the stench of impending doom hung in the air alongside that of rotting fish.

I wrinkled my nose as he pulled me reluctantly inside. I couldn't believe my eyes when I saw the dozens and dozens of photographs sellotaped to the wall. Photos of all sizes — in focus, out of focus, black and white, colour — but they all had one thing in common. They were pictures of me.

Words would not form in my dry mouth. 'I thought this would be a nice surprise and I can see I was right, Kit. Wasn't I?'

I nodded, hiding my hands under the sarong so that he wouldn't see them shaking.

'I've been taking them since that first day.'

I looked closer. There were photos in Samuel's bar, on the lido deck, on the stage — in fact, he'd been taking photos of me all over the ship.

'Now you must look over here, Kit.' His bad egg breath drifted over me as he pointed to the wall opposite. 'These are my favourite photographs, after those of you, of course.'

Alex mistakenly presumed my silence was because I was in awe.

'This is my favourite picture. It's an animated drawing of a typical vertical triple-expansion engine. I know you have an interest in these things, Kit, and I can see that you're impressed.'

His creepy smile made me turn away. Dread twisted somewhere in my gut, but I smiled bravely.

'I will explain more about these photographs later, but right now I want to get on with the reason you're here.' His ice-cold eyes didn't leave my face as he walked to the cabin door and turned the lock. A shudder travelled down my spine.

'You look pale, my darling. Don't worry, it's going to be easy. I could tell at that stupid party that you are a good girl.' He pointed to himself. 'I am a good man. We are made for each other.'

I stifled the cry that formed at the back of my throat. I needed to slow things down. I clawed through the denseness of my mind – maybe David would wake up; maybe he'd come; perhaps he'd find a way to get in. I knew I was clutching at straws.

Alex grasped my hand and held it briefly as though I had an infectious disease, but it was long enough for his volatile body odour of musty sweat and urine to invade my space. 'On the bed now, Kit. I'll get my camera ready. I'm going to use my special camera for this momentous occasion. It has a sensor that uses dual pixels plus a refined cross-type AF sensor. It's fantastic for taking moving engine parts.'

I didn't move. My wild eyes scanned the room for something I could use as a weapon. I couldn't simply go like a lamb to the slaughter without putting up a fight.

'Come, darling. The bed awaits.' Alex fiddled with the tripod and camera that he'd positioned at the bottom of the bed. 'I need to get you in shot so I can put the camera on automatic.'

I moved slowly towards the bed, all the time looking for a weapon. 'Alex, I need to go to the bathroom.' He pointed to the door without comment.

Once inside, I scanned the shelves for something to defend myself. There was a mound of dirty clothes in the shower tray and the lack of soap by the sink or deodorant on the shelf was testimony to the stench of sweat and dirty socks. The only thing remotely suitable as a weapon was an electric razor, but where on earth could I hide that in a bikini?

I held my breath as I opened the door. Alex looked up from the camera and nodded at me before pointing to the bed. Even that small movement quickened my heart rate and I moved at a snail's pace towards the bed. I noticed a tick in Alex's jaw that hadn't been there a few minutes ago.

Suddenly, an ear-piercing shriek hit the cabin ceiling, which sent a fireball running up my spine. Alex punched the tripod and the camera fell noisily to the floor.

'This is all your fault.' He pointed his dirty fingernail at me. 'You've brought us bad luck by arriving too early.'

I flinched, my heart pulsing in my ears. I studied the bed, frightened to look at his face.

'Kit. Look at me.' He raised his voice. 'Look at me, I tell you.'

With trembling lips, I raised my head and, to my amazement, saw a tear slide down Alex's cheek.

I stood inert. Afraid to flee. Afraid to stay.

'You do love me, don't you?' It was a command rather than a question. His eyes dared me to say no.

My body sagged, but I managed the one word he wanted to hear.

He screwed his eyes tight shut, rubbing them with his knuckles, his body joining with the repetitive nod of his head.

I watched him through a veil of caution. My face purposely blank. This might be the only chance I'd get. I had to take it. I broke for the door and started fumbling with the lock, my sweaty fingers sliding as I gripped the key. The surface of the door was flat, no handle, no hinges, nothing to get a grip on. I was angry with myself for being so feeble at what might be my only chance of escape.

The smell told me that Alex was right behind. I made one last effort to turn the key before his hands painfully grabbed my arms and dragged me back into the centre of the room. His voice curdled into mocking. 'You're as bad as all the others. You pretended.'

He threw me onto the bed as though I was a broken rag doll. Then he knelt on my arms, pinning them down against the bed. All I could see was Alex's cold eyes and every glimmer of hope dimmed. I had no choice now; there was no way of escape. My resolve to fight faltered as memories of Tom's terrifying aggression attacked my mind.

I knew I was shrieking and I knew there was no one who would be able to hear me. I closed my eyes and waited, not even feeling the pain I'd inflicted on my own mouth by biting down so hard. As the sweat from his face dripped onto my cheeks, I watched him raise one arm above his head and waited for the blow, pushing myself deeper into the bed.

A knock on the door made Alex bring his hand down heavily over my mouth. The sour taste of dirt and the smell of urine pushed its way between his fingers into my throat.

There was a second bang louder than the first. 'You keep quiet,' he hissed, 'or you'll be sorry.'

I was no longer breathing when a third bang reverberated around the room, followed by pandemonium. I could hear men's voices, shouting, swearing, the sound of heavy feet, yet Alex still knelt on my arms.

'Get out of my room!' he snarled.

'Alex, let her go.' It was a calm command that made my heart light. I knew that voice. He had come.

'Alex. I repeat again. Let her go and you won't get hurt.' David's voice was as slow as a funeral bell.

Baring a gap-toothed scowl, Alex's saliva joined that of his sweat. 'I said, get out of my room. Now! Or I'll call security.'

A deep voice replied, 'Sir, I am security and I advise you to let the young woman go.'

I watched Alex's eyes bulge as he moved his hands to my throat. It was as though the security man's words had lit a fuse, which fizzled like a firework. A tornado of fury erupted as he spat out his reply. 'Never. Never. She's mine.'

David raised his hands in a placatory gesture. 'Alex, you don't want to do this. Kit's your friend.'

'A friend doesn't break another friend's camera.'

'I'm sure it must have been an accident. We'll get it repaired.'

'Don't want it repaired. I want a new one.' Alex swung his body off the bed, releasing me as he did so. He faced the intruders full on. 'Do you hear me? A new one.'

David took a step nearer and nodded. 'I'm sure we can arrange that, Alex. Now, shall we let Kit come and talk to the security man, then she can explain details of the camera that she broke.'

Alex stood rigidly in front of the bed and raised his bottom lip at David for some seconds before speaking, 'You think I'm a fool. I can see through your little game.' He pulled back his arm and, with a tight fist, took a swing towards David.

I watched in amazement as David raised his left arm and blocked the blow. Then, he immediately grabbed Alex's punching arm and twisted it behind him, at the same time sweeping his supporting leg from under him. It was over so quickly.

I looked at Alex sprawled on the floor and the security man moved quickly to put handcuffs on the prone figure. He pushed Alex's body to one side with his foot. 'Alexander Bingley, you're under house arrest. You and I will remain in this cabin until we move you to the ship's security quarters.'

Alex looked at the burly security guard. 'But—'

'You can save all your explanations for the law enforcement at the port.' He turned to me. 'Are you okay, Ma'am?'

I felt David put his arms around my shoulder. I nodded.

'I'm sorry about this, Ma'am. It looks as though you've been through such a lot already, but we're going to need a statement and I'll make you an immediate appointment at the ship's medical centre.'

My voice quavered. 'I don't need a doctor. I'm okay, just shocked.'

The security guard studied my shaking fingers. 'It's for the best, Ma'am. You might need evidence of sexual assault. Everything will be confidential, of course.'

I searched David's face imploringly. He smiled at the guard.

'Perhaps you can give us a little while to discuss this.'

'Of course. Our female security officer will be here very soon. She will talk you through the process of reporting a crime and she'll give you printed security papers to help you.'

David nodded. 'Can you please tell her to meet us in the Starburst lounge in thirty minutes? I'm going to take Kit for a cup of tea to give her time to calm her nerves.'

'The only thing I would say is that if you want the crime investigated, the sooner a forensic medical examination takes place, the better.'

I walked towards the door and as I did, Alex let out a heart stopping sob. 'Kit. Kit. I'm sorry. I love you. I never meant to hurt you.'

'Come on, Kit.' David gently pushed me towards the door. 'Let's go.'

As I looked back, tears welled in my eyes, joining those that were now flowing freely from Alex.

I've no idea how long David and I sat side by side in the Starburst lounge. The tears slowly abated and as my shoulders dropped, I realised I'd been rigid with tension. I can't remember much that the female security officer said, but she left a small pile of papers on the table in front of us, which I'd probably never read.

'How do you feel now, Kit?' David asked.

'I can't believe this has happened.'

'I'm afraid it did, but Alex will be arrested when we reach New York. You'll be safe now.'

I nodded, hearing the words but not absorbing them. A muscle in my calf began to twitch in reaction to what had occurred. I took a few deep breaths, pulling them to the depths of my stomach.

'I give you my word, Kit. Everything's going to be okay.'

'I've been taking part in a nightmare.'

'It's all behind you now.'

'David, this might sound odd, but I feel sorry for Alex. He needs help.'

He stared at me. 'You mean, after all he's put you through, you feel sad for him?'

'He's disturbed. I think he should probably be on medication.'

'Well, maybe so, but what about you?'

'I'll be okay. I've been through worse with Tom.'

'That doesn't mean you should go through anything remotely similar again, though.'

'He didn't rape me, David. In fact, I don't think he'd be capable of it. He's just a man crying out for help. I want to make sure he gets support. That's what I'm going to say on this form.' I caught David's eye. 'I'm not going to press charges. It won't help him in any way.'

'Kit, you're the most forgiving person I've ever met.'

'I'm not sure about that. If Tom walked in here right now, I think I might be able to shoot him.'

'What! Without a gun?'

I smiled for the first time that afternoon.

'Come on, Kit, let's get this form filled out. And next, I think we both need a drink – and I don't mean tea.'

'It's as though I've run a marathon.'

'Then let's both have a nap. We don't have many days left to enjoy ourselves on this liner and tonight I think we should celebrate.'

'Celebrate?'

'Yes. Celebrate us. You and me.'

I smiled and, in that brief moment of happiness, looked at David. My heart leapt. At last I'd met someone I could trust and, for the first time in forever, I was at peace with myself.

DAVID

What the hell was wrong with me? I didn't set out to deceive Kit, but that was just what I was doing. When we met last night, it was all I could do to stop myself from kissing her. I smiled idiotically. I couldn't help it; she was so beautiful, it was difficult not to stare at her.

I'd never felt this comfortable with any woman before. When I was with her, I felt happy, excited, even hopeful and last night I buried the dark clouds of doom that were hanging over our relationship.

My guilt at letting Kit wander around the ship on her own hadn't left me. If only I'd stayed awake, talked with her, tried to take her mind off the meeting with Alex, she might never have been on her own and got locked in his room. Thank goodness the woman on reception believed me when I explained the danger I felt Kit was in. She could just as easily have presumed it was I who was deranged.

I would never forget that terrible smell when the security guard unlocked Alex's door and we rushed into his filthy room. It was all I could do to stop gagging. When I saw Kit lying on the bed with Alex kneeling on her arms, a primeval anger engulfed me and I wanted to kill him. It was a miracle I managed to control my rage.

I had no idea why I ignored the security guard's instructions to keep behind him, but I knew sweat was running into my eyes and my rapid heartbeat boomed in my ears as I spoke to Alex. Everything happened so quickly in the end and Kit and I were both shaking when we eventually sat together in the lounge. The most amazing thing was that Kit didn't want to press charges – she wanted to help him.

I'd never known anyone with so much compassion. She was incredible.

I suggested we had a rest and meet later for dinner, which seemed a good idea at the time, but things didn't turn out quite the way we'd planned.

When I called at her cabin later that evening, it was a pale-faced Kit who opened the door. 'How are you feeling?' I asked.

She grunted. 'Drained.'

'Do you want to cancel tonight?'

'No, but let's have a snack in the café and call it an early night, shall we?'

'Fine by me.'

Our snack was a quiet affair with neither of us saying very much.

We didn't mention Alex and any conversation was of inconsequential things. My suggestion of a nightcap to help us sleep was met with a nod and a brief smile that did not quite reach her eyes.

We walked past by the noisy cocktail bar and the crowded champagne bar, which sounded much the same.

'It's so busy tonight, something must be going on,' she said as we reached the Village Pub, which was also packed.

I was surprised at Kit's suggestion that we go back to her cabin for a nightcap and ten minutes later, the quietness was a panacea to the strange day that would soon come to an end.

She poured two large brandies and we sat side by side on the huge sofa. I wondered whether to broach the subject of Alex; would it help Kit to talk about him? She must have been reading my mind for, at that moment, she placed her hand on top of mine.

'I still feel sorry for Alex, you know. I'm sure he didn't mean to hurt me.'

'But he's caused you so much distress during this cruise, and then today, his cabin, those photos, it's…' My voice tailed off.

'David, he didn't touch me sexually; in fact, I believe he simply wanted to take a photo of us together.'

'But on his bed!'

She rubbed the back of her hand across her forehead. 'I shouldn't have gone to his cabin.'

We sat quietly lost in our thoughts for a while and then Kit suggested we have a final nightcap before I left. She decided to switch on the cruise radio and we sat sipping our drink and melting into the sound of Etta James singing 'At Last'. My shoulders dropped, the unknown tension left and I smiled at Kit. As the dying notes of the music faded away, our eyes locked. I was about to speak but she pressed her forefinger to my lips.

Her face was so close to mine that I could smell the sweet aroma of the brandy she'd been drinking. I wanted her. I needed her. Her smile, her wonderful smile opened something within and I leant towards her lips, hoping yet knowing she would respond. And she did. Her lips were warm and soft. They parted slightly, allowing my tongue to slip inside. My heart beat faster as I squashed the nagging voice in my head, telling me to stop, but I couldn't. Our bodies pressed together heatedly, and we made our way to the bed, undressing each other as we did. I made one last half-hearted attempt to resist, but it was too late.

I felt her arms around me and a rush of helplessness as she kissed me softly at first, and then with a swift gradation of intensity that sent a surging tide of tremors across my body. Our kisses led us slowly towards the floor where we tenderly caressed each other's body. I don't know how long we lay on that floor. I do know that post-coital euphoria had never felt like that before. I felt closer to Kit than I ever had to any other woman; everything was so right that nothing else mattered. The realisation that I loved her took root that night.

The peace that settled over me fooled me into thinking there was a chance for us, but then I came back down to earth, and my throat clogged with the secrets I dared not set free.

KIT

I grinned madly at complete strangers on my way to the Sesha Library next morning, but I was too euphoric to care. Memories of my night with David played in a loop around my head, a loop I wanted to never end. The library was empty and I chose a comfortable-looking chair and picked up a glossy table-top book. However, my eyes refused to focus on the lustrous pictures within. 'Tomorrow, this will be our memory,' David had whispered when our heartbeats had cooled.

Have you ever met someone who was so close to you, so right, that nothing else mattered? That was how I felt about him. I loved him and I wanted us to be together. Today was our last day of this voyage and I was going to tell him how I much he meant to me and my dream of us becoming a family.

I reached for my bag and began to search for a tissue, when I caught sight of the envelope that the captain had given me yesterday. As I opened it, two smaller envelopes fell out. The first one was a mirror image of the one Jess had paraphrased in Captain Hurley's office. I immediately recognised Mother's handwriting on the second envelope and opened it slowly, uncertain about what she was about to say.

> *My dearest Kit,*
>
> *I've many things to be regretful about in my life, but when I look back at the way I treated you, it appals me. I've written to you in my head over and over for many years, but now I realise I must share some things with you before it's too late.*

This letter is the best I can do, even though I've found it hard to express my feelings, and I know my words are inadequate, but confessing one's mistakes is not easy, especially when you care about the person you are writing to.

If only we'd been able to spend more time together in your adult years. We only had those few precious months after you broke up with Tom, didn't we? I managed to keep away from alcohol then, but once you'd left, well, I'm not proud of the way I sank back into my old ways. We didn't have long enough, Kit. It just wasn't long enough.

I was a bad mother: I know that. When I started thinking about this letter, I had intended to paint a better picture of myself but that would've been false. You deserve to know the whole truth. It will be as painful for you to read as it is for me to write, and I only hope that one day you'll be able to forgive me.

My parents gave me all the materialistic trappings of life, but never loved me. When I fell in love at eighteen, I was besotted. I thought he felt the same. It turned out he didn't. At the time he gave me what I thought was love. He also gave me a baby. When I knew I was pregnant, my first thought was an abortion. I knew my father would pay. Scandal in the family would be the last thing he would have wanted. Single mothers were judged harshly back in those days.

I met Henry when I first discovered my pregnancy. I didn't tell him I was expecting another man's baby and fooled him into thinking it was his. He believed me. We married although I can honestly say that Henry and I were never in love. In lust maybe - but never love.

All went well until blackmail raised its ugly head. The father of my baby contacted me, he threatened to tell Henry. I'd no money of my own, although I enjoyed a good life under my husband's roof... one of the reasons I married him, as back then I craved all the glittering trappings of life. I was much older before I realised it was worthless and didn't make me happy.

I only had a few weeks left before my baby was due to be born and I mistakenly thought that if I told Henry everything, he would forgive me and we could raise my baby as though she were our own. I say 'she' purposely because I gave birth to a girl.

It wasn't you, Kit. You were never the firstborn. Henry is the biological father of both you and Jess.

Your father gave me an ultimatum, either I had the baby adopted or he would divorce me. I chose the former and I've lived with the guilt and regret every day of my life since, but I had no money to support myself and I'm ashamed to say I was used to the good things in life. At the time, your father's money smoothed my conscience.

Our marriage went from bad to worse. I promised Henry a son, which was all he wanted from me. He said with a son he'd let me lead my own life and would support me financially. He also said that once a boy was born, he'd find sex elsewhere. I'm sure I don't need to tell you how unhappy we both were.

You came along and were a big disappointment to him, but not to me, Kit. Not to me. However, I'd already started drinking to blot everything out so I wasn't good at being your mother. I saw you and thought of the daughter I'd lost. Now I berate myself for what I did when younger and I take the blame totally. I didn't love you enough. I'm sorry.

So, Kit. You have a sister; I called her Sarah. With your father's money I've had her traced and she lives in New York, although she was brought up in England.

I've been unsure whether to tell you the next part, but it might go some small way to help you understand why I treated you as I did when you were a child.

The morning after your birth, I looked at you mistily between the veils of sleeping and waking and there was this moment between the knowing and the not knowing whether you were my firstborn child. When I realised that you weren't, I wanted to obliterate you from my mind and replace you with her. I longed to hold her, kiss her and let her come back to replace you. I felt bereaved. Please believe me, I'm not telling you this to be unkind or to hurt you, but I want to have everything in the open. No secrets. No lies.

After that first morning, those terrible feelings never returned, but memories of my lost baby became brittle and dangerous and I cast around, seeking more and more ways to ease the pain. As you know, I found it in alcohol.

Even as a child you were far more vulnerable than your brother. Jess was a charmer, always impulsive and good at getting his own way. Your father indulged him simply because he was a boy, and Henry wanted a boy to carry on his business empire one day. It never entered his head that a girl would be equally capable and perhaps even better at carrying out this role.

When your father died suddenly last year, it was a complete shock to me – after all, it was I who'd ruined my body through alcohol. An unexpected sadness overwhelmed me. Henry had supported me, however meagerly throughout my life, and I did trap him into marrying me in the first place. He could have had a much better life if we'd never met.

Upon his death, I was made aware of his will. It seems that as neither of us had remarried and as he'd not bothered to change anything, I was still named as the sole beneficiary in his will. When I met with Mr Jones-Regal, his solicitor, he told me that shortly before he died Henry had made an appointment to see him regarding a new will. However, Henry died before the meeting so the old will is the only one in existence.

You are about to meet your half-sister in New York and then everything will be revealed, but until that meeting I would prefer that Jess knows nothing of Sarah. I know I can rely upon you to keep this secret for a little while.

Mr Jones-Regal has contacted specialist solicitors in New York, and they will be in touch with you and Jess before you disembark the ship. They will also be in touch with Sarah, who knows nothing of the will, neither does she know that she has a half-brother and sister. When she meets you, it's going to be a big shock. Be kind; please protect her from Jess's anger. Although why I write this, I've no idea.

You are the kindest person I know, Kit.

Perhaps you're wondering why I asked you to spread our ashes over the Titanic's resting place. It was always Henry's wish that our ashes be scattered over the ocean — in fact, Mr Jones-Regal told me that Henry would remind him about this now and then. When I learned of it, I was amazed that after all our years apart, he wanted this to happen. Perhaps there was more affection in our relationship than I ever credited.

As you know, your father found the Titanic absolutely fascinating throughout his life, so I thought it made a fitting place for a final goodbye. That, and I suppose somewhere in the back of my mind I hoped you and Jess being incarcerated together for a few days might bring a closeness. I realise that this voyage will have been difficult for both of you. After all, you've not been the closest of siblings.

Well, my darling daughter, I've finished baring my soul to you. I wish I'd loved you better. If only I could turn back the clock, but we know that's not possible. I hope one day you'll find it in your heart to forgive me.

I sat in that empty room, reading Mother's letter again and again. I studied the carpet beneath my feet and read it yet again. My pulse was racing and my world was silent except for the heartbeat thundering in my ears.

Life had been tipped upside down and I was unable to understand my feelings, for they were no longer reachable. I felt trapped in a swirling vortex of emotions, but my eyes remained dry. That Mother had bottled up all this grief and regret for a lifetime, and now it'd finally come to the surface, swept everything from my vision and left me absolutely powerless.

It could have been dawn or dusk, I'd absolutely no idea, and felt totally stunned as the name Sarah bounced around my head. How could I still be breathing when I felt like this?

I gazed around the room with blind eyes and neither saw nor heard David put his head around the door. His voice filled the room as he entered. 'Kit, I'm sorry I'm late. I rang your stateroom...' He suddenly stopped talking and stared at me with an anxious expression.

I held the letter out to him.

He slumped heavily into the chair opposite, running his hand through his hair as he did so. He pulled himself tensely to the front of the chair, reaching for my hand. 'Are you okay?'

I stared at him as though he were speaking a foreign language.

He stood and put his arm around my shoulder. 'Come on. This has been a tremendous shock. I'll walk you back to your stateroom. We'll have a cup of tea, shall we?'

I didn't reply, but in a daze willingly allowed myself to be led through the ship. Upon reaching my room, I looked David in the eye. 'I'm not going to cry.' The words escaped savagely through clenched teeth and as they left my lips, a desolate sob rose at the back of my throat and the flood of tears burst forth.

I was still asleep when the phone rang the next morning and by the time my eyes had greeted the daylight, the room was silent once more. I forced drowsiness from my head and looked at the bedside clock. I groaned. Another late morning, but nevertheless I nestled my head back on the pillow in an effort to delay entry into the new day. I remembered little of yesterday except that I'd spent it in a fog of confusion.

Mother's letter lay on the bedside table and I hesitantly reached for it. Focusing once more on the precious words, I managed to hold back the tears at least long enough to read it to the end.

Slowly, I climbed out of bed and headed for the shower, where threatening tears would be washed away by the soothing water. Thoughts of the sister I'd no idea existed until yesterday were harder to wash away and I viewed our meeting with some trepidation. Would we resemble one another? Would we get on? Would she share Jess's personality? So many unknown answers whirled around my head.

I felt like a rudderless ship with no idea of what to do. It was as I got dressed that memories of Alex hit me like a thunderbolt and added to my confusion.

I was sitting motionless in the chair when the phone rang again. At first, the voice on the other end seemed to reach my ears as though through earplugs. I forced myself to concentrate and realised it was Juan, whose cultured voice was asking whether I wished to have breakfast in my stateroom.

'No, Juan. It's okay. I'm not hungry.'

'Ma'am, it's traditional towards the end of a journey that a very special breakfast is prepared for certain staterooms.'

'I'm not much of a breakfast person, to be honest, Juan. Coffee is my usual start to the day.'

'Then, may I suggest that you have a special lunch in Le Blanc Hibiscus restaurant instead. This can be easily arranged, Ma'am.'

'You're very kind, Juan. Perhaps I can have time to think about it?'

'Naturally. Take as much time as you wish. If you let me know your decision an hour before the time you wish to dine, that will be fine, and perhaps I should have said that this applies to your evening menu, too. When I refresh your room later in the morning, I will leave the special menu choices for you to peruse.'

'Thank you.'

'And may I just add, Ma'am, that these menus are not available to many passengers. I think you'll be delighted with your options.'

'Thank you again.'

Being forced to carry out a normal conversation had restored a little equilibrium. Minutes later, the phone rang again. I hesitated before picking it up, hoping this wasn't going to be Jess. I wasn't ready to talk to him yet.

'Hi, Kit. It's Lou… are you there, Kit?'

'Y-yes, I'm here. It's just a surprise to hear your voice. A very nice surprise, though.'

'I thought I'd get in touch to see whether you fancy meeting sometime today. It's our last day on board and we may not get to meet again.'

'I've been meaning to ring you, Lou. I'm sorry. Life's been a bit full-on at this end. Yes, it would be nice to meet, but at the moment I've no idea how this day is going to pan out.'

'That's okay. I only rang on the off chance. Not to worry.'

'Honestly, I do want to meet you. Can I call you back when I've got myself sorted? It would be nice to catch up.'

'Okay, if you're sure. If I'm not in my cabin when you ring, then leave a message.'

'That's great. I promise I'll ring sometime.'

'Speak to you later then. Oh, and while I think of it, how's the romance going with… um… is it David?'

'It's still going, Lou. Still going.'

'That's great. Tell me all about it later.'

It was as I sat trying to figure out the best plan of action for the day that there was a knock on the door. Surely it couldn't be Juan already.

I opened the door and a voice so quiet, so full of concern, whispered my name.

'David!' We fell into each other's arms and a flood of relief poured over me. I hugged him tightly and his arms encircled me. 'I'm so glad you're here. I was going to ring you.'

'I've tried to ring you, but your line has been permanently engaged.'

Our eyes met and our happiness was obvious. For a fleeting moment, we didn't speak – to embrace each other was enough. I felt no need for words; there was something in David's eyes that was so beautiful, so safe and warm. It was enough.

It was David who broke the silence. 'Did you sleep okay?'

'I slept like a log. I think I must've been exhausted as I awoke late again.'

'Have you had breakfast?'

'No. Not yet.'

'Kit, I've no idea why you're paying for this super-expensive stateroom, you hardly ever seem to take advantage of everything on offer.' David's eyes smiled. 'Come on, Miss Langford, you're going to eat breakfast and then we are going to make our way to the promenade deck. I hear that we might see a pod of dolphins from there this morning.'

'But David, there's so much to sort out. I must talk to Jess, plus Lou rang this morning, and then there's…'

'Whoa, Miss. It's breakfast first, then we'll sort everything else out. Are you ready to go?'

'No. I need to do my make-up.'

'Oh no you don't. You're perfect just the way you are.' And with these words, David leaned in and gently kissed me, before guiding me towards the door.

'Thank you,' I said in a voice barely more than a whisper. 'What for?'

'For being you.' My voice wavered and I felt that now David was here, everything would be fine.

-o-

An hour later saw us standing hand in hand at the rail on the promenade deck, as we scanned the horizon looking for the promised dolphins.

'I don't think we're going to see them this morning,' I said, just at the very moment another passenger yelled excitedly. Before I could even focus on the direction he was pointing, I heard a splash and movement much nearer the ship and suddenly a small pod of leaping dolphins moved right alongside it, churning the sea in their wake. They were so close that I could hear their clicks and childlike cries.

I couldn't take my eyes off them; their speed and grace was electrifying. The spectacle lasted less than a minute, but there and then I decided that nothing could be more fulfilling than watching these magnificent creatures while standing alongside someone as special as David.

'They're magnificent. I'd no idea they were so big.'

'Do you want to stay put in case more appear?'

'I don't think there's time, David. Much as I'd like to. This time tomorrow, we'll be in New York and I've so much to sort out before then.'

'Do you want me to help sort things out?'

'Would you?'

'Right. Didn't your mother's letter say something about a New York solicitor? Has that been arranged now?'

'No. Not yet. Jess and I were promised details before we disembark, so I imagine we should hear very soon. I'm presuming a message will come through via the captain.'

'And I know the very person to sort that out quickly.'

'Who?'

'Your butler. A butler is magic at making things happen – well, at least mine is.'

I nodded. 'You're right, Juan is very efficient.'

'Okay, we'll sort that little problem out in a minute, what's next on the list?'

'I suppose I ought to see Jess. Once we get off the ship, it might be difficult to get in touch with him. He told me ages ago that he and Allegra are staying at some exclusive hotel overlooking Central Park.'

'Ouch. That'll be expensive!'

'Nothing but the best for Allegra, it seems. I think Jess might be paying.'

David frowned. 'Why?'

'Jess believes that Allegra is about to put some very lucrative work his way once they land. He's keeping her sweet and knowing Jess, he'll go over the top to impress her. He told me that he'll probably stay in the States to get it all set up.'

'What about a visa? He'll have no chance of staying without one.'

'Apparently, Allegra will fix it.' I shrugged. 'She's one helluva woman is Allegra.'

'Oh well, good luck to him. It's difficult making any kind of impact in America. I know from experience.'

'You?' I couldn't keep the surprise from my voice. 'Are you involved in American business?'

'Just a little, but we're talking about you and Jess here, not me. Let's return to your cabin, ring your butler and afterwards get in touch with Jess. Does he carry his mobile phone with him on board?'

'I don't know. I can always leave a message if necessary.'

'Right and then is that the end of your list?' David grinned.

'We've got to make time for us on the last full day of this voyage.'

'Well, I've promised to meet up with Lou and I also need to book a hotel in New York. I didn't give much thought to the end of the voyage before I left the UK.'

'I'm sure you had other things on your mind.' He reached for my hand. 'Come on, a phone call to your butler is needed.'

-o-

I noticed that Juan had left the promised exclusive menus on the bed as soon as we entered the stateroom. 'David, did your butler leave you exclusive menus for our last day on board?'

'Yes, he did. I've already studied them because I wasted so much time waiting for someone's phone line to be free this morning.' He smiled. 'I only wish I knew your mobile number.'

'My mobile's in the drawer. I can't seem to make it work on board.'

David's palm gently slapped one eye. 'Oh Kit! It's part of your cruise deal at this level of stateroom. Haven't you used it at all?'

'No.'

'Give me strength! Didn't you read any of the information the cruise line sent you or the information your butler left?'

'Jess had all the pre-booking information and, well, I suppose the honest answer is no.'

He sighed and held out the menus that Juan had left. 'Right, read these. See what appeals to you.'

'What about you? Did any particular dish appeal?'

'I adore scallops, so they're definitely for me, then I thought about smoked eel in Oscietra caviar, or maybe vadouvan John Dory.'

'I know what John Dory is, but what on earth is vadouvan?'

'It's French spices, similar to Indian curry ones.'

'Mr Knowledgeable!' I pushed him playfully.

'It's nice if you like a curry.'

'It sounds as though you wish to choose from these menus.'

'Yes, I would.' He smiled. 'Tonight is our last night on board, let's make it special.'

'Okay, I'll ask Juan to book it in a minute.' I grinned. 'Thanks for helping me sort things out today.'

'All part of the service. Nothing's too much trouble for a good woman.' He threw me a half-smile. 'Now ring Jess.'

Thirty minutes later, almost all of the *to do* list had been accomplished. To my amazement, Jess actually answered his phone and we arranged to meet in the library before lunch. I then arranged to have afternoon tea with Lou in the Victoria lounge.

'Once Juan gives me the solicitor's details, then all I have left to do is find accommodation in New York.'

David's eyes met mine and in that instant I knew what he was about to say. He hesitated before speaking, 'You can stay with me in my hotel if you want. It's fairly central, not overly expensive and it's where I usually stay. I always book the same room; it's big and has got two double beds. No pressure, though. We can see what else is available.'

'Sounds fine. Thank you, David.' I saw surprise register on his face.

'Are you sure? I can call and see whether they have a separate room available, if you prefer.'

'No, I'm happy to share.'

'It's a big room.'

'Yes, you've already said.'

'You don't have to… I mean, it's just a room. There are two beds.'

I was surprised that the usually self-assured, confident man I knew seemed to have taken a step back and in his place was a rather self-effacing person unsure of himself. I was also amazed that in this day and age he hadn't automatically assumed we'd sleep together again.

He smiled softly. 'I'm not good with this kind of thing, Kit. You've probably guessed.'

I tentatively kissed him before speaking, 'I'm not good at it either, David. Every relationship I've ever had went sour. This time, I'm hoping.'

'I'm hoping, too.' His voice became a whisper. 'Kit, there's something I need to tell you -'

As he spoke, there was a tremendous thundering on the door.

'Oh dear, that's got to be Jess. Nobody else would thump a door like that.'

Jess stormed into the room, looking at his watch as he did so.

'You're late,' he announced, ignoring David's presence.

'That would make a change, it's normally you that's late. But for your information, I'm not late. We agreed twelve o'clock.'

He looked at his watch again and thrust his chin out. 'Well, what is it you want to discuss about New York?'

'The ship docks in the early hours and once we leave the ship, I doubt we'll see each other again until we meet at Selby and Cromwell for the reading of the will.'

'So you've got the solicitor's details then?'

'My butler told me just now.'

'Mine hasn't told me.'

'Give him a ring then, but I can let you have the details if you want.'

Jess nodded grudgingly. 'So, what do we need to discuss beforehand?'

'Nitty-gritty things, such as what to do with mother's house. As you know, I've cleared it of her possessions, but it's standing empty. It's bound to be brought up by the New York solicitors.

Do you want it, Jess?'

'Me! Why on earth should I want it? It's run-down, a bit of a dump and in the wrong part of the City, plus I've already got a house.'

'I thought that was Lily's house.'

'It is, but we share everything. No, I definitely do not want to live in mother's old rambling place.'

I doubted that the word 'sharing' had any place in Jess and Lily's relationship, but I said nothing.

Jess smiled disarmingly. 'I think we should sell it and divide the money. Actually, better still, we're about to become quite rich when this will is read. I already have money of my own, as well you know, so perhaps you should have the house? You don't have a house of your own. You could get a builder in and do it up. I gift it to you. There you are - never say that you have a mean brother.'

I smiled to myself, realising that Jess believed he was about to inherit most of the money, which might very well still be the case, but in my mind it was no longer a foregone conclusion.

'That's kind of you, Jess. As you say, I have no house of my own. I think I might accept your offer. Thank you.'

Jess grinned, looking pleased with his generosity. He nodded his head. 'We'll get old Mr Jones-Regal to sort it all out when we're back in the UK. Although I might not be back for some time – as you know, Allegra and I have lots of things to sort out in New York. I'll call him and get him to start the ball rolling once the will has been read, but once you're home you go ahead and move in. It'll save you paying rent.'

'Okay. Will do and thanks again, Jess.'

'My pleasure.'

'I know you and Allegra are going to stay at some upmarket hotel once we arrive. Maybe we should exchange hotel details, just in case. You never know. I've no idea whether our mobile phones will work in New York.'

'You've booked a hotel then?' Jess seemed surprised.

'Yes. I'll phone you details.'

'Okay, Kit. Is that everything? I don't want to rush you, but I've promised to meet Allegra.'

'See you in the Big Apple then.' As I spoke, I felt a little impish glee. The thought of New York filled me with excited anticipation.

In fact, since David had arrived on the scene, I had a good feeling about everything. Nothing that felt this right could possibly go wrong. It just couldn't.

Later, when we were ensconced in a curtain of shimmering fibre optics in the Le Blanc Hibiscus restaurant, I watched the waiter remove the wine glasses that had accompanied our first course. He quickly replaced them with sparkling crystal glasses in readiness for the wine that was to accompany our next course.

I looked quizzically at David, who appeared to be far away. 'This seems decadent. I've never been to a restaurant that has different wines for each course. Have you?'

He looked at me with a vague expression across his face.

'Yes - wine pairing. I've had it a few times, but for me the same wine throughout the whole meal is just as good.'

'Have you noticed my brother sitting over there with Allegra? He's no idea we're watching him.'

David followed the direction of my gaze. 'Jess is a very striking man.'

'He's always known how to make the best of himself, even as a teenager. He was the class heartthrob at school.'

'I can well believe it. Allegra is nothing like I imagined. In fact, she seems a little familiar, but I've no idea why.'

'She certainly gets on well with Jess, although I don't know any female that doesn't.'

Waiters appeared with our main course, which was a temporary diversion to conversation. The tasting of wine and serving of food occupied the next few minutes and it wasn't until we were alone again that we spoke.

'They certainly make you feel special on this liner, don't they?' I said.

'Yes, I could get used to being pampered.' David smiled. 'I'm glad you've got things sorted with the New York solicitor.'

'Me, too. I can't tell you how curious I am about meeting my sister.'

'Did you ever suspect that you weren't the firstborn?'

'No. Never. Until Mother's letter, I'd no idea. Mother always felt distant. I didn't really know her at all - her letter revealed her to me for the first time. She's clearer now than ever.'

'That's good. It must have been very hard for her to write to you.'

'I'm glad she did. It explained so much. I only wish I'd known years ago. It's too late now.'

'No it's not, Kit. She wanted you to know the story behind why she behaved as she did. I believe she thought it would empower you, give you a different outlook on your life and perhaps a new start. Don't let sadness for what might have been fill your heart. She wanted you to be happy and grasp new opportunities.' He changed the subject. 'Do you remember I told you I was born in Almaraz in Spain?'

I nodded as I sliced through the beef on my plate.

'I thought one day I'd return to the town of my birth. Just to see what it's like.'

'What do you know about it?'

'Only what I've looked up on the internet. It's small and it's in the area of Extremadura, which is near Portugal. Its biggest attribute seems to be its nuclear power plant and I believe they're building a solar power plant now as well.'

'You don't make it sound very attractive.'

David grinned. 'I take it you won't be coming with me on this homage to the town of my birth then?'

I wasn't sure how to take this remark and wondered whether he was being flippant and teasing me or if he was fishing to see if I'd be interested in going with him.

Our meal together came to an end. I'd looked forward to these few hours with David, but something had got in the way, although I'd no idea what it was. He seemed distant. It was as though there was something bothering him just beneath the surface.

I think I'd had a little too much to drink because when we stood up to walk to the martini bar, I felt the need to grip David's arm to help me balance. I hadn't wanted the after-dinner Armagnac we'd ordered, but found myself sipping it, nevertheless. Alcohol usually made me talk too much and this night was to be no exception.

'David, have you noticed those two would-be lovers sitting in that alcove?' I looked in their direction so that he could follow my gaze. 'Well, he's just given the girl a red rose and kissed her hand as he presented it to her. I know I've told you a little about Tom, but watching those two has brought him right back centre stage. When I first met him, he was like that, paying me so much attention and treating me as though I was a princess. It was a ploy, of course. He just wanted to get me into his bed and make me his drudge.'

I didn't give David a chance to reply but ploughed on. 'Do you know he lied to me from the very beginning? I was a complete idiot. Did I tell you about the IVF treatment?'

David's eyes widened and he shook his head.

'No, I didn't think I had. I'm ashamed of it, if the truth be known.' I temporarily studied my toes. 'Back then I longed for a baby. I still do. I hope it will happen one day before I get too old. Tom said he wanted a baby, too - and I believed him.'

David watched me with wonder as the story of Tom and the IVF unfolded. 'And do you know what? It was his wife – yes, his wife – who told me he'd had a vasectomy years before. What an idiot I'd been. All the time we'd lived together, he let me go through the pantomime of IVF and hadn't mentioned his vasectomy. He even let me think he was divorced.' David took my hand.

'I don't understand why I've told you this. It's embarrassing.'

'Kit, it's over.' He smiled at me, gently. 'Tom's long gone. He can't hurt you anymore.'

'The hurt's already been done. I'm afraid of it happening again.'

'Oh, Kit.' David studied the floor. I'd obviously made him uncomfortable.

'I've ruined our last night on board, haven't I?' I studied his face; he looked as weary as I felt. 'I think I might have an early night.'

'It'll probably do us both good. We've got to be up very early if we want to see the Statue of Liberty as we sail into New York. I'm more or less already packed and ready to leave, at least I believe I am. To be honest, I arranged with my butler to do it when I was out this evening.'

'Clever you. I didn't think of doing that.'

'Shall we meet at four thirty in the morning, port side, upper deck?'

'Fine. And just checking – port side is on the left, facing the front of the boat, isn't it?'

David chuckled. 'You've been on board all week and you've just called this huge liner a boat and you're still unsure which is port side.'

'Never mind. I'm not planning on being a Brain of Britain candidate,' I replied. 'See you on the upper deck tomorrow.'

It wasn't until I arrived back in the cabin that I realised I'd made my way alone without a single thought of Alex. I silently thanked David and felt a wave of regret that the evening had developed as it had.

I was surprised to find that Juan had already packed most of my belongings. He'd left a handwritten note on the bed, saying that he'd been unable to contact me and hoped that he hadn't taken a liberty by packing my things.

As I clambered into bed, I spied the perfume bottle on the bedside table. Earlier, I'd planned that two bodies would be entwined in this bed tonight and they'd soak in the atmosphere of delicately fragranced sheets. I certainly scuppered that plan.

Tonight, David had had a faraway look in his eyes at times. Perhaps now our voyage was coming to an end he was beginning to see our relationship in a different light. I thought we were becoming closer, but maybe he'd had second thoughts. Had I done it again? Ruined another promising relationship before it had the chance to develop. My heart sank. The positive emotions I had about my future appeared to be in jeopardy.

DAVID

I was shocked when I saw Kit in the Sesha Library. A gaunt expression filled her snow-white face. When she saw me, she covered her mouth with her hand and handed me her mother's letter. It did not make easy reading.

Poor Kit, how much more did this woman have to endure? My lack of honesty had left me plagued with guilt and yet it would be unkind to burden her with yet more desolation by coming clean right now. I hadn't meant for things to develop this far and I wasn't proud of myself.

Thankfully, we had a busy day sorting things out, so there wasn't much time to think. However, by evening, I'd decided I mustn't let Kit go on believing we could have a meaningful relationship. We couldn't and once she knew the truth, she wouldn't want us to continue in any case.

As I showered, it seemed to me that our last night on board would be a fitting end to our liaison. We could look back on this journey as a holiday romance, something to smile about in years to come. I planned to tell her everything after dinner, but whoever said that the 'best laid plans of mice and men often go awry' had it in one. We drunk a fair amount of alcohol, which seemed to loosen Kit's tongue and she didn't stop talking. I couldn't find a suitable pause to start my depressing admission.

Do you know the worst thing of all? Her revelation about Tom and the IVF treatment. I felt my face flush as she relived their journey. It certainly put a stop to any disclosure I might have revealed that night.

Now I didn't know what to do. I didn't want to hurt Kit, even though I knew confessing was the right thing to do. I couldn't let our relationship go on, especially as she so desperately wanted to have a baby. How on earth could I tell her that I'd had a vasectomy on top of all the lies I needed to confess?

It was a relief when she called an early night and now I was worrying about when it would be the best time to confess everything. It seemed heartless to do it tomorrow as we arrived in New York. In any case, what about hotel arrangements? She'd have one helluva job getting an affordable room at such short notice. I suppose I could ring my hotel in the morning; maybe they'd have a spare room available, although I doubted it. At least my room had two beds so I'd just have to make sure we kept to our own bed. Although that would be far easier to say than to do.

JESS

The splashing shower water and Allegra's melodic hum told me that she was preparing herself for a fix – and Allegra's fix, as I well knew, was sex. Lots of it, as frequently as possible. I looked around my cabin and wondered how I'd got myself into this situation. In my lifetime I'd enjoyed my fair share of lust, but Allegra was different. For a start, she'd never give up control; total control had to be hers from the first touch of skin. And no matter which ploy I used, there was nothing I could do to change this. I'd also discovered that even if I was exhausted, turning my back and feigning sleep cut no ice with this insatiable woman. She'd try to arouse me by whatever means possible and it was embarrassing.

The aroma of her perfume wafted through from the bathroom. It wouldn't be much longer now before she entered the room wearing her long red silk negligee, which revealed her ample cleavage in such a seductive way that it immediately drew my eye. Her glance would be sexually inviting and then she'd hold eye contact for so long that I would be forced to look away. Her next move was anybody's guess; I'd learned that it had to be her move and woe betide me if I tried to lead the chase.

I closed my eyes. I'd decided days ago that I hated this woman. I hated being used by her and I hated my weakness for not walking away. All the time, however, at the back of my mind was how useful she was going to be to me once we reached America. Allegra could be my ticket to mega bucks once the will had been read and Father's money was transferred to my bank account.

Even with my eyes closed, I knew she was standing at the foot of the bed. I felt her stroke my feet, rubbing and kneading my skin with gentle thumbs. She'd probably slowly work her way up to my inner thighs. Often she stopped all contact at this point; she was teasing me, playing me, and I loathed her for it.

She moved to sit on the bed beside me and started running her fingers through my hair. Her voice was soft. 'Darling, your Allegra is going to drive you wild tonight, so I need to tie your hands together to make you behave yourself and not be a naughty boy.'

She unwrapped the scarf that was draped around her neck and rubbed it seductively around her breasts before very loosely binding it around my wrists. 'I'm going to do incredibly wicked things, my darling man, until your mind and body explode. Then, I'm going to do them all over again until you beg me to finish.

Agreed?'

I gritted my teeth.

'Darling, your baby is waiting for your reply.' I nodded. It was all I could trust myself to do.

Allegra adopted her breathiest, smokiest voice. 'Aah, I see you're acting cool with your baby tonight. I think I'll change our game play. Tonight, you're going to be my little slave and I want you to do everything exactly as I tell you.' Her sultry eyes held mine. 'First, I want you to lie me down on the bed, kiss my neck, move a little lower, a little lower...'

Every word she spoke fuelled the fire that burned inside. The animosity I felt was acid-burning, slicing and potent. My face flared red; I could no longer swallow my anger. When

Allegra's hand moved to my groin, all rage came out, faster than magma.

I snapped. 'How dare you! Who the hell d'you think you are? I'm not here to fill that sexually dysfunctional emotional need you carry around. Get out of here. Go. Get out of my sight.'

She stared at me open-mouthed and I glared at her with hate. I stood, clenching and unclenching my hands as I marched to the door and wrenched it open. 'Go. I mean it, Allegra. I won't be held accountable for my actions if you don't leave this minute.'

'But I'm not dressed.' Allegra pulled her skimpy negligee around her. 'What the hell's the matter with you, Jess?'

I let the door slam and marched back into the room, grabbing her jacket and throwing it at her. 'Here, put this on and go.' 'You're going to regret this, Jess Langford.' Spittle left the side of her mouth as she spoke. 'You think you can throw me out just like that, do you? You've got a lot to learn and I'm going to make sure you learn it painfully.' With these words, she swept out of the room.

My heartbeat thumped in my ears as I turned my back on the door and stood inert, looking at the empty room. My hand roughly swept the sweat that was threatening to stream from brow to eyes. Like a zombie, I made my way to the bed and in the silence I tapped Kit's number, then immediately stopped the call. What the hell was I going to say? I banged the phone on the bedside table.

My body slumped from sitting to the position of a curled foetus. Suddenly, a growl escaped, which was loud enough to fill every corner of the room. The growl turned into a howl. It sounded just like a wounded animal, which was what I'd become.

'Oh my God! What have I done?' And with these agonising words, my hands flew to cover my face.

KIT

Five o'clock next morning, the Statue of Liberty came into view. The scale of her was staggering, yet despite her immensity, there was something soft about her, something tender, and the fact it was a statue of a woman welcoming people instead of a heroic, manly figure enforced this idea. She looked as though she was reaching up to heaven, her torch showing the path to liberty.

David and I were not the only passengers who'd risen before the sun to witness our liner's arrival in New York. Some were clutching cameras, some takeaway coffees, but we simply held hands as we watched Manhattan reveal itself in its early morning glory. I felt the palpable excitement on deck as more and more people joined us to watch the liner slowly make its way towards Brooklyn.

I grinned. 'I can't believe I'm actually looking at New York out there.'

'It's certainly a sight to see.'

'I keep thinking about all the songs that mention this magical city.'

'You've got a massive job there, Kit.'

'I think Ella's "Manhattan" has to be top of the list. D'you think we'll get a chance to see some of those iconic sights she sang about. The Bronx? The zoo? Mott Street and all that?'

'I thought you didn't know much about New York. You're not doing too bad.'

'I remember song words. Always have.'

'That's a very old song, but perhaps some things will be the same. We'll ask at the hotel.'

'One place we must visit is Strawberry Fields in Central Park. That song always reminds me of John Lennon.' My enthusiasm was bubbling over. 'Look. Isn't that Brooklyn Bridge?'

'No, that's the Verrazzano suspension bridge; it joins Staten Island and Brooklyn.'

'Staten Island. That's in Ella's song, too. Perhaps we can go there?'

David laughed. 'How long are you planning to stay in New York? It'll take a month to see all the things on your list.'

'My visa is valid for about ninety days.'

'I think your shoe leather will wear out long before your visa.'

'Then I'll buy another pair of shoes.'

David grinned. 'Listen. Can you hear a calypso band playing? I seem to remember reading somewhere that a band and champagne would be available as we approached Brooklyn.'

'Where's the band?'

'On the afterdeck, I think.' He grinned. 'The "back bit" to you.'

'So, why are we stood here? Champagne, here we come.'

We passed Brooklyn Bridge standing side by side, champagne glass in hand. I put my arm around David's waist and tilted my face towards his. 'I haven't felt this happy for a very long time.' Then, the thought of Mother crept under my happiness radar. 'Oh David, it feels wrong to be happy so soon after…' My voice trailed away.

'It's not wrong, Kit. Life has to go on. I believe your mother understood that, which is why she wrote you that beautiful letter.'

I stared at the cables of the huge bridge, although my mind was now elsewhere and I wasn't seeing the structure.

David broke the silence. 'We'll be there soon. I thought perhaps we'd get a yellow cab from the cruise terminal to the hotel. Okay with you?'

Ten minutes ago, the mention of travelling in a yellow New York cab would have filled me with glee, but the bubble had been broken.

'Yes. Fine.'

'Good. I'm sure we'll see lots of iconic sights on the journey.'

'Probably.' My smile was forced.

'People seem to be making their way downstairs, ready to disembark. Shall we join them?' I nodded, absentmindedly.

'Or shall we have another glass of champagne and watch the ship dock? I think that'll be much more fun.'

Unfortunately, memories of Mother drove fun from my mind, but nevertheless I stood with David watching our liner slowly ebb its way into dock.

Our yellow cab journey across New York City was a slow, gridlocked affair, but I was too interested in the slowly passing concrete jungle to worry. At first I'd sat quietly, looking straight ahead, but slowly New York seduced me.

'Look at all these people. There's hardly any space for them to walk.'

'Every time I've been here, it's been like that.'

'How often have you visited New York?'

'I don't think "visited" is quite the right description, Kit. I've been here quite a few times – always on business, though, so I'd fly in and out within a few days, and to be honest I didn't do much sightseeing. I'd be locked up in meeting rooms for most of the time.'

'Travelling to New York for work sounds like a dream job.'

David smiled. 'Well, it might sound like it, but it's just work, and work is the same wherever you do it.'

I pointed to a sign saying, 'Times Square'. 'Is that uptown or downtown?'

'It's impossible to answer that one. The people I've worked with here can't agree on where uptown starts or downtown ends. So, we've no chance of working it out.'

'I've always thought Allegra must come from uptown. She seems classy, plus she obviously enjoys the finer things in life. I know she looked down on me.'

'You might be wrong there, Kit. From what you've said, she didn't look down on Jess and you're from the same family.'

I laughed loudly. 'Good heavens. Testosterone-filled Jess could seduce any female, up or downtown. And just wait

until he and Allegra get their hands on Father's money –
there'll be some party going on then.'

'I thought Jess was a businessman and had lots of plans
afoot once he arrived in America.'

'Yes, he is and he has. I think Allegra has plans, too, but
they might not coincide with those of my brother. Jess works
hard; he's ambitious and usually he attains whatever goal he's
seeking. He's similar to our father. His weakness is women.'

'He's got the looks for it.'

'He certainly has. I believe he'd get on fine in New York
without Allegra, but he seems to think that she'll speed
things up and smooth business dealings.'

I could sense the hesitation in David's voice. 'Kit, I wasn't
going to say this and I'm not sure whether I should do so
even now, but I heard a rumour about Allegra.'

I look at him quizzically.

'After you pointed out Allegra with your brother the
other day, I tried to remember where I'd seen her before.
Later, it came to me that they were the couple I'd seen
looking at a bar menu. I'd been sitting on a bar stool making
polite conversation with a stranger, when he spotted Allegra.
Of course, I didn't know her name then and I can't swear
this is true, but this man said that he crossed the Atlantic
numerous times a year on business because he was afraid of
flying and he'd seen Allegra on several sailings.' I watched
David bite his lip before continuing, 'To be honest, his exact
words were: "Look, I see she's got another sucker."'

I winced. As much as Jess and I hadn't always seen eye to
eye, he was my brother and hated the thought of Allegra
taking him for a ride.

'Did he say anything else?'

'He said he believed she was a trickster and conned people out of their money. He also said she was good at it and the unwary could easily be deceived. Apparently, on one voyage, she'd been very subtle and tried to find out this man's business interests, and when he'd played everything down, she quickly lost interest. Once she couldn't smell money, he could tell from her eyes that she'd decided he wasn't important anymore.'

I felt my anger rise. Had Allegra been beside me at that moment, I think I'd have lashed out at her.

David's features were set firm. 'I've no idea how true this is, mind you.'

'Oh, I can well believe it. Poor Jess. I've had my suspicions and I tried to warn him. He doesn't deserve to have a leech holding on to him. Let's hope she doesn't con him out of all his savings, let alone the money that will come to him when the will is read. Stupid man.'

David looked out of the cab window. 'We've already passed Central Park – didn't you mention that their hotel is somewhere near there? I suppose they've arrived at their hotel by now.' I nodded.

'When are you supposed to contact Jess?'

'Tomorrow. But in view of what you've said, I'm going to ring his mobile as soon as we get to the hotel. I want to warn him about Allegra, although from what you say I might be too late.'

'Let's hope not. He's going to have a big enough shock when Sarah turns up at the solicitors; he doesn't need anything else.'

'He certainly is. He'll believe it's unfair if any of the inheritance money goes her way.'

'And what about you, Kit? What do you think?'

'Money has never been a god for me. As long as I've enough to get by, then that's fine. I can understand why Mother might want to do something good for Sarah, though. After all, Sarah would never have been adopted had she had her way.'

Silence filled the cab for the last ten minutes of our journey. We both seemed lost in thought as we gazed out of the windows. As we left the gridlocked streets behind, dread and anticipation filled my heart in equal measure. Would I like Sarah? Would she like me? I could only hope that maybe we'd become proper sisters in time.

SARAH

When I received an official-looking envelope with the names of 'Selby and Cromwell, Wills and Probate Lawyers' clearly marked in the top left-hand corner I was mystified. I'd picked up the mail from the mailbox I shared with the other tenants as I was about to leave for work. The box was always full of money-off flyers or free newspapers. A personally addressed envelope was unknown.

I frowned. Not many people knew my address and of those that did, I couldn't think of a single person who'd write to me. My friends would send a message or email or even a few words scrawled under a Facebook photo.

My amazement increased when I opened the envelope. Why on earth was a New York lawyer contacting me to arrange a meeting? I thrust it into my bag as there was no time to think about it. I needed to get to work.

However, it remained a mystery and was revisited again as I sat on the train to the Rockefeller Centre. I racked my brain to think of a reason why a lawyer should request to see me. When I reached my subway stop, I still hadn't drawn any conclusion.

My heart sank when I saw the queue for the Dunkin' Donuts store just inside the subway entrance. It was only a quarter to six and it looked as though all the world and its dog wanted donuts for breakfast.

'Morning, Sarah,' Ashley shouted when she saw me enter the store. 'Hurry up. I'm sinking under the demand.'

I nodded my head in greeting to my workmate, although workmate was hardly the correct description since our work hours covered different parts of the day. Ashley covered the much quieter twilight hours, but I'd drawn the short straw of early morning and lunchtime cover, which was the busiest period of the day. I'd presumed it was because I was a Brit, but in reality it was more likely to be because I was a temp.

Ashley shouted again, 'Hurry up. Get your butt over here. You're needed.'

I ignored the plea and at my own pace changed into my work clothes in the tiny back room. When I'd eventually donned the brown uniform apron and cap, I stepped out to work beside Ashley during the remaining minutes of her shift.

'You took your time.'

'I'm not on duty until six o'clock. I shouldn't even start for another five minutes.'

Ashley sniffed and turned to the next customer.

Unfortunately, my first customer was not in a good mood. 'Hey, you, I've been waiting online in this queue for hours. Get a speed on, can't you?'

'I'm sorry you've been kept waiting. How can I help you?'

'You're a Brit, aren't you?'

I nodded and waited for his donut order.

'I'll have two chocolate-glazed donuts and a medium coffee with extra cream,' he shouted as he handed over the money.

When I handed back his coffee and the paper bag containing the chocolate donuts, he caught hold of my hand and held it tightly. 'What's up, babe? You wanna come out with me? I'm a guy that's good in the ladies' department.'

I yanked my hand away. 'No, thank you. Next!'

'Don't get your panties in a bunch, Tootsie. A woman of your age is lucky to get an offer. There's plenty of younger fish in the sea, you know.'

Smile, I told myself. *Look pleased.* 'Well, you have a nice day, too,' I countered with a cheesy grin.

A tall woman pushed her way to the counter as the man shuffled away. And so began my non-stop shift. I hated my work, but I needed the money even if I reached home in a collapsed state at the end of most working days. Some days were better than others; it depended upon who I was working with. Some employees moaned non-stop, but on the whole most were okay. My friend, Isabella, was always cheerful even if her timekeeping was atrocious.

'Hi, girl.' I looked up to see Isabella walking into the store. She gave me a wave and made her way to the back room to change.

'You okay?'

I smiled. 'What's your excuse for being late today?'

'I was on the subway and some guy was hitting on me.' She screwed up her face. 'I'll soon be with you.'

Once we were both working the counter, we cleared the queue fairly quickly, but new customers appeared every second and it was some time before I found breathing space to talk to Isabella.

'I've got something I want to discuss with you.' I'd been longing to tell Isabella about my letter from Selby and Cromwell and as the words spilled out, Isabella's eyes widened. 'What d'you think?'

Isabella was prevented from answering by an avalanche of teenagers, who arrived demanding a complicated list of various donuts.

'Tell you what,' I sighed. 'Let's have coffee after our shift and I'll show you the letter. We can discuss it then.'

'It's a bit odd, isn't it? Have you no idea why solicitors might want to talk to you?' Isabella asked as we stood side by side in a sidewalk later that day.

I shrugged. 'No, I haven't a clue.'

'Have you done anything illegal?' There was a chuckle in her voice.

'Like what?'

'Have you got all your paperwork in order to be working in the US?'

'I think so. No, I'm sure I have. My permit says that I can work here for up to a year and I've still got a few months to go.'

'Maybe they've got the wrong Sarah Langford.'

'I suppose that's possible, but it isn't a common name.'

Isabella studied the floor for a few minutes before suddenly raising her voice, 'I've got it. They're not real lawyers. They must be trying to scam you for information fraud and stuff like that.'

I laughed. 'You've watched too many movies.'

'Just trying to help.' She frowned. 'You're not in debt, are you?'

'No. My rent is up to date and I've nothing on hire-purchase. I don't earn enough to think about hire-purchase, even if I was given clearance to apply. Anyway, I only intend to be in New York for a year, so what on earth would I want on hire-purchase?'

'A car. Or perhaps a nice little Dior suit.' Isabella giggled.

'You're crazy.' I enjoyed these moments of banter with my friend; it livened up what might otherwise be a boring day.

'Maybe that place you used to work was sued in a class action lawsuit and you're entitled to a portion of the money.'

'Chance would be a fine thing. I suppose I'll just have to wait and see. The lawyers ask that I attend their office in person on Thursday afternoon, so no doubt I'll find out then.'

'What made you come here, Sarah? I mean, why New York?'

'It's somewhere I always wanted to visit and there was nothing to keep me in the UK, so I thought I'd go for it.'

'And you don't mind working all the hours God gives in Dunkin' Donuts for peanuts?'

'I don't have much choice. Lots of places have absolutely no interest in employing you when you're middle-aged.'

'Middle-aged! You don't look as though you've long turned twenty.'

'I wish. You're being kind, but the truth is I'm almost thirty-five, and once employers find this out I'm viewed as old.'

'Doesn't seem fair.'

'It's life. Who said life was fair? Anyway, I've achieved what I wanted. I got to work in this great city and, moreover, on my free days I see all the incredible tourist attractions. I'm ticking them off one by one.' I smiled. 'It might be noisy, big, brash and all the other things that people say, but I love it here.'

'You won't want to leave.'

'Now, I didn't say that. There are many other places in the world I want to visit so I can't stay here forever. Plus New York is too expensive. I've used a big chunk of my savings just being here; it goes quicker than I imagined it would.'

'I'm glad you're here and I'm going to miss my working buddy when you go.' Isabella puckered her lips. 'Come on, I'll shout you a beer. Let's be tourists and enjoy ourselves.'

I rubbed my hands together in anticipation. 'Right then, we'll mingle with the Times Square crowd, shall we?'

KIT

The hotel receptionist looked at me in amazement when I asked for a map and details of the best way to walk to Times Square.

'Times Square. You can't walk to Times Square from here, Ma'am. Nobody does that. You need a cab.'

'I want a bit of exercise if possible.'

'The subway is about a ten-minute walk from here. That's quite a nice walk.'

I soon discovered that a very different New York was opening out before me on foot compared to that viewed from the cab. For a start, a strange smell dominated the streets, which was no wonder because David and I needed to manoeuvre around the rotting trash on the sidewalks.

I wrinkled my nose. 'I reckon today must be rubbish collection day.'

'Mm. I suppose it gets rancid quickly in this heat. I've never noticed this before, probably because I've usually travelled by cab.' David stopped and studied the map. 'What was it that receptionist said about finding the subway entrance?'

'She said it's difficult to locate because it's squeezed between store entrances, but that we should look for a green-white globe lamp.'

'There's a red globe over there.' David pointed to the other side of the road.

'No, she definitely said green-white.'

'Shall we get a cab? Might be easier.'

'Easier, yes. But we want to experience the real New York, don't we?'

'I suppose.'

It took us ten minutes to find the subway entrance and then ten minutes to work out which MetroCard we needed to buy and that was without figuring out which train to get. By the time we reached Times Square, it was mid-afternoon.

'Did you see that man dressed as a clown juggling umbrellas on the platform?' I asked David as we climbed the stairs to the Times Square exit. 'I thought any minute he was going to let one drop on someone's head.'

He laughed. 'Just as well he didn't. There'd have been mayhem.'

'It's so busy here. It seems worse than London.'

'London's not so smelly, though.'

'D'you think New Yorkers don't notice the smell? Or perhaps they get to like it.'

'Like it! Surely nobody could like it. I expect once the garbage men have been, it's fine again… until the next time.'

'David. Look. We're on 42nd Street.' I pointed to a green sign suspended on a pillar above our heads. 'It says West 42nd Street; is there an East one?'

David chuckled. 'Have you never heard of the New York road grid system?' He proceeded to explain, but I wasn't listening as my eyes struggled to take in the amazing mix of super tall buildings and the millions upon millions of people. Even all the traffic was at a standstill. What a city.

'It's got a buzz, hasn't it?' David asked as he, too, craned his neck skywards.

I grinned with impish glee. 'I'm like a kid in a toyshop. I can't remember when I last felt this excited.'

'So now we're in Times Square, what do you want to do?'

'Everything.'

'Okay, let's grab something to eat first and make a plan while we're sitting down. I'm going to take you to Sardi's. I think it's the best restaurant around Times Square.'

'To be honest, after nearly a week of all that food on board the ship, I'm not that hungry.'

'Neither am I, but we can have a glass of wine and maybe just a savoury dessert to keep us going. Besides which, I thought we'd eat out tonight, nearer the hotel. I know some nice restaurants around there.'

'That's fine with me.'

The list that David wrote was so long that it took us twenty minutes to pare it down to the absolute essentials before we set off. Central Park was the first item on our list and we headed to the subway, thinking it would be faster than a gridlocked taxi.

-o-

I wasn't prepared for the enormous size of this iconic park, nor for the crowds of people that appeared around every bend. But nevertheless I fell in love with its never-ending views and colourful gardens. We parked our hire bikes alongside the Jacqueline Kennedy Onassis Reservoir to study the map.

'Look at all those gigantic skyscrapers around the reservoir. There's one over there with two gigantic towers.' I was aware that I was gushing too much but couldn't help it.

'It must cost an arm and a leg to live in those places,' David said, before turning his attention to our park map. He stabbed his finger on an area too far for my focus to see. 'I think if we cycle this way, we'll get to the Strawberry Fields site.'

'Lead on. I can't wait.'

'I hope you won't be disappointed,' he called over his shoulder as we mounted our bikes.

I wasn't. As we approached Strawberry Fields, I could hear someone strumming 'Imagine' on their guitar and there was a small group of people singing along. I felt goosebumps as we dismounted, and I looked at the solemn faces around me. While it was crowded, everyone was respectful and I watched several people place flowers alongside the many teddy bears on the Imagine mosaic in tribute to John Lennon.

Unfortunately, we stayed so long in the park that there wasn't time to tick off any of the other things on our list, so as the sun set we made our way back to the subway.

David was abnormally quiet on the return journey, which made me uncomfortable. He stared out of the train window and appeared to be purposely ignoring me. Any comment I made, he either chose not to hear or, in fact, was so engrossed in his thoughts that he didn't hear a word.

By the time we arrived at our hotel, I wondered whether spending these days in New York with David was going to be a mistake. Perhaps I didn't really know this man after all.

JESS

As the sun set on my first night in New York, I shook off the mantle of afternoon sleep. On arrival at the exclusive Peter Hotel that morning, I'd taken three paracetamol tablets, drank half a bottle of whisky and collapsed onto the bed. The 'Do Not Disturb' sign that I'd placed outside the door meant that my suitcase stood, still unpacked, on the deep pile wool carpet.

Through blurry eyes, I glanced around the suite and wondered what the hell I was going to do with all this space. From the bed, I glimpsed an ivory-inlaid chest of drawers and guessed that this item alone probably cost as much as my UK house.

I staggered to my feet, holding onto the bed as I did. My eyes swivelled backwards to alleviate the pain in my head, which throbbed even more than it had done when I was horizontal. A leg buckled under me as I hobbled my way to one of the two bathrooms that had been advertised with this apartment. I squinted, dry-mouthed, as I searched for the toilet. The sight and smell of the vomit already in the pan before me, together with my pounding head, forced a taste in my mouth that warned me there could be more to come.

What a stupid state to get into. I ought to shower and get myself together, but it was of no use. The lingering smell increased my nausea, making my only choice to return to bed and retreat under the sheets.

-o-

It was many hours later when I awoke again and my brain was still struggling to recover from the abuse I'd doled out. However, I was now able to stand without swaying as the shower water cascaded down my back.

Taking in the surroundings in a little more detail, I realised it was stupid to pay for this fantastic suite. It was absolutely gorgeous, but if I stayed here for a week, I'd waste so much money and I'd need every penny of cash left for my planned investments, although it would be nowhere near enough. Why on earth had I trusted Allegra?

I picked up the phone in the lounge. 'Hello. I'm in the Rosewood Suite.' I was glad that the little card by the phone informed me which suite I was in – without it, I'd have no idea.

'Can I help you, Sir?'

'Yes. I want to change rooms.'

'Is there an immediate problem, Sir?'

I could hardly say it was too expensive, so I said it was too big.

'You see, it was planned that my fiancée and I would be visiting New York but unfortunately work prevented her from coming.'

The person on the other end of the phone cleared his throat. 'I see.' He paused, momentarily. 'It is impossible to do anything at this precise moment, Sir. There is only a skeleton staff on duty, but if you contact the reception desk first thing in the morning, I am positive we will be able to help you.'

'Aah,' I replied hesitantly. 'What time is it?'

'It's just gone three am, Sir.'

I was sure my intake of breath could be heard on the other end of the line. 'Oh. I'd no idea.'

'It's not a problem, Sir. Is there anything else I can help you with?'

'No, thank you.' I ran my hand through my freshly washed hair before making my way to the heavily curtained windows. I thought they'd been drawn to keep the sun out. As soon as I pulled back the drapes, the twinkling lights of Manhattan immediately assailed my eyes. A backdrop of stars filled the sky like white sugar strewn over dark chocolate icing. It was one of the most beautiful sights I'd ever seen.

I thought of Kit and wondered what her hotel had cost and then immediately felt a tinge of guilt that I'd ignored her warning about Allegra. I hadn't thought much about Kit in any depth for years, but then I'd hardly been in her company for more than ten minutes since we were adults. I resolved it was time to pay more attention to our relationship; she was my only sister, after all. I recalled the disarray she was in after Tom, which, to my mind, was similar to my mess with Allegra.

Allegra, the femme fatale, who'd conned me into letting her use my card on the ship. I'd no idea how I was going to pay off the credit card I'd used to settle the bill or how on earth I would explain this to Lily if she ever found out.

I know Lily only stayed with me because it was convenient. It was advantageous for both of us to parade a partner when work or life demanded it. We were both physically attractive, as well as having an eloquence of speech, so we could help each other charm the most hardened of businesspeople when needed. We were absolutely suited, but our relationship would crumble if I was unable to pay my fair share towards the finer things in life we enjoyed. I could see my business plans ebbing away as I didn't have enough cash to finance them until Father's money was in my bank account and that might take some time.

Allegra's promised networking was like all her promises – candyfloss in the sky. Stupidity hardly described how I had behaved and now I was in this thousand-dollar a night suite without even a free breakfast thrown in. I'd leave immediately, but where would I go? They have my card details in any case, so what would be the point? I was going to be charged for this first night no matter what I did, just like I'd been charged for Allegra's cabin, jewellery, copious new clothes, as well as all the hideously expensive last-minute items she bought on my card.

Perhaps I should contact Kit. Come clean with her; after all, she had seen through Allegra from the start so she might have some good advice now as well. Then, some of our recent meetings came to mind. She had changed. I could no longer visualise the old, dependable Kit I once knew. This new feisty woman would not welcome me with open arms and minister to my problems.

Fully clothed, I crawled back to the bed and laid on top of the silk cover. Tomorrow, I decided, I would sort things out. Then it dawned on me - tomorrow was already here.

KIT

The fashionable bijou restaurant that David had chosen near our hotel turned out to be the perfect place to eat that evening. It was a quaint little place, its bright red tablecloths standing out against the whiteness of everything else, from the walls to the light fittings. I'd chosen to wear my simple black evening gown and felt as though even my silhouette stood out against the snow-coloured walls.

We were seated at a corner table from where we could watch everything going on in the restaurant. It boasted authentic French Provençal cuisine and the food was absolutely delicious. We plodded through a strange assortment of small talk and at the same time worked our way through the Beaujolais. David wore a worried expression throughout and it was obvious he was troubled about something. I wished he'd spit it out; he was making me nervous.

In silence, we walked to the anteroom attached to the restaurant where our coffee and digestif would be served. The waiter poured an intense ginger liqueur over the ice in the glasses set before us and left. I raised my glass to David and was surprised to see a sadness in his eyes that I'd never seen before.

'Kit.' His voice was barely a whisper. 'I've something I must discuss with you. Something I must tell you.'

He had captured my eyes and I stared at him, wondering what on earth was coming.

David cleared his throat. 'I think you know that you are very special to me, Kit, and I respect you immensely. But before we take the next step in our relationship, I need to come clean about my past.'

I swallowed hard but said nothing.

'I know you've been hurt in the past and I know it's been difficult for you to trust another man since. I'm hoping that once I've told you the complete truth about my life, then perhaps you might be able to forgive me and possibly consider there could be a chance for us.'

I placed my glass on the table, but didn't speak.

'When I've finished, you can ask me any questions you want and I'll try to answer as honestly as I can.' David smiled sadly. 'When all's been said, if you prefer that we end our friendship, then that's the way it will be, and tomorrow I will try to get a different room at the hotel. But I hope that's not how it's going to be.

'I'll start at the beginning. That afternoon on the ship when I told you about my marriage – well, I wasn't completely honest. At the time, I was too embarrassed to tell you the truth. I behaved badly back then; I lied to my wife and my girlfriend. I didn't want you to see me in such a bad light, so I lied to you.' His eyes sought refuge in the ceiling. 'I'm sorry.'

I was suddenly fearful of what was to come.

'Kit, I'd no idea I'd develop such deep feelings for you, so at the time I didn't think it would matter if I wasn't entirely truthful. As much as I liked you, I thought we'd be ships in the night. However, these past few days have changed my whole outlook. I want us to go forward together and I hope this is something you might want, too. I don't believe that we can do this unless you know the whole truth: what I did and how badly I behaved.'

I could clearly see the pain on David's face and was unsure how to react.

'If you remember, I told you that I married young and it didn't last long. I said that when my wife told me she was going to divorce me, I took a lover, hoping she'd change her mind and stay with me. That's not quite true.' David sighed. 'It wasn't my wife who said she would divorce me. It was I who wanted to divorce her. You see, I'd already met Carly, who was my lover. Carly became pregnant, but I persuaded her to have an abortion because I didn't want to be a father. It was selfish, I know that now. Once I'd left my wife, Carly became pregnant for a second time, but this time refused to have an abortion and gave birth to Sophie.'

David paused and studied the carpet before continuing, 'My wife begged me not to leave. When I look back now, I realise, with hindsight, that she loved me a great deal and we might have been able to work things out had I stayed. At the time, I was foolish and too young to know what I was doing, so I walked out on her to live with Carly.'

I heard his words as though someone else had spoken them and, in my confusion, I could hear an insistent thump in my ears.

'I'm afraid it gets worse and I'm not proud of this. I told you that Carly didn't put my name on the birth certificate as the father of the child. That wasn't true. She did. I'm officially Sophie's father, so I can have visiting access to her. Carly wanted me to marry her when the divorce came through, but I was frightened I'd make a mess of marriage for a second time so I stalled any decision. Eventually, Carly gave me an ultimatum. We married or we split up. We split up six months later.

'It is true that I see my daughter at Christmas and around the time of her birthday, but I could have insisted on seeing her far more often and I did at first. It was difficult, though.'

David closed his eyes for a few seconds. 'Carly had another man in her life almost as soon as I'd left, and when I spent time with Sophie, it was obvious that she didn't think of me as her father. I was just some man who would take her to the zoo or the cinema every now and then. I should have made sure we met more often, but I didn't. I'm afraid that because of me, my daughter and I have never been close and it's my fault.'

I found my voice. 'What about the maintenance payments; do you actually pay them?'

'Yes. That part is true and they are handed over at a cloak-and dagger meeting. I think Carly doesn't declare this money so it doesn't affect any benefit payments she gets and that's fine by me, just so long as Sophie benefits from the extra money.' David's sigh was resigned and weary as it slowly escaped from his dry lips.

'And do you love your daughter?'

'She's all I have. She's part of me and I feel something very special for her. I'm not sure I'd call it love, because I don't know her well enough to use such a powerful word.' My eyes remained fixed on David's face.

'Throughout my life, my relationship with women has never been good. I made such a huge mess of relationships in my early years. I was a failure at being married, I threw away my relationship, and with it I lost all chance of becoming a proper father to my daughter.' His eyes revealed his sadness, and he slowly shook his head. 'To be honest, Kit, I've never met anybody I truly wanted to be with. Until now.'

I was unable to speak. There seemed no adequate words to say.

The frown lines on David's forehead had grown deeper and deeper as he told his story, but now he looked directly into my eyes. 'Is there anything you want to know, Kit? Anything. You only have to ask.'

'Did you ever love Carly or was it simply a sexual relationship?'

'I thought I loved her. At least, at the time I did. I know better now. As I said, I was too young. Far too young.'

I nodded and lapsed into silence. My mind needed time to process what had been said.

After a couple of minutes, David spoke, 'I'm afraid I have one more thing to add to this confession and this is something I regret tremendously now that I've met you.'

I raised my eyebrows. Surely there couldn't be more.

David bit his lip and roughly wiped the back of his hand across both eyes before continuing, 'When Sophie was a baby, Carly told me she wanted another child so that Sophie would have a sibling. I thought she might trick me into fathering a second child and at the time I was scared. I wasn't ready for fatherhood, besides which I was struggling to support just the three of us.' He lowered his voice. 'I had a vasectomy.'

My skin suddenly felt clammy and numbness travelled from my head to my toes. David's voice seemed to come from far away.

'I've shocked you badly.'

I couldn't answer or even look at him.

His voice cracked. 'I'm so sorry. I shouldn't have lied. But I can't change things and I need to be honest with you.'

I looked around the room with anxiety below my pressed lips. It was some time before I spoke.

'I don't know what to think. Or what to say.'

'There are no more skeletons in my life; you now know everything, Kit.'

'It's not your early life that worries me.' I shook my head. 'Tom lied to me over and over, and I, being naïve, didn't realise. I'm… I'm not sure that I could live with someone who might lie to me again.'

'Oh, Kit.' He momentarily closed his eyes. 'I promise I'll never lie to you again if you give me a second chance.'

'If only you'd told me the truth the first time around.' I stared ahead, my eyes unseeing.

'I know. I know. It was stupid. At the time, I didn't think it mattered.' His hands made fists in his lap. 'I'd no idea you were going to become so special to me. But I'm trying to put things right now. Everything I've told you tonight is the absolute truth. I wish there was some way I could prove it to you.'

The silence that followed moved at funereal pace. My voice eventually cracked as I broke the quietness.

'Maybe now isn't the time to think about these things. We've known each other a very short time and it seems to me that we're such opposites. I'm very ordinary. I work at an ordinary job and have an ordinary life, whereas you… you're clever, you've a powerful job, you travel the world and can…' My voice petered out.

David touched my hand. 'Kit, how can I make it up to you? I'm not comparable with Tom. Believe me.'

'David, I don't want to think about this tonight. The past week has been a roller coaster of emotions and right now I don't want to feel anything anymore.'

'Just tell me that you haven't made any decision yet. Will you sleep on it? Please, Kit.' I nodded slowly.

David dredged up false brightness. 'Let's go back to the hotel, shall we? There's another day tomorrow.'

My feet moved on automatic pilot as we walked back to our hotel. Everything was surreal and the hope I'd cherished about our relationship was fading, slipping further away with every step.

JESS

'Thank you, Sir,' the receptionist said, through a smile that was permanently fixed next to his neatly manicured beard. 'I hope everything was to your satisfaction?'

I nodded. 'Yes, thank you.'

'Shall I call you a cab, Sir?'

'No, thank you.'

I looked at my credit card as I placed it on the reader and hoped my credit limit wasn't about to be reached. I badly need to sit down quietly without a hangover and work out my finances as soon as possible.

'Have a nice day, Sir.'

'Thank you.' I slowly ambled towards the revolving doors, with no idea where I was heading. *This is stupid*, I thought and walked back to the reception desk.

The fixed smile alighted upon me once more. 'Sir. Can I help?'

I realised I had nothing to lose but my pride. 'Would you have a list of other accommodation, perhaps not quite as expensive as The Peter?' I avoided looking at his eyes. 'I'm afraid this city of yours is turning out to be far more expensive than I thought.'

The receptionist nodded, his face now serious. However, I felt sure that I could see a smile swallowed from behind his pinched lips. Before he could reply, the fellow receptionist took charge and quickly stepped in front of her bearded colleague. It was obvious from the way her hand brushed him aside that she was his boss.

'Let me help you, Sir. I've worked in both sister hotels and I can assure you that they are absolutely fantastic, but neither of them is quite as central as The Peter and therefore they're priced accordingly. Is being central important to you?' 'Not necessarily.'

Two glossy brochures were placed before me on the desk.

'Then these might suit you perfectly. If you browse through our brochures, you will see the many amenities that our sister hotels offer. Their accommodation rates are printed on a separate leaflet at the back. If wish me to book ahead for you, just let me know.'

I mumbled my thanks and picked up the glossy brochures before choosing a sumptuously thick armchair in the enormous reception area. Even before perusing the brochures, I had a sinking feeling that these sister hotels were going to be way above the amount I wanted to pay.

As I flicked through the glossy pages, my feeling was confirmed. What would I want with two indoor-heated swimming pools, three á la carte restaurants and a twice-daily maid service? Not forgetting the dry-cleaning service and a whole range of other facilities I didn't want and couldn't afford. All I needed was a clean bedroom and bathroom. I can eat out cheaply and, if necessary, I would wash my underclothes in the sink if there wasn't a laundry nearby. However, I realised there was absolutely no point in aimlessly walking around sidewalks without a plan, so while sitting in the splendid surroundings, I contemplated my options.

After a fruitless attempt at searching my phone for cheap accommodation, my mind racked through any contacts I'd made through work, but eventually I decided it would be foolish to jeopardise my future by contacting these people. After all, if by some slim chance I managed to get my business ideas up and running in the next few weeks, then

I'd need to present a successful business face, not one foolish enough to arrive in New York in need of cheap accommodation.

My thoughts turned to Kit and I wondered how much her hotel cost.

The night crawled past arthritically. I awoke ill at ease and reluctantly glanced towards David's bed. He appeared to be asleep, but I couldn't be sure. I quietly got out of bed and made my way to the bathroom to shower and get ready for the day.

When I returned to the bedroom fifteen minutes later, David was sat up in bed. 'Did you sleep well?'

'Okay, I suppose. What about you?'

'Okay.'

The unsettling atmosphere in the room was palpable and the silence that followed only added to the discomfort I felt.

'I'll have a shower,' David said as he climbed out of bed.

I nodded and picked up the New York guidebook and pretended to read. My head reeled with confusion. I knew my feelings for David had blown hot and cold ever since we'd met, but somewhere deep inside I'd always cherished the idea that maybe at last I'd met someone I could trust. Last night destroyed that sentiment.

I wondered whether the disordered jumble of my mind was made worse because of the bleakness at losing Mother. It couldn't have helped.

David's voice sounded deliberately bright as he re-entered the room. 'Kit, shall we go down for breakfast?'

'I suppose we should, but perhaps we should sort a few things out first.'

David's face crumbled. 'Do you want me to ask about another room while we're down there?'

'I didn't say that, but we can't just pretend last night didn't happen.'

'What would you like to do?'

'At the moment, nothing. I no longer know how I feel about us, about you – in fact, about everything. Death has scrambled my brain and tomorrow I'm going to meet a sister that I didn't even know existed a week ago.'

'You've had a tough time lately. I don't know how you've coped so well.'

'If you'd lived through Tom and come out the other side in one piece, you'd know. Still, I suppose you coped with marriage and Carly – that can't have been easy.'

'That was of my own making. I could have handled things better. None of the terrible things that happened to you was of your doing. You're one strong lady, Kit. You really are.'

'I'm much stronger nowadays. It's a pity that I wasn't the same back then. Anyway, this isn't sorting things out. Do you have any suggestions?'

'I'm in your hands. What do you want to do?'

'Today we have a free day in New York to do whatever we want and I think it would be a shame to waste that opportunity, so, as friends, why don't we make the most of seeing the City? We've got the list we made and we could choose a couple of things and see how it goes.'

-o-

And so it was that as travelling companions we spent our day alongside all the other tourists, who tried to cram as many iconic sights as possible into a short period of time. We started with the Uptown hop-on-hop-off bus tour, which unexpectedly took in fantastic views of Central Park. As the bus made its way along the side of the park, I imagined John Lennon's mosaic strewn with flowers and teddy bears, and the telling words of the 'Strawberry Fields' song lodged in my mind. They described exactly how I was feeling today. A big nothingness… and for me, this day wasn't real, even though I was trying my damnedest to make-believe otherwise. We played sightseers: looking, touching and taking photographs; experiencing the smells and sounds of the City, and the sights of buildings in the instantly recognisable skyline. We were amicable, but the spirit of friendliness was a cover and I knew it delayed the thought of meaningful discussion.

The guide that was taking our small group around the Rockefeller Centre had just enthusiastically embarked on a brief history of Radio City Music Hall when my phone vibrated. I nudged David and pointed to the railings of a nearby stairwell. 'It's
Jess. I'll pop over there and answer.'

The guide had started to move the group on when I rushed back to join them.

'Everything okay?' David asked.

'Yes and no.' I raised my eyebrows. By the time I'd briefly filled David in on my conversation, we were about to be handed over to the Radio City Music Hall's guide for our 'Behind the Stage Door' tour.

'So what's he going to do and what's happened to Allegra?' David probed.

'I told Jess we'd meet him later. I expect we'll hear everything then. I hope that was okay with you?'

'Of course. Maybe I can ring a few of my New York contacts. They might know of somewhere inexpensive to stay.'

I coughed unnecessarily. 'I did say that we could, perhaps, somehow smuggle him into our hotel room for tonight.'

'But there's only two beds.'

'I know, but he's in dire need. I ought to help him.'

'Where will he sleep?'

'He said he didn't mind the floor.'

'Well, that's plain daft. Let's wait and see what he…'

It was a sentence that David never finished as the new guide was obviously not happy to have two of her party chattering. The subject of Jess was obviously something to be discussed later. We fell in with the party and shuffled along with the group, who were silently paying homage to the Art Deco masterpiece of the Great Stage.

Our meeting with Jess at the end of the day forced me to play peacemaker. It was obvious the two men did not get on, but both were endeavouring to be as polite as the situation allowed.

'I'm very sorry about this,' Jess said to a grim-faced David, who was shaking his head at the idea of sharing a room. 'I'm in a bit of a fix and I just can't find a room that is affordable in this manic city.'

'Perhaps had you curtailed your spending on board, then it might be a different case.'

'Yes, I know.'

I watched Jess battling to keep calm as he balled his fists under the table.

'So,' David continued, 'what price bracket do you have in mind?'

'To be honest, as little as possible.'

Eventually, David agreed to ask whether the hotel had a vacant room and, being a regular client, he thought they might make the room rate a little lower. As we watched the receptionist check the computer, Jess quickly added that it didn't have to have a view or anything special, simple accommodation would be fine, which was probably the reason why a small room at the back of the hotel was offered.

'It's rather a dark room, Sir.' The receptionist smiled pleasantly. 'I would prefer for you to see it before making a decision.' She produced a plastic door swipe key and indicated for Jess to follow her.

We waited for his return at the reception desk.

'No matter what the room looks like, he'll take it. I'll put money on that,' David said as he tapped his fingers on the mahogany desk surface.

He was correct, of course, and as soon as Jess had filled in the paperwork, the receptionist handed him a key card, which I quickly grabbed.

'Hey!' was the only word Jess said and, judging by the surprise in his eyes, he'd no idea this was coming.

'What the hell are you doing, Kit?' David glared. 'I'm not going to share with your brother.'

'I'm sorry, David, but this room is mine. Given our relationship, I think it's for the best, don't you?' My eyes told him that this was not up for discussion.

I knew that sharing a room with Jess would be far outside David's comfort zone, but no matter what argument he put forward, I was absolutely insistent that the small room was mine and Jess should have my bed. And so it was.

-o-

When Jess and I met in reception next morning, we approached from different areas of the hotel and David, who originally was going to accompany me to the lawyer's office, was nowhere to be seen. He probably felt too annoyed to be involved in any way whatsoever.

'Your boyfriend's a bit rude, isn't he?' Jess asked as we waited for our cab outside the hotel.

'First of all, Jess, he's not my boyfriend and, second, you should count yourself lucky you had somewhere to sleep last night.'

'But still, this morning I only asked him whether he thought it would be easy to find the offices of Selby and Cromwell, and he looked at me as though I was something the cat brought in and then said he'd no idea. Then he marched to the bathroom and banged the door without as much as a goodbye.'

'If that's all you've got to worry about today, Jess, count yourself lucky. I'm not looking forward to this meeting with the solicitors. I don't think things are going to be as we expect, so if I were you, I'd concentrate on what's about to come.'

The cab pulled up before I'd finished speaking and as Jess followed me towards its door, I could see that my words had given him food for thought. His lips were thin and firm as he scrambled in beside me.

-o-

When the cab dropped us in Park Avenue, Jess stepped back and fiddled with his watch while I paid the fare. I said nothing, but wondered just how much money Allegra had swindled out of my brother. The impressive gold lettering on the black background announcing that we were stood outside the prestigious offices of Selby and Cromwell Attorneys at Law made me feel small and insignificant.

So, this was it. Finally, I was about to meet Sarah, the mysterious sister who'd only entered my life a few days ago. A thousand worries fought for central position in my head. *What would Sarah be like? Would the lawyers ask difficult questions? Would I think of sensible replies? Had I dressed appropriately to meet a New York lawyer?* But my biggest fear was how Jess's anger would erupt when he discovered that any inheritance might be diluted since a third sibling might be involved.

By the time the elevator reached the seventieth floor, my nerves had escaped and my legs were moving on automatic pilot. I felt disconnected from everything but the ever-present sound of drumming in my ears.

We were shown into an empty waiting room by an efficient, well-dressed receptionist who offered us coffee. While I'd no desire for a drink, I decided it would give me something to do with my hands while I waited.

Jess seemed totally relaxed as he made himself comfortable in a deep armchair and started flicking through a glossy Real Estate magazine. He looked at me and smiled. 'Not long now, Kit. After putting us through the circus of the ashes, plus all the other garbage, it's all about to be over. Thank God. Whatever happens today, it'll be alright. I'll make sure you don't suffer. Don't worry.'

I realised he imagined he was about to inherit everything. But I thought it kind that he'd decided I wouldn't suffer.

I jumped when the door from the corridor to our room opened. Although the man that entered smiled and pleasantly wished us both a good morning, my heart was still pounding as he exited by a different door.

Jess reached for my hand and gently squeezed it. 'Don't worry, Sis. They can't eat us, you know, even if they are a group of upmarket New York lawyers. Remember, it's our money that's paying them.'

I smiled and silently berated myself. After all, Sarah would be a woman just like me. It wasn't as though I was about to meet a dragon or anything. My mind turned for the umpteenth time as to whether we would resemble each other either in looks or behaviour.

When the door opened for a second time and a woman of about my height was ushered into the room, I felt that this could very probably be her. I stared much longer than was polite, but the woman seemed not to notice as she scrambled around in her bag and eventually produced an envelope, which she clutched tightly in her hand. She then wriggled back into the comfort of the chair, but didn't seem to relax as the fingers of her free hand slowly drummed the padded arm. At this point, she looked at Jess and me and gave us a disarming smile accompanied with a nod.

A few minutes later, a door opened to what Kit thought must be the lawyer's inner sanctum and a smartly dressed gentleman appeared. His eyes scanned the three occupants before he smiled.

He looked at me. 'Miss Sarah Langford?'

Before I could reply, the woman sitting opposite spoke. 'I'm Sarah Langford.' She stood and walked towards the man, who hadn't moved a centimetre from the doorway.

'Good morning, Miss Langford. I'm John, one of Miss Selby's paralegals, and I've been working on your file. I understand that you have an appointment with Miss Selby?'

'Yes.' She waved the envelope in front of her as though it was proof.

'Will you please follow me? Miss Selby wishes to have a quick word with you before the official meeting.'

Clutching her envelope, she followed John into the inner sanctum and the door closed.

Jess's eyes appeared on stalks. 'Did you hear her name?'

I nodded without comment.

'That's a bit odd, isn't it? There's something suspicious going on here. Why the hell has that woman got our surname?'

I shrugged, hoping that my expression gave nothing away.

Jess towards me and grimaced. 'And another thing, it looks as though our Miss Selby has arranged two appointments for the same time. I've a good mind to complain to that John person. I also imagined the Selby we'd see would be male.'

'Jess, it doesn't matter whether she's male or female, as long as she's good at her job – and I imagine Mr Jones-Regal would have made sure of that, don't you?'

'I certainly hope so.'

'I don't expect they'll keep us waiting too long. There's probably someone else with an appointment after ours. Anyway, we're not in any hurry, are we? We've got the whole day free.'

We sat quietly side by side, waiting for the appearance of John in the doorway for a second time. I couldn't shake the image of the woman who'd recently been sitting in front of us. So that was Sarah. My half-sister. And I'd now learned that we shared the same surname. Her name reverberated around my brain and I wanted to say it aloud to see how it felt on my tongue, but I knew Jess would think me absolutely crazy. I'd no idea what to think or what to feel. I took a deep breath. Did we resemble each other? No, I couldn't see an immediate resemblance and Jess hadn't seemed to notice anything. But that wasn't much to go on, for when did Jess ever notice something like that? Far too inconsequential for him.

I played a guessing game in my head as to why Miss Selby had wanted to see Sarah on her own first and when, fifteen minutes later, Sarah returned to the reception room, I knew that I'd guessed correctly.

Sarah's astonished white face stared at Jess and I intently as she made her way to the unoccupied armchair opposite. She was still staring at me when John returned and bid Jess and I to follow him. As I stood to leave, I made what I hoped was a friendly smile at the seated woman, who returned it blankly. I wondered whether my own face had moved as I'd intended; perhaps it had been more of a grimace. Then, the thought struck me, I'd known for a few days of my half-sister's existence and I was still reeling from the knowledge. How on earth must Sarah be feeling? It was far more monumental for her. In the space of a few minutes, she'd learned not only of a mother who'd recently departed this world, but that she had siblings as well. My heart went out to her.

'That woman's looking a bit weird,' Jess mumbled, as we moved through the paralegal's office. 'Looks like she must have had some bad news.'

I didn't reply but was surprised that even Jess had noticed. It was the kind of thing that usually went way below his radar.

Miss Selby stood and welcomed us into her office and, despite my nerves, I still registered what a beautiful office it was. A desk stood in pride of place. Its high-gloss metallic finish was tinted to a gorgeous grey shade and the curved top and pedestals could only be described as stunning. There was no paperwork hiding the polished top. We were in the office of a very organised lawyer.

Miss Selby swept her arm towards the plush-looking sofa and chairs in the corner of the room. This space alone looked far bigger than my entire flat at home. My well-polished shoes made no sound as I walked across the thickly carpeted floor. I almost felt the need to lift my foot up with each step.

'Please, do sit.' Miss Selby's voice was not as I expected. There was no edge to it, no precise pronunciation of vowels, neither did it make her intimidating.

'I apologise that the sofa is not as comfortable as it might be. I took my eye off the design team and I'm afraid this is what happened. To be honest, the furniture in my working office is far more comfortable than this, but I'm afraid it is a tad untidy. I'd hate for you to see it.' The smile was genuine and for Kit, it was catching.

'First of all, I must apologise for keeping you waiting. Our meeting today is, for Selby and Cromwell, slightly unusual. It is the first time that we've had clients come all the way from the UK for the reading of a will and I'm sure that Mr Jones-Regal, your English solicitor, will have assured you that we're one of the leading companies in New York. Our Estate Attorney Department is excellence, bar none. Your parents' decisions are in safe hands.'

Jess slowly lifted his brow and stared at Miss Selby's smiling face. 'I sincerely hope that this is the case, otherwise our father's wishes will have been made in vain.'

'Rest assured, Mr Langford. It is so. Perhaps now that we have met, we could relax a little and use our first names? The days of formality between lawyer and client are gradually diminishing. My name is Georgina. May I call you by your first name?'

'I'm Kit and this is my brother, Jess.'

'Nice to meet you both.'

Georgina smiled. 'Now, let's get down to business, which, after all, is why we're here.' She pulled out a folder from the top of a concealed drawer in the coffee table. 'Your case is a little different. In fact, I've never handled anything like this before.'

Jess shifted forward to the edge of his chair. I could see that Georgina had his full attention and he was absorbing every word.

'This is going to be a complete shock for you, as it was for

Sarah, and I can't think of any other way to present this information other than to be truthful and say that you are related to Sarah Langford. In fact, she is your half-sister.'

The silence that filled the room was deafening. I looked at Jess, whose face looked as though he'd just entered a nightmare. In that instant, his skin had greyed and his eyes and mouth were frozen wide open in an expression of stunned shock. Unblinking, he stared ahead, shaking his head in disbelief. He'd been rendered speechless, temporarily incapacitated, and sat as if paralysed.

I wrung my hands together. I swallowed hard, trying to persuade some moisture to invade my mouth.

Georgina poured three glasses of water from the silver pitcher that had been placed on the coffee table. She placed a glass in front of both Jess and me. 'I realise that this is an awful shock for you. I'm sure that you would appreciate time on your own before we continue?'

I'd no idea how Jess was going to react and was about to reply yes when Jess suddenly stood up. I sighed, hoping he was fully in control of his feelings, but then he sat down again without uttering a word.

Georgina quietly made her way to the door, although neither of us seemed to notice. We sat motionless for a few minutes before Jess put his hand on my arm. 'Are you alright, Sis?'

I nodded. 'You?'

He shook his head vigorously. 'I don't believe it. I can't. Father would have told us. He wouldn't have hidden something like this all these years.'

'It might have been Mother.'

'If this rubbish about a half-sister is true, that is, but I don't think it is. There is no way I can believe it.'

'I think we need to hear what Georgina has to say.'

'That woman in the waiting room, perhaps she's a money digger. Maybe she's made false claims.' Jess wrinkled his brow. 'I've read about this sort of thing.'

'Maybe, Jess, but how could she know about it?'

'These people are shrewd. They have their ways.'

I felt uncomfortable and wondered whether I should tell him about Mother's letter. However, at that moment, I felt it might stoke the flames even more. It seemed so unfair and I felt guilty for not sharing its contents with him, despite Mother being adamant that I should keep it a secret. She ought to have written to Jess as well as me.

'Jess.' My voice quietly filled the vacuum. 'If you think Miss Langford is a fraud, then we can always demand a DNA test. But I honestly believe we must hear everything that has to be said today before accusing her of anything.'

Jess studied his shoes but said nothing.

It was then that Georgina re-entered the room and sat in the chair opposite us. 'I know this must be a tremendous shock for you both and I'm sorry to be the one to bring such momentous news.'

Jess finally found his voice. 'What I don't understand is why neither of our parents ever told us anything about another sibling? That is, if she is our half-sister. She doesn't feel like a sibling to me. She didn't grow up with us. I know nothing about her.'

'I understand your sentiments. Miss Langford uttered virtually the same thing only a little while ago.'

Georgina reached for the folder and extracted two envelopes. 'This might help begin the explanation process for you both. It's a letter from your mother. She wrote a letter to your half-sister, which I handed to her this afternoon. I believe you might need a little more time on your own to read and digest your mother's words. I'm going to send in a tray of coffee for you and leave you alone for a little while. Miss Langford has been shown into one of our quiet side rooms and she's also been given time to take in what has been written.'

Jess fingered the envelope as though it contained a viral disease he didn't want to escape.

Georgina smiled sympathetically. 'When you've all had time to study what's been written, then I will bring all three of you together, and if you're ready, we will commence reading the last will and testament of your mother. Does that meet with your agreement?'

I nodded, but Jess remained inert, still fingering the envelope and staring at his name, which had been written in Mother's hand.

When I opened my envelope, the sight of Mother's handwriting brought tears to my eyes. I looked at Jess, who was still sat with the unopened envelope in his hand.

'Don't you want to open it, Jess?'

'To be honest, I don't know what I want. It's as though I've entered a nightmare from which there is no escape.'

'I think we need to read what Mother has to say. It might help.'

I scanned the two pages of her letter. It looked as though she'd paraphrased the words she'd used in the much longer version I'd already received. The misplaced love she'd felt for Sarah's father was mentioned and Henry's agreement to provide a home for her, providing she gave up the baby for adoption and gave him a male heir. She told of her sorrow not to have loved us better in our childhood and appealed to us to forgive her and to try to understand that she had no choice and nowhere else to go.

It was good that, at last, everything was out in the open and I felt an immense relief that Jess now knew as much as I did. I wondered how Sarah was reacting to what must be an even bigger shock.

I looked at Jess, whose stunned silence was unnatural. 'You okay?' I whispered, reaching out for his hand.

He nodded, without straightening his hunched shoulders. 'I just don't know what to think anymore. I keep expecting to wake up soon.'

'We're in it together, Jess. Just imagine how poor Sarah must be feeling right now. She must be far more confused than we are.' Jess looked into my eyes, but before he could reply, the door opened and Georgina re-entered the room.

Georgina smiled slightly. 'I'm going to bring Sarah in now. Are you both ready?'

Two nodding heads gave her the permission she sought and, as she left the room, I immediately thought that the next time the door reopened, I'd be meeting my half-sister for the very first time.

Sarah studied the carpet as she walked to the empty chair next to me. It wasn't until she was seated that she turned to glance at me and, not knowing what else to do, I laid my hand lightly on Sarah's arm and whispered 'Hello'. It seemed such an inadequate word, but I was at a loss to know what else to say.

Georgina took command and started by introducing the three awkward-looking occupants of the room to each other. Shaking hands didn't seem the right thing to do, but we did it anyway.

Georgina sighed. 'I'm going to begin by saying that this is the most unusual will I've ever had to deal with. I've never brought together siblings who are unknown to one another and neither have I had clients who have had to travel so far from their native country to find out the contents of their mother's will.'

She looked at Sarah, whose facial expression resembled a blank sheet of paper. 'I know that you're living in New York at the moment, Sarah, but as you are an English citizen, everything I say will apply to you under English law equally as it does your halfbrother and sister.'

Sarah's slight nod conveyed that she understood, but she remained silent.

'Nowadays a will is not read aloud as it was in former times. Normally, a legal document is drawn up that identifies beneficiaries and states what each of them should receive. It determines when and how each beneficiary receives their gifts. Beneficiaries usually find out what they have been given by receiving a copy of the will.' She coughed before continuing. 'Some estate attorneys will gather everyone together to receive a copy of the will if they think there might be some confusion or conflict over the terms of the will. I do not believe that it is necessary for me to read aloud Mrs Sylvia Langford's last will and testament and, if you're all in agreement, I suggest that I give you each a copy to peruse while we're all here together. Afterwards, you may, of course, take the will away to study at your leisure, and if you need clarification on any of the points raised, then you need only contact me. I will do my best to help.'

An awkward moment of silence filled the room before Sarah began to shuffle around the jumble that constituted the contents of her handbag. 'I'm looking for my reading glasses,' she said, meekly.

I smiled at her. 'I get that trouble, too. All the time. Drives me crazy.' We exchanged a moment of common appreciation before I noticed the glare that the only male in the room was giving us.

My hand shook slightly as I opened the large brown envelope that Georgina handed to me. I took a deep breath. *This is it. This is it*, my brain repeated silently and then I exhaled as a picture of Mother took centre stage. A smiling sober Mother that I remembered from the time when, as an adult, I needed her most. I smiled feebly and wondered why on earth I was apprehensive. After all, I knew that whatever was written in the will would cause me no grief.

Georgina gave us time to look at the document and I could hear Sarah and I slowly turning the pages, but Jess was noisily flipping back and forth through them. Eventually, he spoke. 'Georgina. Is this it? Are you sure this is correct?'

'Yes. This is the will that has been entrusted to me by Mr Jones Regal, who I understand is your solicitor in England.'

'Are you sure there's nothing missing?'

'Yes, I am. Why, what are you looking for?'

'From a quick glance, I believe that this will in no way reflects my father's wishes.'

'No, it wouldn't necessarily do that, because your father in his will left his worldwide assets to your mother, who outlived him. So, the scope of this will reflects the decisions of your mother. Not your father.'

Jess glared. 'But leaving everything to my mother was an old will that he made when I was a boy. I know this for sure because he told me. He made a new will and revoked this one.'

'Do you have a signed witnessed copy of the will to which you refer?'

Jess's eyes blazed as he got to his feet. 'Of course I haven't. Do you think I would have come on this charade to New York had I been able to control things from the UK? I presumed old Jones-Regal had it and passed it on to you.'

'Please sit down, Mr Langford. I can check on this. I will get in touch with Mr Jones-Regal and verify facts. The timing difference will be in our favour, so hopefully I will get an answer quickly.'

'Perhaps you could contact him right away. It's pointless for my sister and this woman to believe that this is the correct will.'

'I will do so soon, but first of all I wish to ask everyone in the room whether they have any questions or wish to make any comments. What about you, Sarah?'

'I'm finding it difficult to take everything in, to be quite honest. In the last few hours, I've discover that I have a brother and a sister and I—'

Jess interrupted. 'Half-brother and half-sister, if things can be believed.'

I heard Sarah gulp before continuing, 'I think this will states that I'm going to inherit one-third of my biological mother's estate, after all debts and expenses have been paid. I don't quite know what to say. I'm shocked… I'm…' She shrugged and held her palms upward. 'I don't know what to say.'

'It must be a very difficult day for you.' Georgina smiled sympathetically. 'In fact, it must be difficult for all three of you. You're correct, Sarah, your biological mother in her will has left you one-third of the entire estate. She's also left you the Spanish house that her husband bought—'

A loud voice interrupted, 'That is, Georgina, if this is the correct will. So, I say again, perhaps it would be best if you contacted England right now.'

Georgina fingered the collar of her immaculate white shirt and turned to me. 'Kit, is there anything that you wish to add before I leave the room to contact your English solicitor?'

I paused momentarily. 'Maybe once I've had time to sit down quietly with this document, I can return and discuss things with you if I have questions?'

'Of course you can. You would be very welcome. Though, in a nutshell, you've been left a gift similar to that of Sarah and Jess, except for the Spanish house.'

Georgina's eyes were on the brink of the faintest smile. 'Right, I'm going to try to contact Mr Jones Regal, if he's available. Perhaps this would be a good time to have a break and stretch your legs. There are plenty of coffee stores nearby – in fact, two doors down to the left, there is The Black Cat Coffee Roaster chain. I can recommend their coffee and their cookies are also good. Shall we meet back here in, say, one hour?'

I nodded noticing that Jess had already stomped out of the door. Outside the building, he'd headed in the opposite direction.

Sarah looked at me. 'Jess seems upset. I hope this is not my doing.'

'Jess was close to our father and I think maybe he was promised things that may not happen now.'

'That must be an awful shock for him. And I must be a complete bombshell for you both. I still feel as though I'm dreaming. A half-brother and sister – it doesn't seem possible.'

'Well, it is. Our mother's letters prove it.'

Sarah looked a little sheepish. 'Shall we have coffee together? I mean, you don't have to. It's just, I thought…'

'It's a good idea. Why not? Shall we try the recommended Black Cat?'

'To be honest, there's a Black Cat branch fairly near where I work. I don't rate their coffee much, but they do have nice pastries.'

'Right. Pastry it is then.'

-o-

We sat in the cafe window seats and made those first tentative steps in getting to know each other. Our conversation circled around unimportant trivia, neither of us brave enough to ask the questions we really wished and I think we both felt relieved when it was time to return to Georgina's office.

When we arrived, Jess was already there. He was sitting grim-faced as he studied his copy of the will. He looked up, but didn't speak.

'Okay, Jess?' I asked, meeting his eyes.

He nodded, but didn't utter a word.

Georgina re-entered the room with John at her side. She smiled pleasantly. 'I hope you've had an enjoyable break. I've asked John, one of my paralegals, to join us so that you can meet him properly. Should you wish to get in touch after our meeting and I'm not available, you can be sure that John will assist you in any way possible.'

Jess was the first to speak. 'Did you talk with Jones Regal?'

'Yes, I did. In fact, I spent quite some time talking to him – and to be sure that we have the correct will, he scanned and sent a copy of the will held in his office. I've carefully checked the details of both wills and they are identical—'

'Yes. Yes,' Jess interrupted, impatiently. 'As it is our mother's will that you refer to, then I imagine they would. However, did he confirm that our father made a new will last year in which he states that our mother would no longer be the main beneficiary of his estates?'

'No, he didn't. He double-checked this and called me again a little later. The only will lodged with Regal, Smith and Cooke for your father is the one leaving his entire estate to your mother. And the will we possess here is your mother's last will and testament.'

I looked at Jess, who was sitting rigidly upright, his foot was tapping, his lips pouted and he was repeatedly nodding his head slowly. It was a pose I'd never seen him adopt before.

'So, you're telling me that our mother's will is, as far as you're concerned, the correct will?'

'Since there is no contradictory evidence, then yes I am. This is all we have.'

Jess stood and paced the room for a few seconds before stopping in front of me. 'Sis, I'm going back to the UK as soon as possible. I'm going to speak with old Jones-Regal. We've given him too much free reign already. I'll keep in touch.'

With these words, he marched to the door and slammed it behind him.

Three embarrassed pairs of eyes stared at each other in the silence that followed. The disappearance of Jess suddenly signalled an end to the meeting. A few minutes later, Sarah and I found ourselves stood on the sidewalk outside the office building.

'When do you fly back to the UK, Kit?' Sarah asked. 'It would be nice to get to know you a little before we go our separate ways.'

I smiled. 'Somehow, I think our ways will not be that separate from now on.' I gently placed my hand on Sarah's arm. 'It's lovely to discover I've a sister and it's been great to meet you today. Our mother would've been proud.'

'Mother. It seems odd to hear you say that word.'

'She always loved you.'

'Really? Did you always know about me?'

'Not for a very long time, but when she eventually wrote and told me about you, her words were full of love. And regret. She didn't want to give you up for adoption.'

I could see the tears threatening in Sarah's eyes. 'Is that true?'

I nodded. 'Why don't we have lunch together tomorrow? We've so much to discuss. So many years to catch up. I want to know all about you.'

Sarah rallied. 'Lunch would be great. I should be at work, but I'll take the day off. In fact, I might take the week off if I'm about to come into money. I have to admit this is all very awkward, though. I don't deserve to share this money with you and Jess.' 'Of course you do. It's what our mother wished. She wanted to try to make everything up to you.'

'But she didn't need to.'

'In her mind, she did. It's probably why she left Father's Spanish house to you as well. She wanted to let you know how sorry she was.'

'Oh yes, the house. That was totally unexpected and seems so unfair on you and Jess.'

'Don't be silly. I don't want to live in Spain and I can't imagine Jess spending much time in some Spanish backwater away from the bright lights and buzz of a big city.'

Sarah smiled awkwardly. 'I'd already planned to leave New York in a month or so. Perhaps I'll go to Spain.'

'Good for you. I might come and visit you for a holiday when you've sussed everything out.'

We smiled at each other and I felt this was the beginning of a very special relationship. The warmth of connection embraced me, fragile yet ready to blossom.

We hugged and made arrangements for the next day. As I walked to the cab rank, I silently enthused about the journey to come, a journey that I believed would bring Sarah into my life.

When I saw my hotel in the distance, thoughts of David crushed everything else from my mind. My sigh must have been far louder than I imagined because the cab driver turned briefly to glance at me.

'You okay, honey?' Her friendly voice called over her shoulder.

'Yes, I'm fine. Thanks. I've just remembered something, that's all.'

'Do you want me to continue to your hotel? We can head back if you need to.'

'No, it's not that I've left something behind, it's just that, well, I'll soon have to make a decision about something… about someone and I don't know what to do.'

Why on earth was I telling this complete stranger about David?

'I'm not being nosey, hun, but if this decision involves someone that you care about, and if that someone seems to think a lot of you – in fact, maybe you once loved each other – then you certainly have a big decision on your hands.'

I warmed to the older woman sat in the front. 'Can I ask you something?'

'Sure, honey. Go ahead.'

'Do you believe that people know when true love comes along? It's something my mother believed.'

'Mothers are canny people, hun, but, in all honesty, I'm not sure it works quite like that. It took me years to decide.'

'Really?'

'Sure did. Luckily he hung around long enough for me to make up my mind. Just as well. He's the right man for me, for sure. Been over twenty years now and I still love the guy.'

I could tell by the inflection of her voice that my cab driver was smiling as she spoke.

'If I were you, I'd ask yourself how you'd feel if you saw him passionately kissing someone else? Would it bother you?'

I didn't need to dwell on my answer. I knew instantly, but it was just then the cab pulled up in front of the hotel, so no answer was needed and the business of paying took place.

'I wouldn't think too deeply about these things, hun. Go with your heart.'

The driver gave me a thumbs up sign and smiled before she wound up the cab window and drove away.

I made my way to the dismal little bedroom and sat on the bed. I felt the muscles of my chin involuntary tremble like that of a small child. I reached to turn on the light, as if solace could be found in its glow.

Closing my eyes, I now felt sure of what I wanted. But, oh, the overwhelming emotion. The truth of it was more than I could ever have imagined.

I could almost hear Mother's voice as, with shaking hands, I sent David a text.

His reply was instant and my stomach flipped. I made my way to his room, knowing I was in a trace. My thought processes were utterly incapable of sharp tuning.

'I've come to talk,' I said, anxiously, as he opened the door.

He swept his arm wide and stood back, waiting for me to enter. His face bore the look of a man for whom sleep had been unattainable.

I stood in the centre of the room, wondering how to start. At last, my voice emerged, 'David. I...'

He looked at me with an expression that I could not read. Was it hope or hate?

'David, we've been involved in a cruel farce. Fooling each other. I know bereavement has played a part in this, but it is no excuse. Forgive me. I've not behaved well.'

He nodded sadly. 'Neither have I.' The words seemed to dribble from his lips.

'I know that you've offered me love.' I looked into his eyes as though for the very first time. 'I don't deserve the love of someone like you. The way I've acted. Blowing hot and cold. You'd think a woman of my age would have known what she wanted by now.'

'And… Kit,' he hesitated, 'do you know now?'

'Yes.' My voice became a whisper.

He hurried on swiftly. 'Kit, before you tell me your decision, can I just say something? Please.'

I nodded, not trusting myself to speak.

'I realise I've no right to expect that what I'm about to say will affect your decision, but I've been spending hours online looking into vasectomy reversal and apparently it's possible even after twenty or thirty years. I'm not saying this is our answer, but I know I'm ready for fatherhood now as much as you're ready to be a mother.' His eyes caught mine. 'I would do my best to be a good father this time around and a good husband. Kit, we've got a special relationship. Shouldn't we give it a chance?' He shook his head sadly and looked at his shoes.

I didn't expect to hear the words he'd just spoken, but it didn't affect my decision. I felt my cheeks burn and heard my voice crack as I started the speech I'd rehearsed.

'David, I've been searching for the answers for far too long and I realise I'm not even sure I've been asking myself the right questions. So… do you think we might try…'

Surprise flashed across his face. 'Are you saying what I think you're saying? Do you mean you're willing to give our relationship a chance?'

I nodded and pressed my hands together to stop them shaking. 'I've been afraid to let you into my life. I believe now fate has given us an opportunity. We should take it.'

'Are you sure?' he whispered, his voice breaking.

My smile told him the answer without words.

He put his arms around my waist and pulled me close. The kiss we shared was so soft, so tender. I felt safe. This relationship would last. And as my heart beat wildly, I knew that, at long last, I was in love with the right man.

The story you've just read is part of a trilogy.

Below is an excerpt from **SIBLINGS EMMA'S STORY**, which takes place between Bristol, UK, and New York, USA, spanning from the late 1980s to the present day.

Each book in the SIBLINGS series stands alone and can be read in any order.

-o-

SIBLINGS Emma's Story

2010

LEO

Leo burst into my world on a scorching July afternoon injecting a much-needed dose of excitement into my life. His arrival was like a whirlwind, sweeping me off my feet and into a realm of anticipated adventure. Yet, beneath the thrill, there was always an unsettling confusion about him, a shadowy edge that hinted at danger lurking just below the surface. It would take several months before I fully grasped the nature of that impending danger.

It all began when Cheryl and I decided we needed a third flat mate — not for the company, but because the extra rent money was essential. We placed an ad, and Leo called while I was at work. Cheryl met him that same day and decided he'd be a good fit. Moreover, he was content to sleep in the minuscule backroom we had been using for storage.

He moved in the following Saturday morning and I met him that afternoon when I flung open the lounge door and sent him flying. I looked down at the burly man who lay on the carpet. A child-like smile was escaping from his short beard as he gazed up at me.

'I'm sorry. Are you okay?' I offered my hand to help him up. 'I shouldn't have pushed the door so hard.'

He scrambled to his feet ignoring my outstretched hand and beamed at me. 'And I should have looked where I was going.'

'I'm as much to blame.'

'No. It was my fault.'

Our eyes met and it was an invitation to laughter. My recollection from then on is a bit of a blur. I remember smiling idiotically. I could not help it. The feeling of excitement.

Something new. My hope rising like a star.

He held out his hand towards me. 'I'm Leo.'

'Emma.'

'Nice to meet you, Emma.'

And that was how our relationship started. Even then I knew, regardless of how things turned out, I loved the dance that had begun.

I can't remember what we talked about that July afternoon, but I do recall his mobile rang as I was helping him carry books into his bedroom. He smiled at his phone with ease and made fluid arm movements to exaggerate his speech. I watched him as he nodded in the sunshine that was beaming through his tiny window. His face has not lost traces of boyhood, yet he must be in his early thirties. My eyes are drawn to the muscles that struggle to escape the arms of his t-shirt. I take in his appearance for as long as I dare.

'Emma, that was work. I'm afraid I must go as I'm on call. Thank you so much for helping me. Perhaps we can have a drink together later? I'll get a take away and a bottle of wine on the way back to celebrate moving in. Okay?'

Okay? It was more than okay. It was wonderful. But of course I didn't say that. I nod and give him a little wave as he steps away from the bed which is now creaking under the weight of the books.

I feel sixteen again. This stranger has stolen my heart without even knowing it's in his pocket. Mum once told me that I fall in love too quickly yet all I ever want is a loving relationship. The problem is that until now I've come to believe that hell will freeze over before that happens. Given my past I suppose you'll judge that Leo's going to be another whirlwind romance, but this time it's different. This time it's going to last. Oh please let that be true.

'What d'you think of our new flatmate?' This is Cheryl's first question when she walks through the door after work.

'He seems very nice. And my god isn't he dishy.'

She nods. 'Real eye candy.'

'He's been called back to work but when he returns he's bringing a takeaway and a bottle of wine to celebrate moving in.'

'Now that's the sort of flatmate I like.' Cheryl laughed. 'Pity I won't be here. I've got a date.'

I grin and roll my eyes. 'Who is it this time?'

'Nobody you know, but if all goes well I might not be home tonight.' She winked. 'You'll be able to flirt with Mr Eye Candy for all your worth.'

I give her a watery smile hoping she doesn't read too much into the colour of my hot cheeks.

She raised her eyebrows. 'A-ha. So, you think he's more than just *nice*. Looks like we've got a romance blossoming.'

I push her arm. 'He seems a nice man. That's all.'

She giggles as she walks away. 'Right. He's just a nice man is he? I think I'll definitely not come home tonight. Give you two lovebirds a chance to get this romance on the road. Enjoy the wine.'

ACKNOWLEDGEMENTS

A writer's journey, though often solitary, is never walked alone. I am deeply grateful to the many wonderful people who have supported me along the way.

To my dearest friends: thank you for embracing my stories with enthusiasm and for always encouraging me to write more. Special thanks to my dedicated beta readers, especially those who read the final manuscript—your feedback and thoughtful suggestions have been invaluable.

Special thanks must go to Val Hughes who wrote the poem "White Horses" especially for this book. Such a talented poet ... thank you Val.

I must also express my gratitude to my incredible publishers, The Book Guild, for expertly guiding me through the intricate process of bringing this book to life. Without your skill and encouragement, it wouldn't have made its way into readers' hands.

To my family: your unwavering support and bright smiles have been a constant source of strength. And to my husband, exceptional thanks—for your insight, friendship, and for sharing this beautiful, winding journey with me.

Finally, my heartfelt thanks to you, my readers. Writing this story has been a labour of love and sharing it with you is an incomparable joy. Knowing my words have reached you is a gift that inspires me every day.

If you enjoyed this book—or even if you didn't—I would be so grateful if you could take a few moments to leave a review on Amazon. Reviews mean the world to authors, and your feedback, whether glowing or constructive, is always appreciated.

Thank you, from the bottom of my heart.